Praise for Alan Titchmarsh

'Splendid . . . I laughed out loud'
Rosamunde Pilcher

'Absolutely charming . . . made me understand
a lot more about men'
Jilly Cooper

'A steamy novel of love among the gro-bags'
Observer

'A fine debut . . . great fun, but also sensitive and
sensible with a tuneful storyline. Titchmarsh fans
will lap up *Mr MacGregor*'
Independent

'I admit it, I like *Mr MacGregor*. It's as satisfying
as a freshly-mown lawn'
Daily Mirror

'Humorous, light-hearted and unpretentious.
Titchmarsh's book is strengthened by authenticity.
Ideal for romantic gardeners'
Mail on Sunday

Also by Alan Titchmarsh

ONLY DAD
ANIMAL INSTINCTS
THE LAST LIGHTHOUSE KEEPER
MR MacGREGOR

Alan Titchmarsh

Rosie

SIMON &
SCHUSTER

London · New York · Sydney · Toronto · New Delhi

A CBS COMPANY

First published in Great Britain by Simon & Schuster UK Ltd, 2004
This paperback edition, 2014
A CBS COMPANY

Copyright © Alan Titchmarsh, 2004

The chapter titles and the descriptions of the roses
are all taken from *Classic Roses* and *Twentieth Century Roses*
by Peter Beales, published by Collins Harvill.

Poem on page 300 by Mary Frye.

1 3 5 7 9 10 8 6 4 2

Simon & Schuster UK Ltd
1st Floor
London WC1X 8HB
www.simonandschuster.co.uk
222 Gray's Inn Road

Simon & Schuster Australia, Sydney
Simon & Schuster India, New Delhi

A CIP catalogue record for this book
is available from the British Library

ISBN 978-147114-275-8
eBook ISBN: 978-1-47111-501-1

Printed and bound by CPI Group (UK) Ltd, Croydon, CR0 4YY

For Luigi,
grazie

Acknowledgements

My heartfelt thanks go to Suzanne Baboneau for her tremendous support and understanding during the writing of *Rosie*. Without her forbearance the book would simply not have appeared. Thanks also to Luigi Bonomi, a star among literary agents, for his unfailing help and encouragement, to Hazel Orme for fastidious copy editing which astounds me and makes me smile in equal measure, to Rochelle Venables for organizing things, to Caroline Mitchell for organizing me, and to Clare Ledingham who, as with all my novels, has guided, encouraged and warned. Without their help telling stories would not be nearly so rewarding. Dr. Neil Ashwood patiently advised me on medical matters whenever I rang his number – often at very inconvenient times. His phone-side manner is admirable.

My family, as ever, have waited patiently for me to emerge from my eyrie in the barn and fed me, watered me and cosseted me whenever I needed the attention. They richly deserve my love and gratitude, and I only hope they approve of the results.

Author's Note

Some of the characters and some of the places in this book are real, others are fictional.
The Isle of Wight obviously exists, and so do all the places within it that are
mentioned, except for Nick's cottage, which somehow nobody has yet
found, and Sleepyhead Bay, which is based on a tiny cluster of
cottages in a secluded haven that keen visitors to the Isle of
Wight will know. I felt obliged to change its name to
protect it from being overrun. All the characters
who play an active role are fictional, but real
people and real events are
mentioned and it is up to
the reader to decide
where reality ends
and imagination
begins.

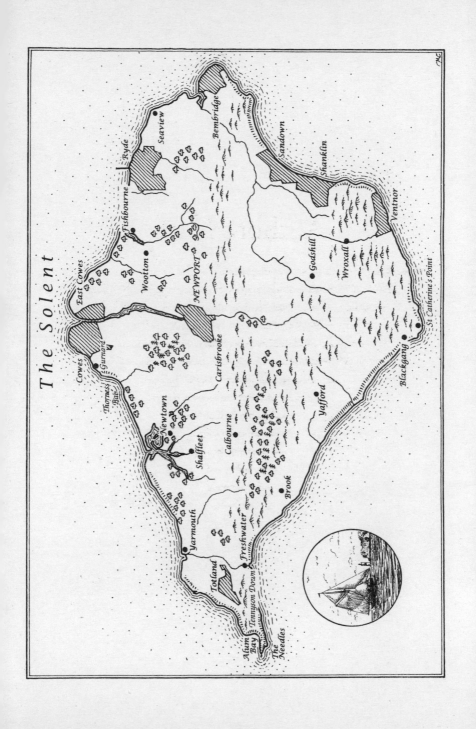

The Solent

Seaview
Ryde
Bembridge
Sandown
Shanklin
Fishbourne
Ventnor
Wootton
NEWPORT
Godshill
Wroxall
East Cowes
St Catherine's Point
Cowes
Gurnard
Carisbrooke
Blackgang
Thorness Bay
Newtown
Yafford
Shalfleet
Calbourne
Brook
Yarmouth
Freshwater
Totland
Alum Bay
Tennyson Down
The Needles

In a characteristic unique to the species, the ageing queen, having seen her progeny into adulthood, performs an energetic sequence of movements in the final hours before her death. These movements, which may become increasingly frenetic and complex, appear to satisfy some inbuilt urge or desire, but are, as yet, not fully understood. They are most usually referred to as 'the queen's last dance'.

Emerich Hummel, *The Russian Honey Bee*, 1918

1
Tour de Malakoff

Vivid magenta flowers flushed deep purple and fading to lilac grey.

'It's your grandmother.'

'Yes?'

'She's been arrested.'

This is not a conversation that many people expect to have. We know that grannies are not what they were, but even allowing for the fact that many are proficient on the Internet, lunatic behind the wheel and capable of doing full justice to the drinks cabinet, the discovery that our own had been detained at Her Majesty's pleasure would, if we are honest, come as a bit of a shock. A shock likely to provoke either disbelief or outrage.

As the policeman at the other end of the line delivered the grave news, in the particularly self-righteous manner that only someone wearing a uniform can, Nick Robertson found himself in the former camp. 'She's been what?'

'Arrested, sir. Well, detained, actually.'

'But what for?'

'Disturbing the peace.'

'Where?'

'In London, sir. She's at Bow Street police station. If you could come and collect her? We don't want to release her on her own and . . . well, I'd rather not say any more over the phone, if you don't mind. We'll fill you in when you get here.'

'But why me?'

'Yours was the name and number she gave us, sir.'

There were many things Nick wanted to say, the first being 'But I live on the Isle of Wight.' Instead he settled for 'Right. It will take me a couple of hours to get there.'

'No problem, sir. We'll keep her comfortable.'

'She's all right, isn't she? I mean, she's not hurt?'

'Oh, no, sir. She's absolutely fine. Keeping my officers well entertained.'

'She would. I'll be there as soon as I can.' And that was it. No more information.

What had she done? And why hadn't she called his mother? She was nearer. But the answer to that was obvious: his mother would have given her mother-in-law what-for. Or his father – her son? No again. Nick's dad would be at the races – or at some surreptitious meeting for his next money-making wheeze. Not much chance of finding him at the end of a telephone: his mobile number changed almost weekly.

Which was why, on a bright May morning, when birds were carolling from the tops of tall chestnut trees, and when he should have been enjoying the maudlin pleasure of staring out of the window and moping about the end of a three-year relationship with a girl now sitting on a British Airways flight to New York, he found himself rattling into Waterloo Station on the eleven fifteen from Southampton. Briefly he pictured his grandmother sitting in a cell, huddled in a corner, cowed and tearful but, if he was honest with himself, he knew that was unlikely.

He wasn't wrong: he found her at the front desk of the police station, regaling a wide-eyed trio of uniformed officers with the reasons behind her forecast for a Chelsea victory over Manchester United the following day. She looked round as he came in and smiled at him. 'Hello, love! Come to take me home?'

He nodded.

The desk sergeant broke away from the group, looking sheepish, negotiated the narrow opening to one side of the counter with some difficulty and beckoned Nick towards the room opposite. 'Would you mind, sir?' As the door closed behind them he heaved a sigh. 'Quite a character, your granny.'

'Yes.'

'I should think she takes a bit of looking after.' The lumbering policeman, whose unnaturally long arms gave him an ape-like appearance, was doing his best not to smirk.

'Well, most of the time she's fine.'

'Lives on her own, I gather.'

'Yes. She's not helpless,' Nick said defensively.

'Oh, I can see that. But it might be worth keeping an eye on her.'

'I do, when I can, but I live—'

'I know, sir. It must be difficult—'

Nick interrupted. 'What's she done? Nothing serious, surely?'

'Well, not serious. Just silly. We're letting her off with a caution. There'll be no charges. I think the embassy was surprised more than anything. It's normally students who chain themselves to their railings. And dissidents. Not that we get many of them nowadays.' Then: 'We don't get many grannies either.'

'No. I suppose not,' Nick said, thoughtfully. Disbelief had been augmented by irritation. There were so many things he could have asked, but in the event he only managed, 'I mean . . . why did she do it?'

'Some sort of protest. Mind you, her equipment wasn't up to much. One of those bicycle safety chains. The sort with a combination lock. We just snipped it off.'

'I see.' He thought about it. It would have been his grandfather's. She wouldn't have sent it to a jumble sale yet or a charity shop.

'The worry is that I think she rather enjoyed the attention. We'd prefer it if she didn't do it again. We've enough on without coping with protesting pensioners.'

'I'm sorry. I'll try to make sure she stays out of trouble.'

'If you would.'

'Can I take her home then?'

'Yes, of course.' He hesitated. 'Can I just ask you, sir . . .?'

'Yes?'

'What your granny was saying. I suppose it's just her funny way, isn't it? I mean . . .' He brought one of the long arms up to tug at his left ear, then looked at Nick sideways. 'She's not really related to the Russian royal family is she?'

'What?' It was one of those defining moments: the sort that make all sounds subside, all movement grind to a halt, and the world seems to take a deep breath. The moment when your granny, whom you've always perceived as adorable and ever-so-slightly . . . *individual*, might have turned a corner that you'd hoped would never appear on the horizon. The policeman must have misheard her. Sounds emerged once more from the corridor. There was movement, too.

Nick shook his head. 'No. I think you misunderstood. Her family *was* Russian. Gran left when there was all that bother with the royal family when she was a baby. She's lived in Britain ever since. Always felt bitter about the revolution, though. I think her mum was caught up in it.'

The policeman stared at Nick for a moment. 'Well, the embassy were very good about it. They had a particularly reasonable attaché on duty today. I suggested to him that your granny was just a bit – well, doo-lally.'

Nick's eyes widened. 'Not within her earshot, I hope.'

'Er, no. I thought it best not to.'

'Wise man.' He smiled ruefully.

'So, if you could just make sure she gets home safely. And maybe keep her away from bicycle chains for a while.' He pointed to the old safety cable lying in a corner, and as the limb revealed its full extent it occurred to Nick that this really was the long arm of the law.

'Yes. Yes, of course. It won't happen again,' he said, and added, under his breath, 'I hope.'

She was standing by the front door of the police station, smiling, silver-grey hair in its familiar soft curls, sensible shoes polished and tweed skirt pressed. Thanks to the morning's excitement, her pale blue eyes sparkled, and she pushed her hands deep into the pockets of the red, woolly jacket.

Nick's greeting came as a bit of a let down.

'Come on, Granny.' Nick's tone was impatient.

She frowned. 'There's no need for that.'

'All right, then – Rosie.'

'Better.'

He sighed. 'Tea?'

'Ooh! Yes, please. Best thing anybody's said all day.'

'I thought police stations were famous for their tea.'

'Yes. But they don't do Earl Grey. Terrible stuff, theirs. Colour of oxtail soup.'

'There's a café across the road. Come on, they'll probably do a range of designer teas.'

She stood quite still and shook her head.

'What's the matter?'

'I'm not having tea there, designer range or no.'

'Where, then?'

'The Ritz.'

'What?'

'As a celebration.'

'A celebration of what?'

'Mission accomplished.'

'What sort of mission? You've just been arrested.'

'I achieved what I set out to do.'

'Which was?'

She pulled up the fake-fur collar of her coat and held it with a leather-gloved hand. 'To draw attention to my life in exile.'

'Oh, Rosie!'

She fixed him with flashing pale blue eyes. 'I mean it.' The stern expression subsided and she grinned. 'Oh, go on, take me for tea at the Ritz. You look as though you could do with a bit of fun.'

He shook his head. 'What are you like?'

She put her head on one side. 'A duchess?'

He felt the same stab of unease that had shot through him when the policeman had mentioned the Russian royal family. He thought it best to shrug it off. Right now an attention-seeking grandmother was not an enticing prospect. 'Just don't push it. We'll go to Brown's, not the Ritz.'

'Cheapskate.'

2

Fairyland

Soft pink . . . borne in large trusses.

'I do wish you wouldn't look so smug.'
Rosie sipped the Earl Grey in the china cup. 'Why shouldn't I? Look, we've even got a tea-strainer.'

'Because you should be ashamed of yourself. Wasting police time.'

'Well, it was all in a good cause.' She sat in the corner of the large chintz sofa, under the towering grandfather clock, looking about her with wide eyes. 'This is nice, isn't it? Classy sort of place. Didn't Agatha Christie set one of her murder mysteries here? I saw it on the box. Lovely costumes.' Her eyes, lively and enquiring, darted around the opulent lounge.

'I think that was Bertram's, not Brown's. Anyway I'm glad you like it. But don't get too used to it.'

'Mmm. Not much chance of that.' She picked up a tiny cucumber sandwich, and popped it into her mouth, whole, chewing it purposefully and scrutinising her surroundings.

'Look at him. Over there.' She gestured towards a small, bespectacled man in a light grey suit. He was systematically putting away the contents of a tiered cakestand, looking around the room from time to time as though he was waiting for someone. 'He looks suspicious. Do you think he's here to meet a lover?'

The reply was impatient. 'I really don't know.'

'Well, he might be. They come in the most unlikely disguises, you know.'

'Who do?'

'Lovers.'

'Like duchesses.'

She avoided his eye, then muttered, mock-absentminded, 'What, love?'

'What were you telling that policeman?'

'Have you finished with the sandwiches? Shall we go on to the cakes?'

'Is this how it's going to be now?'

'How what's going to be, love?' She was examining the cakestand.

'Are you going to carry on being childish?'

She looked hurt. 'That's a bit mean.'

'Is it?'

'Yes. Very. "Childish" is a very mean thing to say.' He saw that her eyes were glistening with tears.

'Oh, don't do that!' He searched his pockets for a handkerchief, found it and handed it to her. 'You know what I mean.'

Rosie blew her nose. 'Oh, yes, I know what you mean. Don't be any trouble. Grow old gracefully. You've had a good life. You're eighty-seven. Why can't you just be a normal granny? The usual stuff.'

'Well, what wrong with that?'

She wiped the tears off her cheeks, and he glimpsed smears of mascara and rouge on the white lawn. 'I'm cross.'

'Why?'

'Oh, I'm fed up – fed up with people.'

'Has Mum been at it again?'

'A bit. But it's not just her.'

'But why the Russian embassy? What do you want to go chaining yourself to railings for? I know you've always had a thing about your mum being left behind, but why bring it all up now?'

'To scare myself.'

'What?'

She blew her nose again. 'To make myself feel as though I'm doing more than just sitting around waiting.' She sniffed. 'That's all it is, really. It's to prove to myself that I can still feel things.'

'Since Granddad?'

She nodded.

Nick reached forward and squeezed her hand. 'I know.'

'I'm glad he's not in pain any more. It wasn't much of a life at the end. But at least he minded. Once. Well . . . I think he did. About me.'

'Of course he did. We all do.'

'Huh! Some more than others.'

'Is that why you didn't ask the police to call Mum or Dad?'

She dabbed her cheek with the handkerchief. 'Not much point was there? Your mum would have given me what for, and your dad wouldn't have been there. No, I wanted you.'

'But you've got to find another way . . . You can't keep getting yourself arrested.'

'It was the first time!'

'You know what I mean.'

'If you mean will I promise I won't be any more trouble, the answer's no.'

'But why should you want to be trouble?'

'Because I want to do something with myself. It's time I had a life.'

'But you've had a life.' As soon as he'd said it he could have bitten out his tongue.

'So, is that it, then? Because I'm eighty-seven I shouldn't have expectations?'

'Well, no, I didn't mean that—'

'Well, what did you mean? I've got a new hip and a new knee. It'd be a crime not to use them.'

'It *is* a crime when you chain them to railings.'

She looked apologetic. 'Well . . . I was upset.'

'That's a blessing. I wouldn't want to think you did it when you were happy.'

'It's just that I don't want to go quietly. To give in. I want to take risks.'

'Like imprisonment?'

She bit her lip, and her eyes brimmed with tears once more. She mopped at them, then sniffed. 'Stupid old woman. I suppose it's hard for you to understand.'

'Not really. In one way, yes, but not in another.' He sat back in his chair. 'I just worry that—'

'That I'm getting dementia? Well, I'm not. At least, I don't think I am. But, then, I don't suppose you realize it when it's happening to you, do you?'

Nick watched as she sipped her tea. She had looked confident in the police station, Nick thought, her eyes shining, enjoying the attention, the thrill of the chase.

Now she looked crestfallen, fearful. He felt guilty: he was responsible for the change in her. He offered an olive branch. 'Tell me about it, then.'

She avoided his eyes. 'About what?'

'This Russian thing.'

'You know perfectly well what it's about.' She picked up another tiny sandwich, nibbled the corner, then finished it.

He spoke gently. 'The policeman said something about the royal family.'

She looked vague. 'Did he?'

'Can you remember what you said to him?'

'I have perfect recall.'

'Well?'

'Not telling you now. Wrong time. Wrong place. One day. When I'm ready.' She eyed the cakestand again and settled on an elaborate cream horn. 'That'll put me right.' She began to dissect it. 'I know what you're thinking,' she murmured, through a mouthful of pastry, 'but I can't be bothered what people think any more. It doesn't really matter.'

'Why?'

'Because people think what the newspapers and the television tell them to think. And, anyway, it's all geared to people under forty. Thirty, even. Get to my age and they think all you want to watch is *Countdown* and repeats of *Miss Marple*. I can remember all the endings, you know.'

'So you do watch them?'

'Only once.' She snapped the end off the cream horn. 'Most of the time people just patronize you.'

'No!'

'Oh, yes, they do. They only want to help you across the street because it makes them feel better. Last week I was standing on the pavement looking at some may blossom. It was so pretty, but before I knew it I was half-way across the road with this man gripping me by the arm and booming in my ear. They treat you as though you're educationally subnormal. And deaf – they always shout at you. And I'm not deaf. Or daft.'

'No,' he said, with feeling.

She was warming to her theme now, and the cream horn was yielding to the pressure of a pastry fork. 'The trouble is, you get used to it. You do! You begin to believe that you *are* past it. You start acting like a child because you're expected to, and before you know it you've given up. It's a slippery slope.

'Take that over-sixties club I went to. What a waste of time. Arguing over the teapot, painting Christmas cards. Being fawned over. Heavens! There's more to life than that. I was twenty years older than most of them and I ended up running round after them – picking up their paints, passing them their coats, taking them to the toilet. It was like being back at school. No, thank you. I've still got a brain – what's left of it – and I still have opinions, but they don't seem to count any more. Who cares what I think?'

'I do.'

She looked at him suspiciously. 'Do you? Do you really?'

'Yes.'

'Even if it means being embarrassed?'

Nick leaned forward. 'I'd prefer to avoid that bit but, on the whole, yes, even if it means being embarrassed.'

Her face brightened. 'So will you help me?'

'Help you with what?'

'To live a bit.'

13

Her request took him by surprise. It seemed so innocent and plaintive. 'Well, I don't know . . .'

'I won't be a burden. I don't want to take over your life or anything. I just need a bit of support. Encouragement, I suppose.'

'I'll try.'

She smiled weakly. 'I know it must look like attention-seeing, but it's not that. It's just . . .'

He raised an eyebrow.

'What?'

She sighed. 'Do you know that Peggy Lee song, "Is That All There Is"?'

He nodded.

'Well, I suppose I just want to keep dancing a bit longer. That's all.'

Nick put his arm round her and squeezed her gently. She smelt faintly of Chanel No. 5. Not like a granny at all.

He eased away and looked into her shimmering eyes. 'Well, no more chaining yourself to railings. Promise?'

She hesitated, then saw him raise his eyebrows in waning. 'I promise. Anyway, I only had the one chain and they cut that. It was your granddad's.' She looked thoughtful. 'I did think about throwing eggs, but that would have been wasteful. Anyway, I'd run out.'

'Thank God.' He sat back in his chair. 'And this Russian thing. You'll talk to me about it when you're ready?'

'Yes. When I'm ready. I never told your dad when he was little. I was waiting until he was older but then I knew there was no point. He was always a bit . . . well . . .'

'Cynical?'

'Yes. No imagination – except when he's dreaming he can make a fortune on some hare-brained scheme or a horse. I told him his grandmother was Russian and that she stayed behind during the revolution when I was brought over here, but that's all. I never told him any more. I've never told anyone. Stands to reason, doesn't it? No one would have believed me.'

'Why not?'

'Not now. Later, when there's more time. And, anyway, there are other things I want to do as well.'

'What sort of things?' Nick asked uneasily.

'Things that nobody else has thought of. Like Marks and Spencer.'

'What?'

She hunched forward conspiratorially. 'I've had this brilliant idea. If Marks and Spencer change the labels on all their clothes, marking them as a size smaller than they really are, more people would shop there.'

'I'm sorry?'

She sighed impatiently. 'You're so slow. Think about it. Women don't like to think they're fat. They want to be a size eight, and most of them are a size ten – or more. All M&S have to do is change the labels on their clothes and then the size-ten women will be able to fit into a size eight.' She glanced about her to make sure they were not overheard, then carried on: 'Stands to reason that Mrs Smith will keep going back there, rather than to Next or Laura Ashley, because she feels better about herself in clothes from M&S.'

'Are you serious?'

'Of course I'm serious.'

'But that would be illegal, wouldn't it?'

'I don't see why. It would if you marked a twenty-eight-inch waist as twenty-six – Trade Descriptions and all that –

but who's to say how big a size eight, ten or sixteen is? Come to think of it,' she went on reflectively, 'maybe they should mark them down two sizes. Imagine a size-sixteen woman suddenly being able to fit into a twelve. Ha! Mind you, if I write and tell them, I don't expect I shall hear anything. Next thing you know they'll be doing it and won't pay me a penny.'

Nick gaped at her.

'Shut your mouth, dear, or you'll catch a fly.' She winked. 'Cakes all gone. Shall we make a move?'

3

Richmond

Very hardy.

As they walked down the street in Richmond towards his grandmother's block of flats with the bare front garden she clung tightly to his arm. 'Come in for a while?'

Nick looked at his watch. 'Just for a few minutes. I have to catch the ferry back to the island.'

'Aah! Doesn't that sound lovely? Almost like an adventure.'

Nick smiled. 'I suppose it does. I still like crossing the water to go home. Makes it a bit special.'

'Yes. And I've always liked the Isle of Wight. Ever since that holiday when you were little.'

'It's a bit quiet now.'

'Oh? I'd have thought it would have been busier than it was.'

'No. I mean quieter for me.'

Rosie looked at him enquiringly.

'Debs has gone.'

She stopped walking. 'What? But you'd been together such a long time.'

'Three years.'

'Oh, love! I'm so sorry.'

'Thanks.' He tried to sound noncommittal.

'What was it? You or her?'

'An estate agent, actually.'

'No!'

''Fraid so.' He sounded pathetic, he thought, and tried to inject a more positive note into his voice. 'But I think it had run its course. Just one of those things.'

'And you feel OK?'

'Marvellous. Raring to go.'

Rosie studied him. 'Really?'

'Yes.'

'Mmm. Not sure I believe you.'

He shrugged. 'Suit yourself.'

'Oh, I will,' she countered. 'Huh. Never liked estate agents. Too smug by half. Wearing cufflinks during the day.' She took his arm and started walking again. 'Was it a shock?'

'Well, it was a bit of a surprise. I thought we were . . . comfortable.'

'I always think that's dangerous.'

'What do you mean?'

'Being comfortable can mean being taken for granted.'

'But you and Granddad were comfortable.'

'Yes, but we'd been married nearly fifty years.'

'So you think I should have carried on playing the field?'

'Well, not exactly – but you could have made her aware of how lucky she was.'

'And how would I have done that?'

'Oh, it's not easy, keeping a relationship fresh, but there are little tricks you can use.'

'Like what?'

Rosie stopped at the kerb, looked right and left, then steered him across the road. Only when they had mounted the opposite pavement did she continue. 'Well, whenever you meet someone who flirts with you, it's no bad thing to let your partner see. I don't mean you have to be unfaithful – nothing as strong as that – but it does no harm for them to be aware that you're attractive to others.'

'Listen to you! You sound like an agony aunt in a teen-mag.'

'Do I?'

'Yes.'

'I wonder if they'd like me to do that. I could write and offer my services. Plenty of experience.'

'You could put it in the post with the letter to Marks and Spencer.'

She elbowed him in the ribs.

'Well, honestly!' he exclaimed.

'Your trouble is that you always undersell yourself,' she told him.

'I'm a realist.'

'No, you're not. You're an apologist.'

'That's a big word.'

'Well, you're a big boy. Look at you – six foot what?'

'And a bit.'

'Good-looking, in a crooked sort of way.'

'Careful!'

'Well, no, you are – you're not George Clooney, but you've got a lovely smile and all your own hair.'

19

Nick winced. 'What is this? Are you starting up a dating agency?'

'Now, there's a thought . . .'

'Don't go there!'

'All right. Too much paperwork anyway. But you're not a bad catch and you're only in your thirties . . .'

'Just coming up for the final year.'

'Oh, yes. I nearly forgot. Still, you needn't worry. People leave it much longer now before they get married. Most don't seem to bother. And if you get someone younger you've still time to have children. Mind you, you'll be sixty-odd when they leave home.'

'If you've quite finished planning my life for me . . .'

She looked up at him, winked and tugged at his arm. 'Sorry. I suppose I'm just an interfering old granny.' She smiled.

'But you mean well.' He smiled back.

'Don't say that! It's the worst possible thing to have written on your tombstone, that is! "She meant well".'

'Better than the reverse.' He was laughing now.

'Maybe. Where's Debs now?' Evidently Rosie felt it was time to move on.

'In the States. She flew out this morning. With her estate agent.'

'Oh. He covers a pretty big area, then?'

'Foreign properties.'

'What do you think he'd describe her as? A country seat or a *pied à terre*?'

'You're incorrigible.'

'Oh, I do hope I am . . . So what now?' she asked.

'I don't know. But I don't want to sit on my arse – sorry,

bum – thinking about it. I'm painting like a lunatic. Trying to get on. You know.'

'You need me to sort you out.'

'I thought *I* was sorting *you* out.'

'Bit of a joint venture, then.'

She let go of his arm and rummaged in her handbag for the key. 'It's in here somewhere.'

'Let me.' He held out his hand for the bag and she shot him a withering look.

'It's the light, not my sight.' She fished out a pair of glasses, put them on and continued to delve into the depths of the cavernous crocodile bag until, triumphantly, she located the key and slipped it into the lock. 'I hate this door. It's so heavy.' She pressed her small frame against it and pushed.

'Here, let me.' Nick hauled the door open. It *was* heavy, even for him.

'How we're expected to cope with that spring I don't know. Like a prison.'

It was certainly different from the house where Nick's grandparents had lived when he was a child. Until widowhood had forced Rosie into a flat, her home had been a modest Victorian terraced house in Cheltenham, but inside it was neither the rebellious teak-filled home of Second World War veterans nor an antiquated Edwardian emporium furnished with chintz and a reproduction of Constable's *The Haywain* on the wall. Instead the walls were barley white and peppered with bright prints and some of Nick's early paintings. His grandmother had bought them from him – for as much as she could afford – when he was starting out. He had tried to refuse the money, but she had insisted, and pressed on him a ten-pound note here, a twenty there, right through art school. The floors were polished boards, part covered with Indian rugs, bright throws to disguise the time-worn upholstery of the sofas. Nick had always liked it.

His grandfather had been easy-going about Rosie's taste: she had been the arty one, and he had deferred to that. He had been content to spend his retirement from the insurance company with the *Daily Telegraph* and the television. Then a stroke had robbed him of movement and speech, and confined him to hospital. Rosie had visited him twice a day for four years, until he had slipped away one evening while she was at home having supper.

She had wanted to stay in the family house, but Nick's mother had insisted it was too large and Cheltenham too far away. Rosie, normally strong-willed enough to stand up for herself, had allowed herself, in the wake of her bereavement, to be moved into a flat in a small, purpose-built block, where her daughter-in-law could keep an eye on her. It was a grudging arrangement on both sides, and while it brought Rosie closer to her immediate family, it distanced her from her friends. When she had finally begun to pick up the threads of her life, she had realized her mistake, but by then it was too late. London was not really Rosie's bag.

'Funny folk round here. Never look at you when you're going down the street. Never say hello. And they don't walk round you, they walk through you.'

Nick watched her hang up her coat and adjust her hair in the mirror, then turn on the lamps in the sitting room, draw the curtains and walk through to the kitchen. Her kitchen had always been painted primrose yellow, and the biscuit barrel from which his grandfather had fed him

Bourbons sat in the middle of the table.

'Coffee?' she asked, filling the kettle.

'Just a quick one.'

'Always a quick one. Why are you in such a hurry?'

'I told you. The ferry.'

'But they run all night don't they?'

'Not quite.'

She squinted at her watch. 'Well, you've plenty of time. It's only a quarter to five.'

'I suppose so.'

She made the coffee, then deftly collected cups and saucers from the dresser.

The events of the day caused him to look at her more critically than usual. Nobody would take her for eighty-seven. Sixty-seven, maybe, or seventy – but not three years short of ninety. She had always been Rosie to him, at her own insistence, never Granny. She was tough and self-sufficient. Eccentric, too, but always grounded. Realistic. Was she finally losing her grip?

Caring for his grandfather must have taken it out of her. Oh, the hospital had done the lion's share of the work, but she had been there for three or four hours every day without fail.

He pulled out a pine chair from the small breakfast table, sat down and looked around the new kitchen. The flat was more sparsely furnished than the house had been and seemed less her home than a staging-post – but there were always flowers: today a handful of dried lavender poked out of a painted jug and scarlet tulips swallow-dived from a square glass vase on the fitted worktop. Nick remembered the painted dresser filled with willow-pattern plates. They'd all gone now.

'Will you stay here?' he asked, curiosity getting the better of him.

'No.'

The answer came so quickly and so decisively that it surprised him. 'Why?'

'Because I hate it. It's awful. And, anyway, I don't need . . . things.'

'What sort of things?'

'Oh, you know – stuff. Possessions.' She brought the cups and saucers to the table. Carelessly. Almost as if she resented them.

'But where will you go?'

'I don't know yet. Maybe back to Cheltenham.'

'But you know what they say about the three most traumatic things in life?'

'I do. Death, divorce and moving house.'

'Well?'

'The first can't happen and the second two already have.' She dropped two spoons into the saucers.

'Rosie, I'm not sure it's wise. Not at—'

'Don't say it! Bugger being wise.'

He had hardly ever heard her swear, and she always told him off when he did.

'If I stay here I'll just sulk and fade away. Let's be honest. I probably haven't long to go.'

'Don't say that.'

She leaned on the back of a chair and the piercing eyes fixed him. 'Now who's not being realistic?'

'It's just that—'

'You don't want to admit it.'

'No.'

'All right, then, we won't talk about it again, so long as

you don't try to wrap me in cotton wool.'

'I don't think I could.'

'Dead right, mister.'

'Normal grannies don't talk like that.'

'Well, I'm not a normal granny.'

He left her at six, and as he kissed her on both cheeks at the door of her flat, he noticed the photograph on a side table. The one that used to be by her bed. The one in the silver frame. It was a sepia-toned portrait of a girl with dark hair, fine features and a clear complexion. A girl whose eyes seemed to shine through the winter cold. She stood in snow, which powdered the front of her high-buttoned coat. A pale scarf was wrapped round her neck, and her mouth was open a little, as if she was catching her breath in the ice-cold winter air. She stood to the left of a small boy in a thick, barathea sailor suit, and a bearded man in a military uniform who was holding a spade that had been used to clear snow. Behind them, the tapering trunks of birch trees stood out against a white sky.

'She's still here, then.'

Rosie turned and picked up the photograph. 'Mama? Oh, yes. She always is. Doesn't she look lovely?'

'She does.'

Rosie replaced the photograph. 'We'll talk about it soon.'

'I'll call you. I can get back next week, if that's OK?'

'Fine.'

As he walked down the stairs she called after him, 'You're not too cross with me, are you?'

'You're not very easy to be cross with.' Then he opened the door and disappeared with a wave.

*

Rosie shut the door. 'But I think you might be soon,' she whispered. She looked again at the photograph and ran her hand over the woman, who was standing in the snow with her father and younger brother.

4

Rose du Roi

Sometimes classified as a Hybrid Perpetual.

The northern coast of the Isle of Wight is divided into two by the Medina river. The eastern half looks towards Portsmouth and Hayling Island, and the western towards Lymington and Dorset. A few miles west of Cowes, between Gurnard and Thorness Bay, there is a craggy, crumbling stretch of coastline opposite the Beaulieu river. Cattle graze the pale green undulating meadows, which slope backwards from the cliff, and ancient wheelless railway carriages in duck-egg blue and tarry black, dusky maroon and peeling white are tucked under wind-grizzled sycamores and garlanded with honeysuckle and bindweed. Once they provided holidays for cash-strapped mainland families. Now all but a handful are derelict, their broken windows allowing access to new families, of robins, wrens and blackbirds.

A snaking pathway cuts its way along the coastline

below them, between banks of blackthorn and quickthorn, brambles and gorse. In winter the salt-laden winds rip through the undergrowth, and heavy rains wash swathes of the greasy grey clay into the waters of the Solent below. In summer, the hedgerows are wreathed in dog-roses and bryony, and clouded yellow butterflies flit over clover and vetches while the song thrush sings in the twisted trees.

For five years, Nick Robertson had lived in a clapboard cottage perched on the top of this bare patch of coastline, just about making a living from painting watercolours and selling them through a local gallery.

His grandmother had impinged rarely on his life. He called her on the phone every week or so, and she would ask how things were going with the painting and his love life – she was never backward in coming forward and always spoke her mind.

His mother, Anna, having raised her three children – Alice, now married and living in South Africa, Sophie, single and travelling in South America, and Nick, the arty one who studied at St Martin's and then decided to 'do his own thing' – was doing an Open University degree in medieval history, and worked at her local library. 'It's my time now,' she had told her family, and proceeded to live an almost independent life. After the children had gone, she had told her husband she wanted out. He surprised her by saying that so did he, then upped and left. Rosie had not been pleased.

Derek Robertson was known to most people outside the family as 'a bit of a lad'. His wife used less endearing terms to describe him. After a moderately successful spell in the City he had cashed in his chips and devoted himself to the turf – often with surprising success. The *Racing Post* was his daily paper, and when he wasn't placing bets on horses, he took a chance on anything vaguely entrepreneurial that came his way. From time to time there were disasters, but Derek was one of those people, said his mother, who would land in a bed of clover if he fell out of the sky.

His flat in Chelsea Harbour suited him nicely, and he could just about keep it going during the winning streaks, which usually came in the nick of time. He loved his daughters, did his best to understand his son, and enjoyed the wheeler-dealer life.

Which explained why, when Rosie was in trouble, she called on Nick, the one member of her family whom she knew she could always contact and would get her out of a spot. Her relations with her son were good-natured but sporadic, and with her daughter-in-law, frosty and matter-of-fact.

Nick sat in his studio gazing at the sea, today the colour of pewter and merging with the sky. The north island – the locals' disparaging name for the mainland – had disappeared from view, as if it didn't exist. He liked the feeling of being cut off. As he was now – in more ways than one.

The parting from Debs had been surprisingly low key. Hollow, even. She had brushed her hand across his cheek and thanked him, almost as if he was a friend rather than a lover. By then the anger had been voiced and the tears shed.

He didn't expect her to call, so when the phone rang he assumed it would be the gallery, enquiring about the paintings that were due for the start of the season, or the garage to say that his van was ready.

It was neither. It was his mother. 'Nick?'

'Hi.'

'Have you seen the paper?'

'Which one?'

'The *Richmond and Twickenham Times*.'

'We don't get it on the Isle of Wight.'

'There's no need to be sarcastic. The front page is plastered with pictures of your grandmother chained to some railings. Do you know about this?'

'Well . . . yes.'

'And you didn't tell me?'

'Well . . . no.'

'Why not, for God's sake?'

'Because I knew you'd be furious.'

'I am! What was she playing at? The Russian embassy, for God's sake! She's not started all that again, has she?'

'All what?'

'About her mother being wronged by the Bolsheviks.'

'What do you know about it?'

'She's clearly not fit to be on her own any more!'

'Oh, come on, Mum. That's a bit much. She looked after Granddad until his stroke.'

'Well, clearly she can't look after herself. And your father's no help.'

'Have you rung him?'

'Don't be ridiculous. Anyway, he'd just laugh.'

'Yes,' Nick agreed ruefully.

'Well, I'm going round there today to find out what it's all about.'

'Don't do that – you'll only upset her.'

'Too right I'll upset her. She has to know that she just can't do this sort of thing.'

He could visualize Anna at the other end of the phone: the grey mane held back with a black velvet alice band, the finely plucked eyebrows, the pearls, the black pashmina draped round her shoulders, the Jaeger tweed skirt and the black tights. 'Just leave it to me, Mum.'

'But what can you do, over there?'

'I can come over. I've already been once, as it is.'

'It's May. Aren't you up to your ears in painting?'

'Well, yes, but . . .'

'I must sort this out before she embarrasses us even more. Thank God I use my maiden name on the OU course. At least nobody will guess I'm related to her.'

'That's not a very nice thing to say.'

'What she did was not a very nice thing to do. I'm going to get some brochures about nursing homes.'

'But she's not ill!'

'Maybe not physically, but you can't tell me she's all there mentally. It will have to be sheltered accommodation at the very least.'

'Look, don't do anything yet. I'll talk to her.'

'It won't make any difference.'

'At least let me try.'

After a few more placatory remarks he put the phone down. It rang again, almost immediately, and the pompous voice at the other end made him smile.

'By my elegant little Cartier watch it's forty-eight minutes past the hour of eleven, which means that you are now exactly eighteen minutes late. As it takes a good half-hour to get to my little gallery in Seaview from your shack in the back-of-beyond that means I shall not see you until lunchtime. Do I take it that you'll be requiring refreshments?'

'Henry Kinross Fine Art' was to be found at the top of a

short flight of worn stone steps by the slipway that sloped down to the sea. It had once been a boathouse, but the bitumen-painted feather-edged boards were now a delicate shade of eau-de-Nil, and scallop shells had been fixed in a double row on either side of the door. As Nick opened it, the bell pinged loudly. The gallery owner was holding a dreary seascape and frowning at it through half-moon spectacles. 'Look at this! Drive a man to drink. Or a couple of Nurofen.'

Nick glanced at the picture. 'Mmm.'

'Typically noncommittal.'

'Well, what do you want me to say? That it's crap?'

'It would be accurate.'

Henry Kinross was not a small man. He had a sizeable belly, short legs, and the sort of face that looked as though someone had sat on it. His hair was grey, his cheeks the colour of a Victoria plum, and his voice refined with years of claret. The painting would have been crushed into matchwood had he clenched his fat fists. Instead, he laid it on the white-painted table in the centre of the room and took off his glasses. 'Time you got a new motor.'

'They reckon they've fixed it this time.'

'Serves you right for buying British. Why don't you get yourself a reliable foreign car?'

Nick ignored the jibe. 'Do you want me to bring them in?'

Henry waved at the blank wall at one end of the gallery. 'It'll look pretty bare if you don't. How many have you got?'

'About a dozen.' Nick propped open the door and began to carry in the framed watercolours.

'Wonderful. That should keep me going for a couple of weeks.'

'God! Longer than that, I hope. I'm not a machine.'

'Bloody artistic temperament. You'll never make your fortune at this rate. John Piper could turn them out much faster.'

'John Piper had had more practice.'

'Ah, yes, but you have better luck with the weather.'

Henry began to line up the paintings against the wall. 'No gratitude, that's your trouble. Not everyone sells like you do, you know. Look at old what's-his-face.' He nodded in the direction of the grey seascape. 'That'll never shift. Too depressing.'

'Accurate, though,' Nick told him.

'If people want accuracy they can take a photograph.'

'Maybe mine will start to get a bit more dreary now.'

'Ah.' Henry put down with the others the painting he was carrying and straightened, with some effort. 'She's gone, then?'

Nick nodded.

'And you're feeling sorry for yourself.'

'Guess so.'

'Mmm. I know the feeling. Can't say I blame you. She was a nice girl.'

'I don't need reminding.'

'I suppose not. But you probably need cheering up.'

'Oh, I wouldn't bother if I were you, Henry. Bit of a lost cause at the moment.'

'Well, let's change the subject or I shall be put off my lunch, and I don't remember the last time that happened.' He stood back to take in the row of Nick's paintings – some large, some small. 'I like that one – good sky. And the Needles. I can sell those little bits of white rock as fast as you can paint them. Where's the church?'

'Shalfleet.'

'Oh, yes. Dumpy tower. "The Shalfleet poor and simple people, Sold the bells to build the steeple."'

'It hasn't got a steeple.'

'It fell to bits. Waste of time selling the bells, if you ask me.' He wrinkled his nose. 'Not a bad lot, Mr Robertson. Well up to par.'

'Thank you.'

'Oh dear, oh dear. Come on. Let's get out of here and into some food. Starving artist and all that.'

'I'm not hungry.'

'Well, I am, so you'll just have to watch me. Come and have a glass at least.'

Henry prodded Nick across the road and into the bar of the Red Duster. He ordered a bottle of the house red and two glasses. They planted themselves, on Henry's instructions, at a table just opposite the door. 'Cheers, old bean! First of the day.' Henry took a gulp of wine and sighed with satisfaction. 'Oh, little grape, how great thou art! Now, then . . . we'll wait to order food. Someone else is joining us.'

'Oh?'

'Artist. Wants me to take her stuff. I'm interested to know what you think.'

'What – here? In the pub?'

'No. Thought you'd like to meet her first and then we'll go back and look at her paintings.'

'No fear.'

'What do you mean?'

'I'm happy to meet her, Henry, but I'm not going to sit in judgement on her stuff – certainly not in front of her. One artist criticizing another?'

'That's all you lot ever do, isn't it?'

'In private, maybe, but not to each other's faces.'

'Suit yourself.'

The uneasy silence that might have followed was pre-empted by an almighty clatter outside the pub. All conversation stopped, and there was a general movement towards the door. Nick and Henry were first on to the pavement, followed by the barman and a couple of local builders.

'Bloody 'ell.' One of the builders had summed up the scene neatly, if not with clinical accuracy. In front of them, where earlier Nick's Morris Minor van had sat by the pavement, was a hybrid vehicle, half Morris, half Fiat, with no visible distinction between the two.

A dark-haired girl was sitting at the wheel of the Fiat, her head in her hands. Nick tried to open the car door but it refused to budge. He ran round to the other side and tugged at the passenger door, which yielded. 'Are you all right?'

The girl lowered her hands.

'It's OK. Don't worry. Come on, let me help you get out.'

She gazed at him apologetically. 'It was my brakes.' Then she began to shake.

'Best get her out,' offered Henry.

'Yes, come on. Can you slide across?'

She swivelled her denim-covered legs across the passenger seat and got out on to the pavement. She was slight, about thirty. Her long dark hair had been pinned back, but was now falling over her face – fine-boned and olive-skinned, but pale with shock. He put his arm round her to steady her. The baggy pink and white sailing shirt she wore made her appear waif-like, as though a sea breeze might blow her away.

'I tried to stop, but nothing happened,' she said.

Nick glanced at the fused vehicles. 'No.'

'God, what a mess!' said Henry, and the girl burst into tears.

'Thank you, Henry. We can see that.'

Nick eyed his van and realized that their long association was at an end. Then he looked at the Fiat. Not much hope there, either. In the back of the car, he spotted a tangled mixture of blankets and canvas, and grasped that the girl must be the artist Henry had been so keen for him to meet.

'Come inside,' he said to her. 'Let's get you a drink.'

By the time they had walked through the door of the pub and sat down at the table, a large Scotch had appeared courtesy of the barman. But the girl shook her head. 'Just water, please. Tap.' She reached into her pocket for a tissue, pushed back her hair from her eyes and tried to smile. 'What a way to start.'

'Do you feel OK?' asked Henry. 'No bones broken?'

'I don't think so. Just a bit stiff.' She wiped her eyes with the tissue and thanked the barman for the water.

Henry took a gulp of his wine. 'I think I'm going to need this.'

'I don't know what state my paintings will be in.'

'Don't worry,' said Nick, 'we'll sort them out later.'

'What about the cars?' asked the barman. 'Shall I call the Old Bill?'

'Not unless you want to?' Nick directed his question at the girl.

'But whose is the van?' she asked.

'Mine.'

'You'll want to claim on your insurance.'

Nick shook his head. 'I wish. The garage told me this morning that she was on borrowed time. I think she's just passed away. Not worth losing my no claims. But what about yours?'

'Same.'

'Shall we just call the breakdown truck to clear them away, then?'

'Are we allowed to?'

'Don't see why not. If we're quick.'

Within an hour the only trace of the collision was a scattering of dried mud and a bucketful of broken glass on the road. Passers-by had been hurried along, and the police – who were probably busy on the congested Newport Road – had failed to put in an appearance.

Henry never did get his lunch. Instead, he helped salvage the paintings from the Fiat, and carried them into the gallery.

It was a good half-hour before Nick discovered the identity of the girl who had written off his dear old van. Her name was Alexandra Pollen.

5

Alchymist

Black spot can be troublesome.

She turned out to be nothing like as frail as he had thought. But, then, you can't make judgements about anyone's character on the basis of having pulled them out of a crumpled car.

Over tea in the back room she explained that she'd discovered Henry's gallery the previous year on a day trip to the island. She had thought he might like some stuff that wasn't run-of-the-mill, and that her oils might be just that. She'd been confident enough to win Henry over on the phone, but he had warned her that anything too esoteric was unlikely to sell.

Nick admired her nerve, if not her paintings. They were vivid and simplistic, not at all his style, but they did have a raw energy.

'Can you sell them, do you think?' she asked Henry.

'Well, there's only one way to find out.' He looked across

at Nick. 'What do you think?'

'I told you, I never comment in public on another artist's work.'

'But as you're here . . .'

Nick did his best not to glare at Henry for putting him in such a position. 'I think they're . . . exhilarating.'

Alex wasn't fooled. 'Diplomatic,' she said wryly.

Nick shrugged.

'Well, I can't expect everyone to like them. But I'll be happy enough if you'll give them a go, Henry.'

The remaining conversation was polite. Then it was time for Alex to leave, and the question arose as to how that might be achieved.

'Well, I'd run you to the ferry, dear, except that I don't drive,' said Henry. 'Not since the, er . . .' He nodded at a bottle of claret on the desk. 'What about you?' he asked Nick.

'I'd better hire a car . . . until I can do better.'

'I'm so sorry,' Alex said.

'There's no need. You probably just moved things on a bit.'

The greater truth of his statement quite escaped him.

A call to a friendly local garage resulted in a car being delivered to the gallery within the hour, and Nick dropped Alex at the Wight-Link ferry terminal at Fishbourne. 'Where's home?' he asked.

'Portsmouth.'

'Handy.'

'Very. That's why I wasn't too worried about getting home. I can walk from the ferry at the other side.'

She got out of the car, then leaned in through the

driver's window and smiled. 'Thank you for being so good about the car. I really don't know what to say.'

'Don't worry.'

'Just in case you change your mind.' She handed him a piece of paper on which, in italic script, she had written her name, address and telephone number. 'I expect we'll meet again soon. I like coming over to the island.'

He motored home, deep in thought, considering an Austin A30 – and Alexandra Pollen. He was not considering Rosie. Until he saw her standing in the doorway of his house.

'What the . . .' He leaped out of the car and strode up to her. 'What are you doing here?'

'Getting away.'

'From what?'

'Your mother.'

'What do you mean?'

'She came round this morning. Did you tell her?'

'I didn't tell her anything. It was in the local paper.'

'Damn.'

'Well, it's not surprising, is it?'

'Wants to put me in a home. Told me, there and then. Even had some brochures with her. I mean, I ask you!'

Nick looked at her, laden with a small suitcase and two carrier-bags. 'How have you managed?'

'I got a taxi – both ends.'

Nick unloaded her. 'Come on. Let's get you inside.'

Rosie glanced down the path to the road. 'Where's the van?'

'In a scrapyard somewhere near Bembridge.'

'Oh dear. Has it finally given up? Never mind – perhaps you can get a sports car now instead.'

'Will you stop changing the subject?' He fumbled in his pocket for the key, and ushered her in.

Over tea and biscuits the story tumbled out. 'She didn't even ask if I was all right.'

'I don't suppose she needed to.'

'Didn't care, more like.'

'Oh, now, stop feeling sorry for yourself.'

'I'm not. I'm just cross.'

'Well, you know what Mum's like.'

'Huh. Only ever worries about herself and about what her friends will think.'

'That's not quite true.'

'Doesn't worry about me.'

'And neither is that.'

Rosie looked at him pleadingly. 'But to put me away!'

'She doesn't want to put you away, she wants to make sure you're taken care of. That's all.'

'Dreadful expression! Taken care of! Makes me sound senile. Just so that I don't get in her way.'

Nick realized this particular conversation was going nowhere. 'Why have you come here?'

'Because you're the only person I can trust.'

He smiled. 'You sound like a secret agent.'

'Mmm.' She paused. 'That would be fun.'

He shot her a look.

'I thought it might be a bit of a break,' she went on. 'Do me good. A spot of sea air. There isn't much of that in Richmond.'

'Have you booked somewhere?'

'No.'

'Where will you stay, then?'

Rosie looked about her.

'Oh, Rosie! There's no space.'

'There's the little bedroom.'

'But it's full of painting stuff, and it's tiny.'

'You'll hardly know I'm here – and it won't be for long, just till I get myself organized.'

Nick could think of a million reasons why it wouldn't work, and why he really ought to put Rosie into the car right now and drive round the island until they found a reasonably priced hotel that would take her for a week or two.

'I can cook for you while you're painting. I won't get in the way.'

'It's not that I don't want you here, it's just that, well . . . it's not really big enough for two.'

'But you lived here with Debs.'

'That was different.'

'You mean you loved her . . .'

'Yes. No. I mean . . . it's not the same.' But when he looked into her eyes he knew he had lost: she wasn't going anywhere. And he was, as she had known he would be, a soft touch.

He sighed. 'I'd better clear out the little bedroom.' He bent down and kissed her cheek.

'Thank you, sweetheart. You're a life-saver. And it's just till I get sorted. Then I'll be out of your hair.' She squeezed his hand and walked over to the window. 'What a wonderful view.' Then she turned round to face him. 'What a lark, eh?'

Many things might have happened over the next few days: she might have irritated the pants off him; she might have been demanding in her requests for food, drink and entertainment; she might have fussed over him and driven him mad. In the event, she did none of these.

Over the first day she observed him at work and noted his *modus operandi*. By day three he worried that he was not looking after her enough. She had breakfast just after he did, then washed up and put away the china. Then she pulled on a pair of soft boots and a windcheater and went out. He didn't see her again until early evening when she joined him for supper. The conversation was pleasant, and she was not inquisitive, as though she were on her best behaviour. She went to bed early.

He was concerned about her walking along the cliff unaided, so he bought her a stick. She was indignant, until he explained that all proper walkers carried one like this, a modified ski pole. Then to his relief, she grudgingly accepted it.

By day four he was nervous of her amenability, and over supper he pushed her a bit. 'Are you managing?'

'Yes, thanks. Are you?'

'Yes. Surprisingly.'

She unwrapped a Nuttall's Mintoe and popped it into her mouth. 'You see, I told you I wouldn't be much trouble. And I'm not, am I?'

'Not so far, no.'

'Hmph!'

He avoided asking when she thought she would go back. It was only three days, after all. 'Have you got enough clothes and things?'

'Oh, yes. I think so. I thought I might have a bit of an expedition, though. Get myself some new bits for the summer. There's some nice sailing stuff in Cowes.'

He grinned at her. 'Don't tell me you're thinking of going sailing.'

'Oh, yes. I've booked the course.'

He nearly choked on his coffee. 'What?'

She rolled the peppermint around in her mouth. 'At the sailing academy.' She saw the look on his face. 'It's for five days.'

'But you—'

'They've had older people than me doing it. The man said so.' She noted his look of wide-eyed astonishment but carried on, savouring the moment. 'I've always fancied getting out on the water, but your Granddad never liked it, so we never did.'

'No.' He was staring at her, astonished.

'Only little dinghies. Toppers, I think they're called. Quite fast, though.'

'Yes.'

'Should be all right as long as I can remember to keep my head down.'

His jaw dropped.

'Catching flies again?' she asked.

He closed his mouth hastily. 'You crack me up. You really do.'

'What a lovely thing to say. I must remember that.' As she went towards her room he heard her chuckle to herself, then murmur, 'You crack me up, you really do!'

Between his concern for his grandmother, his need to complete more paintings, his thoughts of Debs and a new van, Alex kept drifting into his mind. He toyed with calling her. To see if she was all right? To ask her out for supper? No. There was too much to think about without that.

And so he found himself staring at the grey Austin A30 van in the second-hand car dealer's yard in Newport. He liked old vans: they were characterful and practical: you could get a lot of paintings into the back. Difficult in a sports car. That was what Rosie wanted him to buy, of course. Something more racy. He shook his head, and felt a little embarrassed that it was he who was unadventurous while his grandmother was the fast lady.

''Sgoin' for a song, mate. Only twelve 'undred quid.'

'Twelve hundred?'

''Sa collector's item, that is.'

'What sort? A debt collector?'

'Discerning.'

'Well, maybe I'm not discerning enough.'

'Suit yerself. It'll go.'

'But not to me.'

He cursed himself on the way home for being pathetic and indecisive. And for being walked over, first by Debs and then by Rosie. It was time he put his foot down. But how could he? He couldn't simply turn her out. She might look a tough old bird, but he had seen her moved to tears in the last week, and he didn't want to dash her spirits when she seemed to be on the mend.

He turned into the gravel path at the front of his cottage. 'The Anchorage', said the small slate sign. He couldn't help thinking that, as far as Rosie was concerned, the name was appropriate.

He walked along the veranda at the front of the house, between the forest of bright green montbretia leaves, and glanced into the tiny boxroom next to the front door. It was the one place where he could tuck a computer, without it taking over the place. The desk lamp was turned on, and Rosie was hunched over the keyboard.

Nick let himself in through the front door and poked his head into the little room. 'What are you doing?'

Rosie almost leaped out of the chair. 'You made me jump!'

He glanced at the screen, and then at his grandmother. 'When did you learn how to use a computer?'

'At night-school when your granddad was ill. It took my mind off things.'

'You didn't say.'

'Well, I don't have to tell you everything I do.'

'Of course not. Sorry.'

Then she said brightly, 'I've found you a car.'

'What?'

'A new car. I've found one on the Internet.'

'What? An Austin A30 van?'

'Don't be ridiculous. It's an MG.'

Nick sighed. 'But I don't want an MG. You can't get pictures into an MG.'

'Yes, you can. You can have a special rack on the boot lid over the spare tyre. I've checked. And, anyway, your pictures are quite small. Most of them would fit in the footwell at the front.'

'What about when it rains?'

She looked at him through narrowed eyes. 'It does have a hood, you know.'

There was nothing for it but to look over her shoulder at the advert on the screen.

'You see?' she said. 'Perfect. Very sporty. Bit of fun. Take you out of yourself.'

'I thought it was you we were taking out of yourself?'

'Oh, don't worry about me. Just a minute – I'll print it off.' And then, evidently fearful that she had overstepped the mark, 'You don't mind, do you, about me using the computer? I haven't touched anything I shouldn't.'

Nick shook his head. 'No. Not at all. I'm just surprised.'

'And pleased? A bit pleased?'

'Yes. And pleased.'

The printer whirred and Rosie picked up the piece of paper and handed it to him. She stood up and indicated the finer points of the car. 'It's British racing green – you can't tell that from the printout – with a red radiator grille. And the hood is black. It says it's in its original condition and has had the same owner for the last thirty years.' Her enthusiasm was infectious. 'I've always loved those old MGs. Our doctor used to have one. He'd jump over the door without opening it. Smoked a pipe. We used to think he was very dashing . . . Well-mannered, too.'

Nick read out: '"MG TC, 1949. Mechanically this car is superb. The engine, when being driven, has an excellent oil pressure and is entirely sound." Well, they would say that, wouldn't they?'

'Read on,' said Rosie.

'"When on 'tick-over' the engine can hardly be heard. The gearbox, and all other parts related to the chassis, like brakes, steering, et cetera, are also in excellent working order. No visible signs of rust." Probably been resprayed.'

'And it has the original logbook, showing owners back to 1963, and all the bills and receipts for the last thirty years. It was bought in 1969 for a hundred and fifteen pounds.'

'How much is it now?' asked Nick, his eye drifting down to the foot of the page. 'Bloody hell! Eleven thousand two hundred and fifty quid! Not a chance! I've just turned down a van for twelve hundred. This is almost ten times that.'

'Yes, but look what you're getting. It's a very pretty car!'

'But I haven't got that sort of money.'

Rosie's eyes lit up. 'I have!'

'What?'

'*I* could buy it.'

'Don't be silly.'

'I'm not being silly. I could buy it as an investment. I've got plenty saved up and nothing else to do with it. The banks aren't paying much interest. Much more fun to have a sports car. That way, you can drive it and I can come out for a spin occasionally. Can't I?'

'Well, yes. But no! I mean, this isn't right.'

'If you're worrying about your sisters and their inheritance, don't. I've sorted all that out.'

'But I want a van!'

'Don't be ridiculous. Can you hear yourself? "I want a van"! What a feeble thing to say when you could be spinning around in that.'

Nick looked back at the printout. It was indeed a lovely car. 'I don't know . . .'

'Do it for me?'

He folded his arms. 'And if I don't?'

'I shall be unhappy.'

'Where is this flash car?'

Rosie pointed out of the window. 'In Portsmouth. We could be there in an hour.'

6
The Doctor

Should not be allowed to vanish into oblivion.

It was love at first sight. Oh, how could a man get so excited about a heap of metal? The rolling wave of the mudguard. The neatly spoked wheels. The crimson-reeded radiator grille. The gleaming chrome. Nick ran his hand over one of the bulbous, glistening headlights and Rosie knew he was enslaved.

They hardly needed to take her out for a test drive. Nick knew how she would feel. Strong, but nimble. Spirited, but of a certain age. Obliging, as long as she was handled sensitively. The car had a lot in common with his grandmother.

He felt embarrassed when she wrote out the cheque, and tried not to look like a little boy who had just been indulged by his granny. Which, of course, he had, although he tried to tell himself that *he* was indulging her.

*

The salesman waved as they drove away, like an excitable couple of newlyweds. From her position deep in the bucket-like passenger seat, Rosie glanced at Nick as they sped towards the ferry. He was beaming from ear to ear. She had not seen him so happy for a long while. It made her smile, too.

And then she remembered how it had felt to be taken for a spin in a fast car by a good-looking young man. She had been twenty-two. Her hair streaming out behind her, she was laughing and looking sideways at the handsome doctor, who brushed her knee lightly with his hand. For a month they were barely apart. Then he was called up, and she never saw him again. Six years later they engraved his name on the war memorial.

'Can we stop for a minute?' she asked.

Nick had been lost in his thoughts. 'Sorry?'

'I just wondered if we could pull up for a minute. My eyes are watering.'

He drew in to the side of the road. 'Yes, of course. Are you all right?' He watched her reach into her pocket for a tissue. 'Are you sure?'

'Oh, yes. Just remembering.'

'Happily?'

'Very.'

He leaned towards her, and kissed her cheek. 'Thank you.' He tapped the steering-wheel. 'She's lovely.'

'Oh, she's a she, is she?'

'Of course.'

She pushed the tissue back into her pocket, pulled out a brightly patterned headscarf and tied it firmly under her chin. 'Come on, then, or we'll miss the boat.'

He started the engine again and the car growled softly out of the lay-by, then down the slip-road to the Isle of Wight ferry. For some inexplicable reason, Nick felt as though he was driving there for the first time.

At six thirty the following morning he found himself leaning out of his bedroom window gazing dreamily at the car parked below. How long would Rosie want to stay? He enjoyed her company – which was just as well: she'd shown no sign of wanting to go home.

He looked up at the sky, which was flushed with the amber glow of a clear morning. The sea was glassy calm, and there was no sound, except the distant kleep-kleep of half a dozen oystercatchers on the shore. He'd take himself off to Tennyson Down. No, it might be too breezy up there. He'd go to Sleepyhead Bay, find himself a quiet corner by some rocks, then paint the cottages and the little café. He hadn't felt like taking out his brushes for the better part of a week. Today he was anxious to get started.

'Will you be all right?' he asked later, as he loaded his bag into the passenger side of the car.

She was standing by the front door. 'Of course I'll be all right. Perfectly capable, you know . . . now that I've got my stick.' It was only a mock admonishment, acknowledging their little joke – that everybody thought she needed taking care of, even him, but he was the only one who didn't fuss, who let her live her life.

'What will you do?' he asked.

'Pace myself.' She grinned. 'That's the secret. Go for a little walk. Catch a bus somewhere. Not sure.'

'Well, take care. Don't go too far.'

'That's what I used to say to you.'

'Well, you know how it feels, then. I'll be back late afternoon. We can have supper together if you want.'

'That'd be nice. I just fancy a bit of fish.' She waved, and went indoors as he steered the car down the track towards the village and out across the island.

With his board on his lap, he was sketching the scene before him – the towering cliff, the neat row of cottages tucked in beneath it, the apron of rocks, girdled by shallow pools, and the children dipping for shrimps and crabs with their bamboo-poled nets. A couple of small yachts played nip-and-tuck half a mile out, and the lobster fisherman was carrying his catch up the steps to the little café. Nick had picked a good day.

He did not like being watched while he painted, but out here, especially during the school holidays, it was an occupational hazard. He had just finished the sky when he became aware of a child at his side. 'That's nice,' she said. Her dark hair was tied into plaits, and she was leaning on her shrimping net to examine his work.

'I'm glad you like it.'

'It's better than my mum can do.'

'Does she paint?' he asked politely.

'Yes. She tries to sell them.' The child shrugged, dismissive.

'So do I.'

'I bet you sell more than she does.'

'Oh, I don't know.'

'I do. She hasn't sold one yet.'

'Oh. I see.' He laughed.

'Would you like to come and see her painting?'

'Well, I'm a bit busy at the moment.' He frowned, hoping she'd leave him in peace.

'She's only over there. And she'd probably appreciate some advice.'

He gave in, amused by the child's conversation, which was older than her years. She was nine or ten, and was wearing a white T-shirt and a pair of baggy yellow shorts. Her feet were bare, and her toes, with chipped red varnish, were bent into the rocks for support. Her skin was honey-coloured from the early summer sun, and her turned-up nose was dusted with freckles. She had the darkest eyes he had ever seen.

'What's your name?' she asked.

'Nick.'

'Nick what?'

'Nick Robertson. What's yours?'

'Victoria.'

'Victoria what?'

'I'm not going to tell you. My mum says I shouldn't – in case you're not very nice.'

Nick grinned. 'Quite right, too.'

The child pointed her shrimping net to the other end of the cove. 'She's over there. Will you come and look? Please?'

He could see that he would not get any peace until he did as she asked, so he put down his board, anchored it with a rock, and followed her as she picked her way nimbly through the sharp stones, using the shrimping net to keep her balance. Occasionally she would raise one leg in the air, looking as though she were about to topple into one of the small pools, then she would recover her balance and tiptoe quickly ahead.

Around a particularly large and craggy outcrop they came upon a woman seated on a smooth, round boulder, with a stubby easel jammed among the smaller rocks in front of her. She was dressed like the child – in T-shirt and shorts – with her dark hair pinned up at the back of her head.

'I've brought someone to look at it, Mum.'

'Oh, poppet, why do you think . . .?'

The woman looked up. It was Alexandra Pollen.

Nick laughed.

Alex scrambled to her feet. 'Hello! Fancy meeting you here.'

The child looked from one to the other. 'Do you two know each other?'

'Well, yes,' Alex said, and coloured. 'This is the man whose car I crashed into.'

'Oh!' Victoria turned to Nick. 'I expect you're pretty cross with us, then.'

'No. Well a bit. But not much.'

'We've got another one.' She prodded the net into the pool at her feet. 'It's not very good. Worse than the last one, actually. But it was all we could afford.'

Alex brushed down her shorts and shifted from one foot to the other. 'Sorry about this. She's a bit annoyed with me for pranging the car.'

'Not your fault when your brakes fail,' said Nick.

'It hadn't got an MOT,' Victoria chipped in.

'Oh. I see.'

Alex lowered her eyes. 'Sorry. I should have said . . . only I was due to take it in to the garage the following day. I hadn't noticed . . .'

'Daddy came round and she got in a bit of a state. She always does.'

Nick felt uncomfortable. 'I'd better get back to my painting.'

'Fancy a coffee?' Alex pointed towards the café.

'I really should get back. The light . . .'

'Ah, yes. The light,' she teased.

He saw the look in her eyes and gave in. 'Just a quick one.'

Alex turned to her daughter: 'Shall I bring you back an ice-cream?'

'No, thanks.' She was concentrating on the rock pool, and bent down to pick something out of her net. 'I'd rather have a drink. Diet Coke, please.'

'OK.' Alex shot Nick one of those apologetic looks used by parents who are embarrassed by their children, and by children who are embarrassed by their parents, and began to walk towards the café.

'She's quite a character,' he remarked.

'You can say that again.'

'How old is she?'

'Ten, going on twenty-nine,' she said, with a smile, as they crossed the warm sand.

'I had no idea you had children.'

'Yes. But it's just Victoria and me. I'm a single mum.'

'Oh?'

'Most of the time anyway. He keeps coming back – or trying to. We're over here for a few days to get a break. A breath of air.'

Nick said nothing, unsure how to respond.

Alex covered the awkward moment. 'Oh dear! This is all getting rather intense, isn't it? Too much information.'

'No – please, go on. I wasn't . . . I mean . . . well . . . Would you like that coffee?'

She laughed and broke the tension. 'Yes. And I'd kill for a biscuit.'

He ordered two coffees and some tartan-wrapped shortbread biscuits, then sat down opposite her at a little table on a sun-bleached deck among some old fishing-nets. 'Shall we start again?' he asked.

'Third time lucky? Sorry. You must think I'm a complete wacko.'

He tilted his head from side to side. 'Only a bit of a wacko.'

'And Victoria?'

'Oh, she's far more sensible.'

'Enough sense there for both of us. Good thing, too, I suppose.'

'Have you had a difficult time at home?'

'Yes. It's better than it was, but it's still a bit iffy. I hope he got the message this time.'

'How long have you been together?'

'Eleven years, off and on. Classic, really. We married too young and stayed together because of the child. He's not a bad guy, but we're just not suited, and the rows seem to get worse.'

'What now, then?'

Alex shrugged. 'Who knows? Next week he's going abroad on business for a few months. I thought if we came here we'd be out of the way until he's gone.'

'Won't he come and find you?'

'Oh, I don't think so. It was all pretty final this time. I wanted to be out of the way. Have a change of scene, and I like it over here.'

He looked out towards the sea. 'Nobody knows about it, really.'

'About the island?'

'England's best-kept secret.'

'It's supposed to be for old folk, isn't it? White-haired ladies and men with fawn anoraks.'

'Who says?'

'Public opinion.'

'Well, we all know about public opinion. I love it here. But, then, I'm not your typical thirty-something.'

'That's a relief.' Alex grinned.

'Thank you!' He sipped his coffee.

'So what are you?' she asked.

'Almost thirty-nine.' He grinned.

'And never been kissed?' she asked with a wry smile.

Nick frowned. 'Another disaster area, I suppose. Not much to tell. Just come out of a long relationship – well, not as long as yours, but three years. Debs went off to the States last week to see a bit of action. Too quiet for her here, I think.'

'Oh, I'm sorry.'

'Me too. Bit of a bugger, really.'

'What does she do?'

'Human resources.'

Alex stirred her coffee. 'Are you in mourning?'

'Not really. A bit fed up. And hurt, I suppose. That life wasn't exciting enough for her. But then there doesn't seem to be much excitement around at the moment.'

'I see.'

He realized what he'd said. 'Apart from this, of course,' he added.

'How very polite.'

'No. Honestly.'

'Are you committed to staying here?' she asked.

'For now, yes. I love painting on the island – and I love it in winter when there's nobody about.'

'I think you're just a loner, really,' she told him.

'Maybe. Not always though. How about you?'

'Just the reverse. I hate being on my own. Not that I am.' She looked round to check that Victoria was still in view. 'She's been my life-saver.'

'That's funny.' He smiled, as if to himself.

'What is?'

'You don't look like a mum.'

'What does a mum look like?'

'Well, not like you.'

'What do you mean?' She sounded irritated.

'I meant it as a compliment,' he assured her, and she relaxed.

'I'm sure your mum would appreciate that,' she said.

'Don't remind me.' He pushed a shortbread biscuit across the table. 'Another?'

'No. I'll wait until lunchtime. Are you staying?'

'Well, I've got a painting to finish . . .' He hesitated.

'Why don't you have some lunch with us? You can meet Victoria properly, and you can give me some advice on my painting.'

'I wouldn't dream—'

'Well, I'll settle for a bit of company, then . . . if you don't mind?'

7
Vick's Caprice

Unusual . . . taking an upright stance.

He watched them as they pored over the menu, Victoria leaning over Alex's shoulder. They were like sisters, each advising the other on the best choice in front of them.

'You should have that,' said Victoria, pointing to 'freshly fried fish and salad'.

'What about you?' asked her mother.

'That.' Victoria darted a finger at 'Pint of prawns with brown bread and butter', then slipped the straw of her Diet Coke into her mouth and sucked.

'Can you peel them?' asked Nick.

Victoria nodded, without looking up.

'She's been able to peel prawns since she was little. We had a holiday in Spain, and she learned when she was three. She loves seafood.'

'Expensive tastes,' said Nick.

'Yes. She gets it from her father. I'm very low maintenance.'

'Must be the artistic temperament.'

'It doesn't work for Elton John.'

'No. I suppose we should be grateful it works for us.'

Victoria sat back in her chair. 'How long are we going to stay here?'

'Until I've finished my painting, sweetheart. Probably about four o'clock.'

'I meant how long are we going to stay on the island?'

'Just for the week,' Alex told her. 'Then we'll go home.'

'We can't see it from here, can we?'

'Not from this side of the island, but we can from the north side.'

'I prefer this side.'

'Why's that?' asked Alex.

'Because there's more sea.'

'Do you like the sea?' asked Nick.

'It's not that. It's just that it takes longer to get home from here.'

'Well, we can come back lots if you like,' her mother told her.

'Yes, please,' and with that Victoria returned to her drink.

Victoria finished her prawns, leaving a neat pile of shells on her plate, while Nick and Alex were still eating. She excused herself from the table and went back to her rock pool. They watched her concentrate on fishing.

'How's she coped with it all?' asked Nick.

'Not bad, on the whole – but how can I tell? She tries to be grown-up about it, but it obviously hurts.'

'Does she get on with her dad?'

'So-so. He spoils her rotten and he's not badmouthed me. At least I don't think he has. She's never said anything that makes me think so.'

'Will he still be able to see her?'

'Oh, yes. But if this new job takes off he'll be away quite a lot, so I shouldn't have to grit my teeth too much.'

'You really get on well with her.'

'Most of the time, yes. There is the occasional tantrum.'

'Well that's growing up, isn't it?' He smiled ruefully.

'That's what I tell myself. And I'm the only one she can let off steam with.'

'Grandparents?'

'No.'

'That's a shame.'

'Yes. It would help. Give her a greater variety of company. I think she must get pretty pissed off with me sometimes. Moody. You know.'

'You're a bit hard on yourself.'

'I deserve to be. I don't like cocking up, and I've made a real mess of things so far.'

Nick pointed to Victoria. 'Not with her.'

'No,' she said softly. 'Bless her. I'm just determined that things will get better, you know? That's what keeps me going.'

'Is that why you're painting?'

'Partly. It's a bit selfish, too. Hopefully it'll raise some money to help with Victoria's schooling, but it also makes me feel good. I can escape when I'm painting. Go somewhere else. Be someone else. Not like before.'

Nick watched as Alex traced patterns on the table with a finger. 'So you're not a career painter?' he asked.

'Oh, come on! You knew I wasn't when you saw my canvases.'

'They're lovely!'

'Don't be patronizing.' She leaned back in her chair and frowned.

'No. They really are. God! They're better than a lot of professional stuff I've seen.'

'But you knew I wasn't a professional painter.'

'Only because of the way you acted.'

She looked worried for a moment. 'Do you think Henry knew?'

'Probably, but he doesn't care as long as things sell. He thinks you're worth a punt.'

Her face lightened again. 'Well, that's something, I suppose. A start.'

'What did you do before?'

'I was an English teacher. Then Victoria came along and I didn't want to be a part-time mum so I gave it up. But I can read a cracking bedtime story.'

'Lucky girl.'

Alex looked out to where her daughter was absorbed in her own world. 'Oh, I hope so. I really want her to have a good life. That's the most important thing, and I don't feel I've done very well for her so far.' She gazed at her daughter wistfully for a few moments, then asked, 'What about you?'

'Well, no kids. Two sisters, both abroad. And a granny.'

'No mum and dad?'

'Yes. But the granny's the one who takes up most of my time.'

Alex laughed. 'Why?'

'She's a bit of a liability. Eighty-seven. Sharp as a razor but she has her moments.'

'How?'

'Oh, she's just taken it into her head that she hasn't lived enough so she's starting now, which is very nice in one way but a real pain in another.'

'Good for her.'

'Are you taking sides?'

'I'm all for anyone who refuses to give up. Who refuses to "go gentle into that good night".'

'But there are limits.'

'Why? What's she done?'

'Oh, it's a long story. She's staying with me at the moment.'

'Here? On the island?'

'Yes. You ought to meet her.'

Alex hesitated. 'She sounds a real character.'

'Oh, she is. Why don't you come for supper one evening?' Then he worried that he had pushed himself too much. 'But perhaps . . .'

'No. I mean, yes. It would be lovely,' she said.

They sat quietly for a few minutes, looking at the sun glinting on the water.

Then Nick got up. 'I'd better get on. Painting to finish.'

'Yes.'

'Look . . .' He pulled a stubby pencil and a scrap of paper out of his pocket. 'This is where I am. I've promised my grandmother supper tonight, so if you two want to come you'll be very welcome. It would be good for her, too. And Victoria. They might be a match for each other.'

She took the note, glanced at the address and the map he had sketched. 'Are you sure? We're a bit of a handful.'

'I'm positive.' He leaned forward and kissed her cheek.

She smelt of Johnson's baby powder. 'And thank you.' He turned and walked away across the rocks.

'My pleasure,' she whispered, as she slipped the note into the pocket of her shorts.

'What sort of company?' asked Rosie.

'Female company,' said Nick.

'Ooh!'

'There's no need to say it like that.'

'I didn't say it like anything.'

'Well, that's all right, then.'

'Do I get a clue?' Rosie asked.

Nick sighed and looked up from chopping the salad. 'An artist and her daughter.'

'That's nice.'

'And you're to be on your best behaviour.'

'And not embarrass you?'

'Oh, you won't embarrass me. Just don't get on your hobby-horse, that's all.'

'I'll try not to,' she said, as he tipped the salad into a glass bowl. 'Anything I can do?'

'Well, you could lay the table. Do you know where everything is?'

'I think I've worked it out.' Her sarcasm, she could see, was lost on him.

Rosie put knives, forks and spoons, napkins and place mats on the scrubbed pine table that stood in the tiny bay window. She liked his little cottage. It made her feel as though she was living in a dream. The outside walls were black-painted clapboard with yellow window frames, and inside, the wooden panelling was white. Everywhere there was light. Nick's taste was minimalist without being cold:

there were pieces of gnarled driftwood and shells on the doorstep, cream linen curtains at the windows, and white-painted furniture on which he had grouped feathers, shells, a bird's egg, a fishing float.

The two bedrooms were warmer: brightly coloured quilts covered the mattresses and dried flower wreaths hung over the brass bedsteads. Painted wooden fish hung from hooks on the walls, and the bathroom sported a tiny bath on ball and claw feet. It was the perfect seaside bachelor pad, and Rosie felt like a lucky interloper.

She finished the table by placing a small bowl of wild flowers in the centre – dog-roses, campion, grasses and buttercups. 'Where did you find those?' he asked.

'On the clifftop. I nearly got blown away picking them.'

'They're lovely. Thank you.'

'Well, I haven't done much since I came.'

'Er . . .' He pointed to the car outside.

'Oh, that's different.'

'Yes. A lot different from a van.'

Rosie smiled at him fondly. 'Now tell me about this artist.'

'Oh, don't go getting ideas. I've only just come out of a relationship and I'm not ready to go headlong into another. Anyway, there are two of them to think about.'

'Oh, I see. Responsibilities.'

'Look, this is just a meal!'

'Well, I only asked you about her so that I didn't put my foot in it.'

He told her about the crash outside the pub, about Alex's paintings, and about meeting her at Sleepyhead Bay. He told her about Victoria and about the child's father. About how Alex had turned from being an English teacher to being a painter and about how she was hoping to change her life.

By the end Rosie couldn't suppress a grin.

'What's the matter?'

'Nothing.'

'Why are you smiling?'

'Because you're so happy. Happy to talk about her. And there's another reason, too.'

'What's that?'

'She has the most wonderful name.'

'Pollen?'

'Well, yes, that's lovely, but I was thinking more about her first name.'

'Alexandra?'

'Yes. Very Russian.'

Nick frowned in admonishment. 'So how come you were called Rosie?' he asked.

'To put people off the scent when I was smuggled out of Russia. It's not my real name.'

'What *is* your real name?'

'Alice Marie Xenia.'

'That's a bit of a mouthful.'

'All family names.'

He flopped into a chair. 'When are you going to sit down and tell me everything?'

'Whenever you want. It's time somebody knew.'

'Well, not tonight. Let's keep to lighter topics.'

'Like the weather?'

'Yes.'

'That'll be interesting.'

'Rosie, there is one thing, before we get off the subject.'

'Yes?'

'If you're so pleased that Alex has a Russian name, why on earth did you christen Dad Derek?'

'Your grandfather put his foot down. I wanted to call him Alexander, but your granddad said it sounded too snooty. He was a lovely man, your granddad, and I didn't want to upset him.'

'But why Derek?'

'Because it was the name of a very good friend of mine. Someone who was killed in the war. A doctor.'

'And me? Was Nicholas your idea?'

'As luck would have it, that was your mother. All I had to do was sit quietly and smile to myself. Mind you, I was a bit worried. There was a point when she thought she might call you Torquil. Tricky for all of us, that was.'

Nick winced. 'It would have been even trickier for me.'

'She saw sense in the end. But your father had the last laugh.'

'With my middle name?'

'Yes. I thought your mother must have been a bit dim not to understand, but your dad managed to pull the wool over her eyes – until after the christening at least.'

'Well, thankfully I don't have to use it, and by the time I got to school most people didn't understand anyway.'

'I did think he was taking his love of the horses a bit too far. Naming you after a Grand National winner.'

'It could've been worse.'

'Worse than Nicholas Silver?'

'Yes. If I'd been born a few years later I could have been called Red Rum.'

Rosie laughed. 'Sometimes you really crack me up,' she said.

8
Royal Blush

Soft blush pink.

'I don't know whether to feel guilty or relieved.' Alex was looking at the MG parked outside the house.

'Oh, think of yourself as a catalyst,' said Nick, a twinkle in his eyes.

'You do say the nicest things to a girl.'

'It's a way I have.'

'Are they all right in there, do you think?' Alex looked towards the house, where Rosie was showing Victoria Nick's treasures, like the ship in the bottle and the stuffed gannet.

'Oh, yes. She's had lots of practice.'

Having over-indulged the child during supper – with three helpings of ice-cream – Rosie had slipped into great-grandmother mode while Nick and Alex drank coffee on the veranda.

'She'll be reading her a bedtime story next.'

'Talking of which . . .' Alex looked at her watch.

'There's no rush,' said Nick. 'It's a lovely evening.'

He gazed at her sitting in the cane chair, feet curled under her. Her dark hair was still pinned up, but she had changed into a pale pink shirt and jeans. He could see the candlelight reflected in her dark eyes as she gazed out across the water.

'It's the most perfect spot,' she said. 'You're very lucky.'

'I suppose I am.'

'So did . . . I can't remember the girl's name.'

'Debs.'

'Did she live here with you?'

'Some of the time – when she wasn't abroad.'

'She travelled a lot?'

'A fair bit, yes. That's why it fizzled out, really.'

'For you or for her?'

'Both of us, I think. It came as a bit of a shock to admit it to myself. I felt miserable about it, but I knew I was feeling sorry for myself rather than missing her.'

'What about her?'

'Absence made her heart grow fonder . . . of somebody else.'

'Over the water?'

'Yes. In a manner of speaking – Southampton.'

'How was it? The ending, I mean.'

'Strangely civilized. Scary, really.'

'Oh, don't be scared of civility. It's better than the other option.'

'I guess. But it's not very passionate, is it?'

Alex grinned at him mischievously. 'And are you a passionate man?'

He was about to reply when he became aware of another voice: it was Rosie's and she was getting into her stride. 'And then the princess met the most wonderful man.'

'How was he wonderful? Was he good-looking?' Victoria asked.

'Not especially.'

'But was he fit?'

'Well, I suppose he was quite healthy.'

'No. I mean . . . was he fanciable?'

'Oh, yes. Definitely.'

'And *did* she fancy him?'

'Oh, I think so. She certainly wanted to get to know him a bit better.'

'And did she?'

'Well, yes, I suppose she did . . . You see, the princess lived in a country that was very large, and a lot of the working people didn't have much money. This meant that they didn't like the princess's family because they had too many lovely things, like Fabergé eggs and suchlike.'

'What's a Fabergé egg?'

Suddenly Nick grasped the drift of their conversation, and sprang up. 'Rosie!'

'Yes, darling?'

'What are you talking about?'

Before she could reply, Victoria said, 'A princess and a . . . What was he?'

'A pauper. Well, not exactly a pauper, dear, but certainly a commoner.'

Nick endeavoured to steer her away from what to him were uncharted waters and a possible source of embarrassment. 'Don't you think it's a bit late for stories?'

'Yes,' Alex put in. 'We really must be going.'

'No – I didn't mean—' He looked pleadingly at his grandmother.

She beamed at him innocently. 'It's only a quarter to ten – and they are on holiday.'

Alex stood up and slipped on her shoes. 'No. You're quite right. It's way past Victoria's bedtime. It's been wonderful, but we really must be going.'

Nick tried to retrieve the situation. 'Don't go. It was just that . . .'

'It's all right. We've had a lovely time. Perhaps we'll see you again before the end of our holiday. Say goodnight, Victoria, and thank Rosie for a nice evening.'

'Oh, do we have to? I want to hear the end of the story.' Alex shot her a look.

'OK.' Victoria sounded resigned. 'Goodnight, Rosie, and thanks for having me.' She stretched up to give Rosie a peck on the cheek. 'Goodnight, Nick.'

'Goodnight, Victoria. Thank you for coming.' He was embarrassed now. He turned to Alex, but she was collecting Victoria's jacket from the back of her chair and did not meet his eye.

As they walked down the veranda steps together he tried to make amends. 'I'm sorry.'

'Oh, never mind.'

'No. I mean about . . . just then . . .'

'It's fine, really. Thank you for a lovely meal.' She squeezed his arm, then walked round the battered old Ford, let Victoria into the back seat and belted her in. 'Have a good rest of the week,' she said, and before he could say any more, the little car slid down the stony track and away into the night.

Nick watched the scarlet tail-lights disappear. How had

he managed that? How could a perfectly pleasant evening have soured so quickly? It was only minutes since he and Alex had been sitting on the veranda, enjoying the moment, sizing each other up, and now she had left without . . . well, without anything.

He stormed inside. 'You promised!'

'Promised what, sweetheart?'

'Not to go on about your past.'

'But I didn't. I was only telling her about the princess and the pauper.'

'Oh, yes? A princess who had Fabergé eggs and lived in a large country where the poor people didn't like the princess's family.'

'Well, I was only embellishing it a bit with things I knew.'

'And look what's happened! They must think I'm rude and—'

'Inconsiderate?'

'Don't push it, Rosie!' His voice was raised.

'Well, you shouldn't treat me like a child.'

'Then don't behave like one. You've ruined a perfectly good evening.'

'I didn't ruin it. You did. I was just . . .'

'I know what you were doing.'

Rosie sat down and looked away, blinking back tears.

Nick thumped a chair-back. 'Oh, please! This isn't fair! Come on!'

'I don't understand why you're so cross with me.'

'Because I worry about you.'

'But if you worried about me you'd care, and if you cared you'd listen, instead of doing what everybody else in the family does and treating me as though I'm stupid.'

'But most of the time you're not. It's just that every now and then you get this bee in your bonnet, and then you're like a different person.' He was kneeling beside her now. 'You don't seem like you when you do this – you're almost a bit . . . well . . . doo-lally.'

'I'm not!' she wailed.

'No, no . . . I didn't mean you're doo-lally, just . . . different.'

Rosie shook her head. 'I might as well give up. Nobody really knows. Or cares.'

'That's not true. Look.' He squeezed her hand. 'Let me get you a drink. What do you want? Tea? Coffee?'

'Scotch.'

'Scotch it is. And then you can tell me, if you want to.'

She looked up at him. 'Depends if you want to hear.'

'Of course I do.' He poured her a large Scotch, and one for himself, then went over to where she sat and handed her the glass. 'Are you sure you've never told anyone before?' he asked.

She picked up on the note of disbelief in his voice. 'I told you, your father would have laughed and your mother would have had me committed.'

'Well, I'm all ears.' He sat at her feet, and tried to look sympathetic, still wondering what Alex was thinking now as she drove to her hotel. The first few words washed over him, but then he was listening as Rosie told her story.

9
Royal Highness

At its best in fine weather.

'I didn't know anything about it until I was twenty. Until then I just thought my parents had given me away when I was a baby. They were poor and couldn't afford to keep me. They had five children already – one more mouth to feed would have finished them off. I was brought up by a couple in Cheltenham. They told me I was properly adopted when I was about seven, but they just said that my real parents hadn't wanted anything to do with me once I had been handed over.'

'And you accepted that?' asked Nick. 'You never felt curious?'

'Oh, I was curious all right, but in those days you had no right to see them. I did have a friend at school who somehow managed to meet her real parents and it had all gone wrong. She was torn this way and that. In a real state. So I thought, no, I'm not doing that. Then my father died when I was fifteen. It was so sad. He had a stroke, and Mum and I nursed him for months before he slipped away.'

'Like Granddad?'

'Yes, but it was worse in a way. I was so young. At least your granddad had had a good life. But it taught me a lot. Made me stronger, I suppose. Then, when I was twenty, Mum was taken ill. I was desperate for her to get better. She was all I had left. There were no uncles and aunts, or cousins that I knew of – anyway, they wouldn't have been mine.'

'What was wrong with her?'

'Cancer, I suppose. I didn't know at the time, but I came to realize later. Something to do with her tummy, anyway. She lay in bed getting paler and thinner and I remember knowing one day that she was going to die. Just before the end came – a couple of days before, it must have been – she said she had something important to tell me. Something I ought to know about my real family, but that it might be better if I kept it to myself. I was a bit scared. I didn't know what she was going to say. All sorts of things went through my mind – that they might be criminals or something. Murderers, even.' She paused.

Nick squeezed her hand. 'Go on.'

'She told me I hadn't been born in Cheltenham, as I had always been told, but that I was born in St Petersburg and smuggled out of Russia as a baby to avoid a scandal. You can imagine how I felt. It was like a dream – a fairy story. I mean, I lived in Gloucestershire, I was a Cotswolds girl, always had been. I thought she must be rambling but she kept on. She said I had to know, that it was only right. She said that back in 1917 there had been some sort of group of people – what do you call it? You know, when they send diplomats and things.'

'Delegation?'

'Yes. That's it. A delegation was sent to Russia from Britain – to do with King George the Fifth and the Tsar. They were cousins, you know. Very alike, too. They used to be mistaken for each other.' Rosie's eyes were misty.

'And?'

'The Tsar had five children. Olga and Tatiana were in their early twenties by then, Anastasia and Marie were in their teens, and their son, the Tsarevich Alexis, was about twelve.'

Nick watched her intently. There was an almost trance-like quality about her face. This old lady of eighty-seven was reciting history with a calm lucidity that belied her years – almost as though it were a mantra.

'There was a young diplomat in the delegation. My mother didn't know his name, only that he came from a good family. Apparently he'd got on a bit too well with one of the elder daughters, as a result of which she became . . . well . . . I was the result.'

'*What?*'

'That's what she said.'

'But if it's true, why were you shipped out?'

'There was enough scandal in the Russian royal family already. Some of the Tsar's cousins had been a bit . . . loose in the years leading up to the revolution. At that time it was just a year away. For one of the Tsar's daughters to have an illegitimate child would have been unthinkable.'

'But why didn't they just . . . get rid of you?'

'Abortion? Too risky. Imagine if anything had gone wrong. It was out of the question.'

'But you're not . . .'

'No. No, I'm not. The Empress, the Tsarina, was the

carrier. She was one of Queen Victoria's grandchildren. Her mother, Princess Alice, was a carrier too, and so was the Queen. The Tsarevich was the only one of the Tsar's children who was a haemophiliac.'

'But how did they keep the pregnancy secret?'

'My mother's clothes would have done the job until the last three months or so, and after that I suppose she was simply kept out of the public eye.'

'When did all this happen?'

'In the summer of 1916. I was born in 1917, just before the revolution, and spirited away.'

'How?'

'I've no idea. By diplomatic means, I suppose. Probably in a diplomatic bag. With a bottle.'

'What does it say on your birth certificate?'

'Not much. Two fictitious names were given as my parents.'

'How do you know they're fictitious?'

'Because I tried to trace them.'

'When?'

'About six months ago. I'd always thought the names must be made up, so I went to check at the Public Records Office – the National Archive, they call it now – in Kew. It's just down the road from your mother. They have no record of any married couple called George Michaels and Matilda Kitching.'

'Maybe they weren't married.'

'I thought of that, so I tried that avenue, too. I could find a George Herbert Michaels, but he was the wrong age and lived in the wrong place. I couldn't find any Matilda Kitching.'

'So they were just made up.'

'Yes. By the people who smuggled me out, I suppose.'

'But you said your real name was Alice Marie Xenia.'

'That's what it says on my birth certificate, but my mum – the one who adopted me – always called me Rosie because she didn't want people to start asking questions.'

'But wouldn't it have made sense for whoever sorted out your birth certificate to have called you Gladys or Doris rather than Alice Marie Xenia?'

'Oh, they could pass as British names. I like to think someone was being kind to me about my heritage.'

'And after you came over here?'

'They were all killed. But you know that – if you know your history.'

Nick nodded.

Rosie took a deep breath. 'I can remember the dates off by heart. The Tsar abdicated on the fifteenth of March 1917 and on the sixteenth of July 1918 the whole family was assassinated. I can't think of it without feeling terrified. It was at Ekaterinberg. In the House of Special Purpose. Isn't that a dreadful name?'

Nick saw Rosie's fist tighten and her knuckles turned white.

'Wasn't there something about one of them escaping. Anastasia?'

'She was an impostor. Her name was Anna Anderson. The Tsar's cousin – another Grand Duchess Olga – escaped to Britain with her sister Xenia on a British warship, and she met all the impostors. She knew Anna Anderson was a fraud. No. They all died. They were herded into a basement room and shot. All of them. Even little Alexis. And my mother's dog.'

'So you know which one was your mother?'

'Yes.' Rosie got up from her seat and walked into her bedroom. For a moment, Nick wondered if she would come back. A few minutes later, she returned, the tears wiped away and her lipstick refreshed. She held the framed photograph that had always stood in her hallway, of the man in the army uniform, the boy in the sailor suit, the girl with the wonderful eyes and the clear complexion.

In a moment of realization, Nick knew what she was going to say. The photograph was so familiar, but he had failed to make the connection. The obvious connection. Until now, it had always been just a man with a beard, a pretty young girl and a small boy, playing together in the snow.

'That's my grandfather, the Tsar, my uncle the Tsarevich, and my mother, the Grand Duchess Tatiana.'

Nick took a deep breath. 'And you believe all this?'

'Oh, yes. I know it's true. I can *feel* it's true.'

Nick stared at her.

'But why should anybody want to believe me, an old woman from Cheltenham? I mean, I don't look like a grand duchess, do I? And I certainly don't sound like one. It's the most ridiculous story they've ever heard. It's the most ridiculous story *I*'ve ever heard. But I loved my mother – the one who adopted me – and she wasn't a liar. I could see how frightened she was when she told me, but she wanted me to know. It was so important to her.'

'But who told her?'

'I don't know. Someone who was involved, presumably.'

'So if it's true, it means . . .' He was trying to make sense of it all.

Rosie brightened. 'Yes. It's funny, really, isn't it?'

Nick stood up. 'It's not funny at all. It's unbelievable. I mean, if your adoptive mother was right, then I'm . . .'

'Yes, love. You're in the line of succession to the Russian Imperial Throne. After your dad, that is. But somehow I don't think Tsar Derek has the right ring to it. Do you?'

10
Gloire de l'Exposition

Loose and untidy.

Nick didn't sleep much that night. Well, you wouldn't, would you, after being told you were an heir to the Russian throne? Early the next morning, he lay in bed scrutinizing the planking on the ceiling and wondering if he really had gone mad. There were a hundred unanswered questions in his head. Had Rosie really told no one else the full story? Was she telling the truth, or was she simply unbalanced? She certainly seemed convinced. Had his parents any idea at all? Why had the details never surfaced before? Enough stories were being dug up about the Tsar and his family, why had this one not been unearthed?

He got up, showered, and went out on to the veranda with his bowl of cereal. A skein of mist hung over the sea and a watery sun was doing its best to break through. The echoing cries of seabirds floated up from Thorness Bay. He shivered in the morning chill. It was six thirty. In half an hour Rosie would be up and about. He would leave early, give himself time to think – although half of him thought there was little point. It was just a story. How could it be true? Rosie's adoptive mother might have believed she was telling the truth, but in the delirium brought on by morphine who could think straight? She might have been well meaning, but that didn't necessarily make her story accurate. Rosie had probably been born in Russia and smuggled to Britain, but that was about it. She had no proof even of that.

It was ludicrous – laughable, even. But he couldn't bring himself to laugh.

He looked at the car in the lee of the house wall. He would have to clear out the old boathouse to make room for her. Keeping a Morris Minor van out of doors was one thing, but a drophead MG wouldn't stand up to the elements quite so well. Salt spray had done for the old Morris over five years, and it would probably polish off an older sports car even more quickly. Tonight he would start the clearance operation. But his thoughts refused to be marshalled into the mundane.

He wished he could talk to someone about the events of last night, someone who might help him straighten out the tangle of thoughts in his head. Debs would have told him to get himself sorted. Snap out of it. But Debs wasn't there anymore.

Henry? No. And, anyway, Henry was the island's most accomplished gossip. What Henry heard one week, the *Isle of Wight County Press* reported the next. He meant well, but no. Not Henry.

Alex? He would call her and make amends for the night before. But not yet. It was too early.

He loaded his painting bag, board and paper into the car and folded down the hood. Then he released the hand-brake and let her roll down the track before starting up out of Rosie's earshot.

The mist was clearing. He drove on past green fields and light woodland, the stumpy tower of Shalfleet church, then turned right on the narrow lane that led to Newtown Creek. He drew up on a rough gravel car park, took out his bag and board and made his way along the boardwalk that crossed the narrow inlets. The tide was on the turn, beginning to fill the muddy arteries that glistened in the early-morning sun.

He found a spot for his folding chair and easel, and set to work, trying to keep his mind on what lay in front of him: a pallid sky, humps of wetland turf, and the slowly filling miniature estuaries, linked with their planked bridges. Three small boats bobbed gently in the river, their owners still asleep below decks.

Newtown had always been a special place. It was where he and Debs had come on their first date. Supper at the New Inn, then a walk across the creek. Now he tried not to let it put him off the place. It was too ancient and beautiful a spot to be given up for sentimental reasons. Although if he had really loved her he wouldn't want to be here and reawaken all those memories.

Maybe he would never fall completely in love. He'd never experienced the earth-shattering, life-changing force that was supposed to infuse your every fibre and prevent you thinking of anything else. And if it hadn't happened by the time you were thirty-eight, what was the chance of it happening at all?

Anyway he wasn't sure he believed in it. If brainless teenage pop stars could do it on a daily basis what value was there in it? True love – *real* love – wasn't like that. It was a known fact. People stayed together for a long time because they got on. Because they were friends. Because they liked each other. Not because they were 'in love'. That sort of love didn't last. There was enough proof of it all around him. You could have one thing or the other: loving friendship for keeps, or a short-lived mind-blowing passion.

Look at Henry. A couple of years ago he'd been besotted by a young art student from Derby. He'd taken her paintings, then her body. Then she had taken him for ten grand and disappeared. Poor Henry. Soul-mates, he'd said they were. But the girl gave her soul to someone else and left Henry with a hole in his pocket.

For three hours he worked on the painting, until the light had changed too much. Then he packed away his paints and walked back to the car. The three boats were hauling up their sails to catch the breath of wind that was ruffling the surface of the water. Now the muddy creeks were turning into rivulets, swirling into hollows by grassy banks.

He drove through sleepy Calbourne and sprawling Carisbrooke to Newport and went into a bookshop. Under the section headed 'European History' he found what he was looking for: a book on the Russian royal family. He looked around as he bought it, just in case someone was observing him, then felt embarrassed at his own stupidity, and watched the shop assistant drop the book into a carrier-bag with his receipt. She clearly hadn't rumbled him, which was a relief.

By the time he had returned to the Anchorage Rosie had gone out. He made some coffee, and opened the book.

Three hours later, he closed it and sat back in his chair, strangely apprehensive. He was now acquainted with the Tsar's family – he still couldn't begin to think of it as *his* family. He knew about Rasputin, Lenin, the Bolsheviks, and the murderous Yurovsky. He had read about Olga, the eldest of the sisters, shy, with long chestnut hair, bookish and close to her father. Tatiana was the most elegant, tall and willowy with grey eyes and auburn hair, an accomplished pianist, full of energy, and regarded by the rest of the children as their unofficial governess. She was devoted to her mother, often washing and dressing her hair, always attentive to her needs.

There were the two younger daughters: Marie, the prettiest of all, whose dark blue eyes were known as 'Marie's saucers', and the dumpy, mischievous Anastasia. She had been the tree-climbing tomboy, the practical joker who had hidden stones in snowballs until one had knocked Tatiana out cold and brought Anastasia to her senses.

And then there was the Tsarevich, Alexis, known in the family as Alexei. The haemophiliac child had been next in line to the Imperial throne, and was a martyr to the disease, which caused regular internal haemorrhaging, made his joints painful, and a nosebleed life-threatening. Nick felt sorry for him.

He had read of the Tsar's mishandling of power, and of Alexandra's devotion to him. From what he could remember of history lessons, the Tsar had been portrayed as an autocratic tyrant, but his reading led him to wonder if that had really been so. One authority in the book had suggested that he was every bit as effective a ruler as his cousin George V, but what had been seen in George as positive attributes were regarded in the Tsar as weaknesses.

Would he ever know? Did it matter? But whether he was related to them or not, the story was compelling, and the way in which the Imperial family had met their end was shocking and inhumane.

He looked at his watch. Half past one. Alex would probably be out painting. He had her mobile phone number but was reluctant to call. Then his own phone rang.

'Hello?'

'Is she with you?'

'What?'

'Is Rosie with you?'

'Yes.'

It was his mother. She was not calm.

'Bloody typical! I've arranged for her to see two lots of sheltered accommodation and she's buggered off.'

'Well, did you ask her if she wanted to see them?'

'I arranged it with her the other day.'

'Yes, but did you *ask* her?'

'I told her I'd—'

'Yes. You *told* her.'

'Well, what do you expect? She's eighty-seven, for God's sake.'

'But she still has opinions.'

'Yes. And look where they got her. Honestly, Nick, I'd have thought you'd more sense.'

'Than what?'

'Taking her in and encouraging her to think she can be independent.'

'But she can. It's just that she gets a bit upset now and again. It's not surprising, is it?'

Most daughters-in-law would have been only too willing to relinquish a relationship with their mother-in-law on the breakdown of their marriage. Not so Anna Robertson. Rosie was a loose end, and loose ends had to be tidied up.

'Well, she'll have to come back and look at these two places. I've made appointments.'

'Unmake them. She's here for a while now.'

'How long?'

'Not sure. Till she feels better.'

'What she regards as "feeling better" is hardly likely to be much of an improvement, as far as I can see.'

'Well, cancel them for now.'

'Only if you promise to send her back.'

'I can't do that. She's not a child.'

'Now, listen, Nick—'

'No, Mum. *You* listen. She's getting on and she's a bit unreliable, but that doesn't mean you can shut her away.'

'I'm not shutting her away. These are lovely places and they'll look after her.'

'Well, I'm looking after her at the moment so that's all right, isn't it?'

'But how long can you carry on?'

'I don't know. But, quite honestly, I'd rather she was with her family than stuck in some home that smells of pee with chairs all round the walls.'

'That's disgusting.'

'Exactly. And she's having fun here. She's even booked to go on a sailing course.'

'What?'

'It's OK. She says they've taught people older than her.'

'Maybe, but I bet they had all their marbles.'

'And you don't think she has?' asked Nick.

'Do you?'

He changed the subject, careful to ask the question offhandedly: 'What do you know about her family?'

'Oh, it's quite ridiculous. She's got it into her head that her mother was somehow caught up in the Russian revolution.'

'How?'

'I've no idea. She thinks she was smuggled out when she was a baby.'

'Who were her parents?'

'Russian peasants, probably.'

'Does Dad know?'

'Well, if he does he's never bored me with the story. Look, I haven't time to talk. I've a lecture in five minutes. Just let me know the moment she leaves so that I can arrange these meetings. OK?'

Nick felt reluctant to commit himself – or Rosie – to such an arrangement. 'We'll see.'

'Nick!'

'I promise to look after her and see that she doesn't get into any more trouble.'

'Well, I'm relying on you.'

'Mmm.'

'Speak soon. Must dash. Oh, and don't let her spend any money. Apparently her bank account is overdrawn.'

11
Danse de Feu

So bright, this rose almost screams.

Troubles are like buses: they come in convoys. Nick had quite a collection now. His grandmother's presence, his grandmother's state of mind, his grandmother's apparent lack of funds, Alex's opinion of him (which could not have been high) and the prospect of being a future tsar of Russia.

To his credit, he was relatively rational about the last, and put it out of his mind. But, as troubles go, it was never going to be one that he would get his head round. The choice was simple: incredulity or insanity. Wisely, he opted for the former. But the matter kept drifting into his mind and gave rise to an uncomfortable sensation in the pit of his stomach.

All of the above would probably have resolved themselves sooner rather than later had not two more buses turned up. They were clad in charcoal grey suits and wore dark glasses. They stood on the doorstep of the Anchorage looking strangely out of place.

'Mr Robertson?'

'Yes.'

'Mr Derek Robertson?'

'No. I'm Nick.'

'Are you expecting us?' asked the shorter of the two. They were both sturdy men with close-shaven heads and no necks. The sort of men you'd find wearing twirly earpieces and standing outside a nightclub called the Matrix. One even had the habit of pushing up his chin to free his non-existent neck from a collar two sizes too small.

'No. Should I be?'

The taller one looked down at the smaller one, then at Nick. 'This is the Anchorage, isn't it?'

'Yes.'

'But you're not Derek Robertson?'

'No. I'm his son.'

The small one cut in impatiently: 'The son of Derek Robertson?'

'Yes. Look, this is getting silly . . .'

'Only your father said we'd be expected.'

'Well, I'm afraid you're not.'

'Your father hasn't been in contact, then?'

'Not for a week or two.'

'So you haven't got the package?'

'What package?'

The shorter hulk looked up at the taller hulk and frowned, then looked back at Nick. 'Look, son, this is serious. We've come all the way across here because we were told that this was where it would be.' He slipped his hand inside his jacket, after the style of Napoleon. 'Don't tell me we're wasting our time.'

'I'm sorry, but I really don't know what you're talking about. Is this some sort of joke?'

'No,' said the big hulk.

Nick felt uneasy. 'Well, I can call my father, if you like, but he keeps changing his mobile so I'm not sure he'll still be on the same number.'

'No,' said the shorter man. 'That's the trouble.'

Nick felt an overwhelming urge to push them down the garden path. But he thought better of it. It might have been something to do with their size, or that their suits had unidentifiable bulges in unexpected places.

'Look, I'll get in touch with him somehow and tell him you called. Have you got a number where he can reach you?'

At this, the larger man took a step forward, almost crushing Nick against the door frame. 'We don't mess about, you know.'

'Hey! Look! What the—'

'Don't piss us around,' growled his accomplice. 'We've come a long way.'

'Well, I don't have what you want so I don't see what I can do.'

Nick squeezed out from between the man and the door frame, then took a deep breath.

'Hello, I'm back,' said a voice. 'Had a lovely walk right along the cliff path. Oh, hello – I'm Nick's granny.' The two men wheeled round in time to see Rosie hold out her hand. They didn't take it. They just stared, while Rosie twittered on: 'Shame it's not brighter, isn't it? I expect you needed your sunglasses when you set off, but it's a bit threatening now.' She looked up at the sky. 'Quite cloudy.'

The two men froze as though they had been anaesthetized. They were clearly used to younger bodies than the fragile frame that had addressed them.

'Are you staying for lunch? I think we've some salad left over from last night. And a tin of tuna. I can certainly put the kettle on.'

Nick made to stop her, but the shorter of the two men spoke first: 'No, thanks, lady,' he said, his tone bemused. 'We've got to be going.'

He turned to Nick and partially recovered himself. 'We'll come back. You'll have it by then. We hope.' He gestured his companion towards the path, then nodded at Rosie. 'Take care, lady.'

Nick and Rosie watched as the pair lumbered down the path and out of the gate. They heard a car start and drive away. Then Rosie asked, 'Did I do all right?'

'What?' asked Nick, dazed.

'I'm quite good at playing the harmless old lady. Did it help?'

'I'll say.'

'What was it about? Who were they? Are you in some sort of trouble?'

'I have absolutely no idea.' And then, trying to sound casual, he said, 'When did you last hear from Dad?'

'About a fortnight ago. You don't think they're anything to do with him, do you?'

'No, no. I just wondered if he was still on his last number or whether it had changed again.'

'Only one way to find out,' she said.

'Yes.' So he tried. The number was unobtainable.

*

The lighthouse at St Catherine's Point winked out over the sea as Alex and Victoria ate their picnic lunch on the clifftop, huddled in windcheaters.

Victoria was nibbling an apple. She broke the silence: 'Are you cross with me?'

'Why should I be?'

'Because of last night. You know. With Nick.'

'What do you mean?'

'Do you fancy him?'

Alex looked at her admonishingly. 'What's it got to do with you?'

The child shrugged. 'Just wondered.'

They sat in silence for a while longer.

'What if I do?' asked Alex evenly.

Victoria examined her apple core. 'Don't you think he's a bit quiet?'

'Not at all. He's just . . . well . . . thoughtful.' Alex took a bite of her sandwich.

'I think he's quite nice.' Victoria put her apple core into an empty crisp packet. 'Will you see him again?'

'Who knows?'

'Don't you want to?'

'Oh, yes. I'm just not sure . . .'

'If he wants to?'

Alex nodded.

Victoria stood up. 'You can go without me, you know. I don't want to cramp your style.'

'*What?*' Her mother looked at her hard.

'I don't mind if you want to be on your own.'

Alex patted the ground next to her. 'Come and sit down.'

Victoria flopped on to the plaid car rug beside her

mother, leaned against her and gazed out over the sea. Alex stroked her hair. 'You've never cramped my style – understand? Never. And I don't want you thinking you have to keep out of the way. It's you and me in this, OK?'

Victoria raised her face to her mother's and nodded. A few moments later she said, 'I liked Rosie.'

'Yes. Me too.'

'She's fun. And not old. Well, I mean she *is* old, but she doesn't *seem* old, does she?'

'No. But some people are like that. They don't fit other people's preconceptions.'

'What are they?'

'Preconceptions? Oh, like prejudices.'

'Like Mr Darcy had?'

'Sort of. People don't always fit into boxes. It doesn't do to make hasty judgements. Sometimes they surprise you.'

'I don't like surprises.'

'Oh, the right sort of surprises are nice.'

'Do you think Nick might be surprising?'

'Too early to say, I suppose. Maybe.'

'So you will see him again?'

Now Alex stood up, and brushed the crumbs off her jeans. 'For someone who thinks he's a bit quiet you seem very anxious that I should.'

'Maybe I have a pre-, a pre-thingy.'

'Preconception.'

'Yes.'

'We'll see. Anyway, we've only a few days left here so there may not be time.'

'Do we really have to go back? Couldn't we just stay here?' Concern was etched on Victoria's face.

Alex folded up the rug. 'We're only just across the water. We're not far away.'

'I know, but it's different here. Quiet.'

'So, quiet can be good, then?'

Victoria nodded.

'Not boring?'

'No.'

'Well, you've got school next week.'

The child pushed her hands deep into her pockets. 'They have schools here, too.'

Alex put out her arm and turned Victoria to face her. 'Don't you think we're being a bit premature?'

Victoria shrugged.

'And you do know what that means, don't you?'

'Too soon.'

'Yes. Let's just take our time, shall we?' She handed Victoria the carrier-bag that contained the remains of the picnic and began to walk across the grass to the car.

'Mum?'

'Yes?'

'What does playing hard to get mean?'

Henry Kinross had had a good day. He had feared the worst when he opened the gallery that morning. The weather was pleasant, which was not what he needed, but then the clouds had come over and the wind strengthened. It turned into the sort of day when people were happy to shelter in an art gallery. Much better.

He had sold seven paintings: four of Nick's, one of the gloomy canvases that he and Nick had disliked (purchased by a taciturn couple from Chalfont St Giles), and two of Alex's brightest creations had been snapped up by a young couple from Fulham. He felt vindicated for having given her a chance. He had a new *protégé*. An attractive one at that. Perhaps he should ask Alexandra Pollen out to lunch. Butter her up a bit. Or maybe he was being a shade optimistic. And Nick seemed to have taken a shine to her. It wouldn't do to fall out over a woman. After the last time . . . well, maybe it was safer to stick to the St Émilion. You knew where you were with a bottle of claret.

When it came to the opposite sex, what he needed was a mature woman, someone with a bit of conversation. Companionship was just as important as sex, for God's sake. The sad thing was that both were in short supply.

The sound of the bell broke in on his musings. He looked up to see Nick standing in the doorway with a bright-eyed lady on his arm. 'Henry, can I introduce you to Rosie?'

'Dear boy! Of course!'

12
Breath of Life

Rich, but not dazzlingly so.

She was rather older than Henry would have liked – she must be nearly seventy, he thought – but she had a certain sparkle – and some indefinable quality that he found particularly engaging.

Over a bottle of claret in the Red Duster, Rosie and Henry became better acquainted. After a few minutes, he realized that, had she been a few years younger – well, a good few – she would have been the woman of his dreams. She was startlingly knowledgeable about art, easy to talk to and surprisingly coquettish for someone of her advanced years. He could still not work out how old she was, but that made her all the more interesting.

Nick was listening to the two of them, and marvelled at his grandmother's ability to adapt her personality to suit present company. She could find common ground with anybody, whoever they were, raise her game, or lower it, to suit the occasion.

Her eyes shone like pale sapphires when she was being made a fuss of. She didn't simper, she flirted, which, in a woman of eighty-seven, came as a bit of a surprise – to Nick, and, apparently, to Henry too.

Nick watched as she put away a couple of glasses of claret and a plate of steak and Guinness pie. She glanced at him occasionally, but Henry had her full attention, and she his.

Nick felt a little left out, then saw the funny side. But not for long. His problems surfaced and spun in his head. Should he broach the subject of Rosie's financial status? Was it any of his business? Well, as far as the car was concerned it was. And what was he to do about the Russian thing? What *could* he do? And there was the matter of the two men who had turned up with menaces. And what about Alex? He would call her and invite her out.

Alex's suspicion that Nick was a loner had been understandable but was not well founded. He needed space – as all creative souls do – to paint and think, but that didn't stop him believing that, one day, he would find the perfect person with whom he could spend the rest of his life. Mind you, there were times when he thought it improbable. His relationship with Debs had proved that: he'd thought she was the one. But he had also admitted to himself that while he had loved her he didn't believe in being 'in love'. Not a good start for someone seeking a lifelong soul-mate.

Here he was, living on the Isle of Wight, with a handful of dalliances and one major relationship behind him. He was nearly thirty-nine, reasonably tall, still predominantly dark and moderately good-looking in a lop-sided way, with just about enough to live on and the hope that things might get better. In short, he had enough of the dreamer in him to be assured of a bright future, once he realized he was just as capable as the next man of falling in love.

By eight o'clock Rosie was living up to her name: her cheeks were brightly flushed. She was noticeably giggly, too, and a little wobbly on her pins. Nick saw the warning signs and decided to take her home.

'Oh! Do we have to go? I'm having such a lovely time.' She didn't slur her words, but there was a slight over-enunciation.

Nick looked at Henry, whose countenance almost matched the liquid in his glass.

'Stay for another bottle, Rosie,' he said. 'Don't let this dauber take you home yet.'

Nick raised an eyebrow at his grandmother, and for once she took the hint: 'No. He's right. We'd better be going. Things to see, people to do, you know. Ha-ha.' She pushed herself up, steadied herself on the table, then walked gingerly to where Nick waited with her coat.

Henry stood up. 'Well, it's been a pleasure. Perhaps we can do it again some time.'

Rosie beamed. 'Oh, I do hope so. Thank you for your company.'

Henry ambled over to her, bent down and kissed her cheek. 'Take great care, precious lady.'

She beamed. 'Oh, to hell with that! Life's for living, and I'm going sailing tomorrow.' She took Nick's arm and walked out of the Red Duster, swaying gently from side to side in a decidedly regal sashay.

*

The silver Mercedes with the brand new numberplate completely blocked the track to the Anchorage.

'Bloody hell!'

'Language, Nicholas!' his grandmother admonished him.

'Well, look at that! Blooming holidaymakers! Think they can park anywhere.' He manoeuvred the MG on to the verge beside the track. 'Can you walk from here?'

'Of course. 'Snot far, is it?'

Her speech was sibilant now. He suppressed a grin. 'Only fifty yards or so. You can take my arm.'

'Oh. Thank you. Don't mind if I do.'

He walked her up the final curve of the track, and his heart missed a beat as the veranda came into view. Someone he had not seen in months was sitting on the step: his father.

'Hello, Nick! How ya doin'?'

'Dad! What are you doing here?'

'Come to see you and Mum. Hello, old girl.'

Rosie screwed up her eyes. 'Derek! Who told you I was here?' And then, with a note of anger in her voice, 'You've not come to take me away, have you?'

Derek Robertson got up. 'What would I want to do that for?'

'Because of Anna. She wants me in a home.'

Nick's father shrugged. 'Nothing to do with me, old love. I'm happy as long as you are.'

They stared at each other for a few minutes, until Derek asked, 'Can we go inside, then? It's a bit nippy out here.'

Nick handed his grandmother over to her son, unlocked the front door and let them in. He put on lights, motioned Rosie and Derek to take a seat and asked his father what he would like to drink.

'Scotch, please, old lad.'

'Some things never change,' said Nick, wryly. He left his father and grandmother while he went into the kitchen to fix the drinks.

Derek Robertson could not have looked more different from his son. For a start he lacked height, and his manner of dress, while not exactly shouting 'spiv', had a showy look, from the slip-on buckled loafers to the black shirt and brown suede blouson. He even had crinkly dark hair and a thin moustache. If you had seen him walking along the via Condotti you would have taken him for an Italian with Mafia connections.

Nick watched as his father sipped Scotch and enquired after his grandmother's health. Rosie was doing her best to concentrate, but the alcohol was taking its toll, and she could barely keep her eyes open.

After ten or fifteen minutes she excused herself. 'I'd love to sit up and talk to you, Derek, but I'm afraid I must go to bed. I'm completely done in.' She giggled. 'Knacked, I think, is the word. Yes. That's it. I'm completely knacked.' She pushed herself out of the chair and tottered elegantly towards her son, who rose to meet her. 'Goodnight, dear.' She pecked him on the cheek and wobbled unsteadily. 'Oops. Steady the buffs.'

'Goodnight, old girl. Look after yourself.'

'Oh, I don't need to. I've found somebody else to do that.'

Nick tried to butt in.

'And it's not my grandson. I met a very nice gentleman today. In the pub. Henry. Art dealer. Lovely man. Very good company. Mmm. Lovely big hands.' Without a backward glance she walked carefully in the direction of her bedroom.

Derek looked at his son. 'Is she behaving herself?'

'Depends what you mean.'

'Always done her own thing, Rosie. Never been one to conform. Know what I mean?' He winked.

'Yes.' Nick paused. 'Dad?'

His father was knocking back the remains of his Scotch. He put the glass down. 'Any more in that bottle?'

'A drop. Are you driving?'

'Only a small one, then.'

Nick poured a little of the amber fluid into his father's glass and continued the conversation. 'Dad . . . I had two guys here today asking for you. Something to do with a package.'

'Oh, shit.'

'What?'

'I told them it wouldn't be here till tomorrow. They never bloody listen.'

'Who don't? And what won't be here till tomorrow?'

Derek Robertson knocked back the contents of his glass in one and reached down the side of his chair. He lifted out a small padded envelope.

'What's that?' asked Nick.

'You don't need to know,' replied his father. 'When those guys come back tomorrow just hand it over to them, will you? They won't give you any trouble now.'

'But why can't *you* give it to them?'

'Because I won't be here. I've got a plane to catch.' Evidently he recognized Nick's confusion and irritation from the look on his son's face. 'No, don't worry. They won't do anything stupid as long as you give them that envelope.'

'Dad!'

'I know what you're thinking, but it's all above board. It's just better if I'm not here, that's all. I wouldn't do anything that would put you at risk – or Rosie. It's just safer for all concerned if you do the handover.'

'Of what?'

'Of . . . what's in the envelope. You don't need to know what it is.'

Nick folded his arms. 'I'm not doing it.'

'It's nothing to do with drugs, if that's what you're thinking. You know I don't do that sort of thing.'

'I don't care what it is. You've no right to ask me to do this.'

'Of course I haven't. And I wouldn't unless it was really necessary. It all sounds odd, I know, but it's perfectly straightforward.'

'Dad, you can't just swan in here like some shady character, pull out a package and expect me to hand it over to a couple of thugs without asking a few questions.'

'Look, I know it seems suspicious—'

'You can say that again.'

'Well, I'm asking if you'll do it. You'll have to trust me.'

'Have to?'

Derek sighed. 'I'd like you to.'

'I'd like to as well, but I haven't got much to go on.'

His father laid a hand on his shoulder. 'Will you or won't you? Just say yes or no and I'll be out of your hair.'

Nick struggled with his conscience. 'You promise it's nothing illegal?'

'Good God, no. It's just . . . well . . . private. That's all.'

'But you can't do it yourself?'

'If I do it there might be a lot of questions that I don't

want to have to answer. Yet. If you do it, there won't be. They know it's nothing to do with you.'

'Oh, they know me, then, do they?'

'Well, I've told them about you.'

'You told them where I lived as well.'

'I had to. Look, son, I'll tell you one day, when it's all sorted. For now I just need you to do this one small thing for me. OK?'

Nick shook his head. 'I don't believe this is happening to me.' He stared at his father.

His father stared back at him. They had reached an impasse. Then he played his trump card: 'It's to help Rosie. But I can't tell you any more.'

Nick threw his hands into the air. 'Oh, come on!'

'It's not what it seems.'

There was a silence. Nick was annoyed with himself for having been cornered. He had little choice. And his father knew it.

'OK – but I must be mad.'

'And I must be going. Those ferries are a bugger – never turn up when you want them to.' He slapped Nick on the back and made for the door.

'Dad!'

His father turned.

'When will I see you again?'

Derek Robertson shrugged. 'Not sure. Probably later rather than sooner.'

He swung out of sight, and Nick ran after him, calling in his wake, 'What do you know about Russia?'

His father stopped dead in his tracks half-way down the lane, then turned to face him. His expression was serious, with the merest hint of alarm. 'What do you mean?'

'Rosie's past. What do you know about Russia?'

'Oh, that.' He looked thoughtful. 'Bloody big country, Russia. Lot of people.' He got into his car, slammed the door and drove off into the night.

13
Belle de Crécy

At best, can be one of the most beautiful in its group; at worst, horrid.

How she had managed to be up and out of the house before him was a mystery. He knew she hadn't had that much to drink, but it had affected her. Why wasn't she stumbling around with a hangover?

Nick was rattled by her apparent self-sufficiency, and that he had not asked more about her sailing course. Where was she? Who was she with? When would she be home? Then the absurdity of the role-reversal struck him, and he felt slightly ashamed.

He ruffled his hair in some attempt to increase his cranial circulation and, therefore, his grasp on life, yawned and gazed out at the sea. She had chosen a good day to start: perhaps a force three – enough wind to fill her sails, but nothing strong enough to give trouble.

The ship's clock on the kitchen wall told him it was

eight thirty. He went to fill the kettle, and saw an envelope propped up against it. He opened it and found his birthday card. He had quite forgotten. He was thirty-nine.

But the card lifted his spirits. It was not of the 'Happy Birthday to My Favourite Grandson' type, with a couple of verses of Patience Strong to see you gaily through the coming year, instead it bore a black-and-white thirties photograph of a man in a suit holding the hand of a delicate-featured girl who was staring, rather distractedly, off-camera. The caption above it, in purple, read: 'Emily is told that "Philip's 12 inch" is, in fact, his television'.

He opened it and read the inscription: 'Sorry! Thought this might make you smile! Thanks for putting up with me. You're one in a million. (Or rather more, actually.) All my love, Rosie xxx'.

He looked at the front of the card again and laughed out loud.

The United Kingdom Sailing Academy nestles alongside the river Medina in West Cowes. It is a modern building with a slipway that leads down to the water; boats carrying sailors of little or no skill can be safely launched there. In the small classroom Rosie looked about her. She was the oldest by a good twenty years and felt rather smug. There were half a dozen teenagers, three forty-something married couples, a single man and a single woman in their sixties.

In her new baggy sailing shirt, pink cotton trousers and deck shoes she felt very much the part. She'd left the stick at Nick's.

Within a few hours she would be out on the water, and a lifetime's ambition would have been fulfilled. She thought, fleetingly, of her grandson, and hoped he would have a good birthday. But today the painter that held her attention would be made of rope.

The padded envelope sat, tantalizingly, at the end of his bed. He stretched out a hand and felt it, in the same way that a child feels a Christmas stocking, in an attempt to gauge the contents. The package gave nothing away. He got up and looked out of the window again. The sun was glinting on the water. It was the perfect May day. The perfect day for a birthday.

What a joke. Here he was, with half the troubles of the world hanging round his neck, plus a mad granny who thought she was a cross between the Empress of Russia and Ellen MacArthur, and a package of heaven-knows-what waiting to be collected by a couple of heavies who would probably break his legs. His car was likely to be impounded at any moment by a debt collector, his father arrested for trafficking in stolen goods, and himself banged up for perverting the course of justice. Even the most optimistic soul would have to admit this was not a promising way to celebrate the end of your fourth decade.

And then he saw her walking up the lane, Alex, with a packet in her hand. She saw him at the window and waved. She was alone.

'Hi! Come in.' He was at the open door to welcome her.

'You look happy.'

'Don't be deceived by appearances.'

She leaned towards him and kissed his cheek. 'Happy birthday.'

'How did you know?'

'Grannies talking to ten-year-olds.'

'Ah!' He smiled apologetically.

'You not having a good day, then?'

'Oh, just things.' And then he felt guilty for not welcoming her properly. 'But it's my birthday, so I'll put on a show.'

'Oh dear! All a bit too much for you, is it?'

'Rather a lot's happened in the past few days. And I'm sorry about the other night. I was a bit impatient with Rosie. I shouldn't have been but . . . well . . . Anyway, coffee?'

'Please.'

Once inside, she turned to him and held out the packet. 'We made this for you, we girls. Victoria's holed up with her friends, or she'd have come as well.'

He looked at the home-made envelope, which bulged at the seams, and at the scraps of coloured paper and feathers stuck to it. 'What is it?'

'You may well ask. Open it.'

Carefully he pulled at the seams of the home-made envelope, and tipped out the contents on to the kitchen table.

'Oh! Treasure trove!'

'It's silly, really. Beachcombers' booty.'

He gazed at the objects that had tumbled from their paper wrapping: a tiny starfish, the black purse of a dog fish egg, green and blue glass shards washed smooth by the sea, two shiny razor shells, a piece of bleached white coral and a dozen or more shells that were no bigger than his thumbnail in creamy white, soft purple and dusky pink. 'They're beautiful.'

'And very expensive.'

'What a wonderful present.' His eyes darted over the treasures. 'Thank you so much.'

Then he looked up at her in her loose white shirt and calf-length jeans, the shiny dark hair held back today with a tortoiseshell clip. He stepped forward, put his arms round her and gave her a hug. 'That's the nicest thirty-ninth birthday present I've ever had.'

She grinned. 'I'm glad.'

He bent down and kissed her forehead. 'I don't suppose you fancy a birthday supper, do you? I mean . . .'

'Just the two of us?'

'Well . . . if that's all right.'

'I'll have to ask permission,' she teased.

'Of course.'

She laughed. 'I'd love to.'

Over coffee they talked of Rosie's foray into the world of spinnakers and mainsails, and of Victoria's day on the beach with the friends she'd made in Sleepyhead Bay. Then Alex said she'd better be getting back before Victoria outstayed her welcome with her holiday chums, and he arranged to pick her up that evening. They parted with a double-cheeked kiss on the veranda.

He came back inside and picked up the padded envelope again. He stared at it, then squeezed it. It was fastened with staples. It would be a simple job to bend them back, open the end and examine the contents. Half of him wanted to, the other half urged restraint. The first half won. After all, if you're going to get yourself into trouble, you might as well know what for.

Carefully he slipped the blade of the kitchen knife under each staple, prised back the teeth, then popped back the flap and eased out the contents. The self-sealing polythene bag seemed to be full of cotton wool. He pulled it open, and tipped out the contents on to the kitchen worktop, lifted away the soft wadding, and out fell four stones that glittered and dazzled in the light from the lamp.

He had never seen such astonishingly beautiful diamonds.

He felt sick. Quickly he put them back into the wadding, careful to avoid marking them with fingerprints, then slipped it back into the polythene bag, the bag into the padded envelope, and nipped the jaws of the staples into place. The whole operation had taken no more than a couple of minutes.

He put the envelope under a cushion in the sitting room and sat down to think. His heart was hammering and his mind raced. Were the stones stolen? Surely not. His father had always lived on his wits but had never been on the wrong side of the law. And yet he said he was leaving the country by plane. Why, if he had nothing to hide? And why couldn't he hand over the diamonds himself?

It was all so ridiculously unreal.

For a moment he toyed with replacing the stones with something else, then banished the idea. If he did so the men would be back and he would be more deeply involved in something that, with any luck, would simply go away once he had handed over the envelope.

What were they worth? He'd never seen diamonds of that size before. They'd fetch thousands.

His hands shook.

A knock at the door brought him to his senses. He looked up and saw the silhouettes of the two burly men. They had come for their packet.

It was six o'clock when Rosie returned, her cheeks flushed with fresh air and excitement, but her eyes betrayed her tiredness. She flopped into a chair and said, 'Oh, yes, please!' when Nick offered her a gin and tonic. 'What a day. I don't remember when I last enjoyed myself so much. And the instructor said I was wonderful. He couldn't believe I'd picked it up so quickly. He says I'm a natural.' She took a sip from her glass, then looked up at him. 'How are we celebrating your birthday?'

'Ah.' A pang of guilt caught him. 'Well, er, I've arranged . . . to go out.'

'Oh. Oh, I see.'

He heard the disappointment in her voice.

'With Alex. You could come if you like.'

Her face was like that of a spaniel who has just been chastised. Then she smiled. 'And Granny came too? I don't think so. You go and enjoy yourself, love. I'll have an early night. We sailors have to be up in good time – decks to swab, ropes to coil, that sort of thing. And we're sailing at Gurnard tomorrow.'

He crouched in front of her and rested his hand on her knee. 'I'm very proud of you, you know.'

'That's sweet of you, but you've saved my life, love, when all around me were thinking only about theirs.' She patted his hand. 'You go and have a lovely time. Just don't make a noise when you come in.'

'You're not overdoing it, are you?'

'I'm pacing myself. I told you.'

'Well, make sure you do. It's hard work keeping up with teenagers – and I should know. I'm thirty-nine, after all.'

'So you are! And that reminds me. Could you nip into my bedroom and fetch the little packet that's on my bedside table? I'd go and get it myself only my grandson tells me I have to be careful.'

112

He went to her room, thinking it had been quite a day for packets, and returned with a small parcel that was, perhaps, three inches square. He gave it to her, and she handed it straight back to him.

'Happy birthday, my love.' She took another sip of her gin. 'Just a little something.'

He fingered the parcel, and his unease about her financial status was reawakened. 'You haven't done anything silly, have you?' he asked.

'Of course. Old lady's prerogative.'

He pulled off the wrapping to reveal a small box. For the second time that day, his heart thumped. He hoped she hadn't been ridiculously rash. He lifted the lid of the box. A diamond winked at him.

It was the same size as those he had seen earlier in the day.

'What's this?'

'Your present.'

'Well, yes . . . but . . .'

'Now, stop making a fuss and just admire it.'

'But – but – what am I going to do with it?'

'Keep it for a rainy day.'

'Where did it come from?'

'What's that got to do with you?'

'But, Gran – I mean, Rosie, you've bought me a car, and now this and – I mean your bank account—'

Rosie raised an eyebrow. 'Someone's been talking.'

'Yes.'

'Your mother?'

'Yes.'

'I wondered how long it would be before she found out.'

'But how could you afford—'

'By being careful for the best part of eighty-seven years.'
Nick flopped down in a chair. 'I don't understand.'

Rosie took a restorative sip of her gin. 'I got the idea from the Queen Mother.'

'What idea?'

'Getting rid of my assets.'

'What do you mean?'

'Well, she did it. Gave everything to her grandchildren. That way you can avoid death duties.'

'Are you sure?'

'Provided you live for seven years after you've handed the stuff over.'

Nick looked at her with a plaintive expression on his face. He was sure he'd read something about 'gift tax' or 'capital gains'. His thoughts were cut short.

'Oh, I know what you're thinking,' Rosie said. 'I'm eighty-seven, am I likely to last until I'm ninety-four.'

'No!'

'Don't interrupt. I looked at my bank account, and at how much interest had built up and it was pathetic. Did you know they charge you 7.8 per cent interest when you want to borrow money, and they'll give you 2.5 per cent when you invest it? Pathetic! Shouldn't be allowed. It's fraud. So I got to thinking that it wasn't worth leaving all that money in the bank, and having the taxman take his cut when I died. He's taking enough from me while I'm alive!'

Nick was listening to her, mouth open.

'Catching flies again, dear?'

He closed it.

'So I looked at the papers every day – you know, the financial pages – and worked out what the best investment was. It's a risky business. What do they say? "Interest rates can go down as well as up." I decided I needed to sink my money into something that was unlikely to be so . . . er, volatile, I think the word is. And the financial experts seemed to think it was the right time to invest in diamonds. So I emptied my bank account and bought a few. This one's yours.'

'But . . . what's—'

'What's it worth? Oh, at the moment about twenty-five thousand. Hopefully a bit more in a few years' time.'

'And what about Sophie and Alice?'

'Don't worry; I've taken care of your sisters. They have one each as well.'

'I see.' Nick gazed at the stone. 'It's beautiful,' he said, as though in a trance.

'Yes. I'd take it to the bank and leave it there for a while, if I were you. Until you need to cash it in. Then you can take it to a dealer. Shop around. I've written down some instructions so you can get the best price.'

Nick shut the lid of the box and looked at his grandmother. 'We've just got to make sure you live for another seven years, then?' His lips curled into a grin.

'Oh, I wouldn't worry about that. As far as the government's concerned I've just spent my money. No need for them to know where. I probably lost it on the horses. It's yours now.'

'Rosie! Is that legal?'

'Probably not – but it's no more wicked than taxing old ladies so that they can't afford to live on their savings, is it?'

'So how are you going to—'

'Live?'

'Yes.'

'Don't worry, angel. I've a little left in the building society and that should see me out.'

'Don't say that.' He hated it when she talked about the end.

'Just practical. We sailors are, you know. Anyway, hadn't you better be getting ready to go out for dinner? Don't want to keep Alex waiting.'

She winked at him. As he smiled back at her he thought that, royal or not, she was the most amazing person he knew.

14
Nuits de Young

. . . one of the best . . .

The butterflies in his stomach were obviously due to recent events. At least, that was what it suited him to believe as he eased the MG along the narrow lanes of West Wight. If he were honest with himself, though, he knew that his dinner date was at least partly responsible for them.

A vision of her had floated into his mind countless times that day, and he had done his best to banish it. Not because he didn't want to think of her, but because he didn't want to imagine feelings that weren't there. On her part as well as his. As excuses go, it was pretty futile.

He had arranged to pick her up at the end of the lane on the Undercliff, a hundred yards from where she was staying. He drew in at the appointed spot, but there was no sign of her. The hood of the car was down, and he looked up at the trees, now fully decked in late-spring finery. The early-evening sun slanted between the sap-green leaves of sycamores and beeches. He checked his watch. She was late, but only just. He drummed his fingers on the steering-wheel and craned his neck to see round the corner.

Then he heard running feet, and she rounded the bend, a pale blue sweater draped over her shoulders and tied loosely at her neck.

She greeted him breathlessly. 'Sorry. Bedtime story took a bit longer than I thought.'

He leaned over, opened the car door, and she slid in beside him, kissed his cheek and said, 'Blame it on inheritance.'

'What?' he asked.

'We've finished *Pride and Prejudice* and we're on to *Sense and Sensibility*.'

'What's that got to do with inheritance?' He started the car and drove down the lane.

'Have you tried explaining to a ten-year-old girl why in 1811 a father's estate was bequeathed to the son of his first wife and the three daughters of the second wife got nothing?'

'No.'

'Well, if you had, you'd find it took longer than you'd think.'

Nick frowned. 'Did you manage to convince her?'

'Not really, no. She's furious – thinks it was completely unfair. Or, to use her word, minging.'

'Hang on, let me get this right. It's a truth universally acknowledged that a single man in possession of a good fortune must be in want of a wife as long as she's not minging!'

Alex laughed. 'Something like that.'

'Isn't Jane Austen a bit ambitious for a ten-year-old?'

'You'd think so, wouldn't you? But ever since she saw one of them serialized on TV she's been nuts about them. She's even decided she wants to change her name to Dashwood because it sounds better than Pollen.'

'Victoria Dashwood . . . It does have a bit of a ring to it. But it's not as delicate as Pollen, which makes you think of flowers.'

'Why, thank you kindly, Mr Robertson.'

'Robertson's a bit dreary in comparison, isn't it? What does that make you think of? Jam? Which reminds me. Are you hungry?'

'Starving. Where are we going?'

'Well, there's a little bistro at the back of the George in Yarmouth. I've booked a table there – if that's all right?'

'Fine.' She leaned back in the seat and looked skywards as they drove along the coast. 'I'm looking forward to this.'

They were given a corner table in the dusky, cream-painted restaurant, candle-lit and secluded, and ushered to it by a girl in her teens. Nick ordered a bottle of Rioja, and she brought it to their table rather hesitantly. Nick noticed that her black shoes were huge, almost like clogs, at the end of her sparrow-like legs.

Alex had followed the direction of his gaze. 'Surprising she can lift them, isn't it?'

Nick shook his head. 'I must be getting old.'

'Steady on! If you really want to feel old you should start mixing with girls half her age.'

'Well, if it's all the same to you I'll stick with the thirty-somethings.'

Alex smiled. 'Very sensible.'

'Cheers!' He lifted his glass of wine and clinked it against hers.

'Happy birthday! And lovely to spend it with you.'

They sipped their wine, and then he asked, 'It must be hard going out when you're a single mum.'

'Is this where I sound sad? I don't manage it as often as I'd like.'

'Can't think why,' he said warmly.

'Where are you leading, Mr Robertson?'

'Nowhere. I can't believe men aren't falling over themselves to take you out.'

Alex spluttered into her wine. 'Either you are the most ridiculous chatter-upper I've ever met or you don't understand the effect that a child can have on a potential relationship.'

'Ah, I see. It is a truth universally acknowledged that a single woman with a child will find it difficult to get a man.'

'You know, if anybody else had said that to me I'd have told them where to go, but as it's you . . .'

'Sorry. Will you let me off?'

'Just this once.'

Nick could not recall anyone, apart from his grandmother, to whom he found it so easy to talk. Even with Debs he had not relaxed as much as he did with Alex. He watched her animated face over the glow of the candle. Her flashing eyes seemed almost jet black.

She wore a loose-fitting white shirt and a pair of black trousers that hugged her slim figure. Her hair, fastened back with the tortoiseshell clip, shone like ebony. He was entranced.

She told him of her childhood on a farm in Devon, of losing her parents when she was in her teens, of her marriage to Paul and their broken relationship, her hopes for Victoria.

'And what about you? What do you want?' he asked, over coffee.

'Oh, that's a big one. Don't really have time to think about me.' She looked away. 'I'm a bit scared, I suppose.'

'Why?' he asked gently.

'Got it wrong once. Might get it wrong again.'

'So why bother trying?'

'There's a bit of that, I suppose. Don't want to rush into something that might not work out. I can't mess it up any more for Victoria.'

'There she is again.'

'You see? It's impossible for any man to understand my responsibilities.'

'I think you might be underestimating any man.'

'You think so?'

He looked into her eyes. 'I think so.' He laid his hand on hers. 'Don't sell yourself short,' he said.

She wrapped her fingers round his. 'Are you just being kind?'

'Oh, no. I'm not being kind at all.'

Alex looked wary. 'You're funny.'

Nick looked serious. 'Funny? Why do you say that?'

'Because you're not like other men.'

'Oh, I see.' Nick was puzzled.

'No. I mean, you listen.'

'Don't other men?'

'No. Only when they want to get you to . . . well . . .'

'And I don't?'

'I don't know.'

He squeezed her hand. 'Sorry. I didn't want to embarrass you.'

'No?'

'No.'

She squeezed back.

Their eyes met. Then the silence was broken by a plaintive voice: 'Was everything all right?' asked the waitress.

Nick began to speak, but Alex beat him to it. 'Oh, yes. It was lovely.'

He opened the car door for her, then walked round to the driver's side and slid in. The engine roared into life and he steered the MG out of the car park. They said nothing, but he could feel her sitting closer than before. He caught an occasional whiff of her perfume. Suddenly it started to rain heavily.

'Oh, God!' He swerved into the side of the lane, beneath the shelter of the overhanging sycamores. 'It won't take a minute! Hang on!' He leaped out of the car and fought with the hood. It took several minutes to fasten it in place, during which time Alex shrieked, at first from the shock of the freezing deluge, but then with hilarity as he battled with the canopy and its collection of poppers and zips that seemed to bear no relation to the fittings on the car. Eventually, she jumped out to help, and soon the car was shielded from the worst of the elements by the ancient black shroud that passed for weatherproofing.

'Get in! GET IN!' Nick roared, as he ran round to his side and stumbled into the damp interior.

Alex did her best to obey. 'I can't! My door's stuck!' she

yelled. He got out again, ran round to her side and applied masculine pressure to the handle, which finally yielded. Nick tumbled into the driver's seat and was greeted by a drenched Alex, laughing until tears and raindrops were running down her cheeks in tandem.

'You silly man! What a ridiculously impractical car.'

He was watching the rivulets coursing down her face, her bright eyes, the droplets of water on her dark hair.

'Me? Look at you!' he exclaimed, and wiped the water off her cheek. As he did so, he leaned forward and kissed her. Her scent filled his nostrils as he felt the softness of her lips on his. Gently his tongue crept into her mouth. She made no move to resist, and he slid closer to her, in spite of the gear lever.

For a moment she saw the hilarity of the situation, and let out a brief laugh, which turned into a sigh, and rested her head on his shoulder, inhaling with him the aroma of wet leather and damp clothing. 'Wow!' she said softly.

'Yes,' he replied. 'Wow!'

He stroked the back of her head, then turned her face towards his and kissed her again, tenderly and with an unexpected longing.

She began to breathe faster, as the rain beat down on the car's hood. He laid a hand on her shoulder and felt the heat of her skin through the soaking cotton shirt. He kissed her lips, cheeks and chin. Her eyes were closed now, and she sighed with pleasure.

He felt himself becoming aroused by her closeness, her warmth and her perfume. He stroked her arm, then moved his hand down to her waist. She let out a whimper, put her hand on the back of his neck and drew his head towards her breast. He nuzzled into her, then he lifted his head and gazed into her eyes.

Neither of them said anything as he undid her buttons and eased apart the translucent white cotton that covered her brown body. She was not wearing anything beneath the shirt. With the back of his hand, he delicately traced the outline of her breasts, then bent forward and feathered them with kisses. She arched her back with pleasure until, finally unsure of being able to control herself, she drew away with a gasp.

'No.'

He raised his head and looked into her eyes, then leaned across and kissed her forehead. 'Sorry.'

She shook her head. 'No, no. Don't be sorry.'

He rested his head on her shoulder until their breathing had returned to normal, then started the engine and drove her home.

15
Magenta

Frustratingly temperamental.

The following morning he was lying in bed, listening to the rain pounding on the roof. He replayed the events of the previous evening over and over again in his mind. He had not expected to be so affected by her, and wondered if she felt the same. Where was she now? What would she do today? Not go out painting, that was for sure – not in this weather.

They had not made any arrangement to meet again. It was as if they both needed breathing space. There seemed to be fear on both their parts. He needed to take stock of his emotions and understand whether it had been simply an evening of easy passion. And what of Alex? She had seemed willing at first, but had pulled away. Too much too soon? Or had she not wanted to get involved?

He slid out from under the duvet and padded across to the window. A stiff breeze was blowing the rain in diagonal sheets across the steel-grey sea and into the cliff face. Battalions of droplets rattled against the window of the cottage and trickled down the panes. Not a good day for sailing. He pulled on a bathrobe and went into the sitting room, expecting to find Rosie in her dressing-gown.

She was fully clothed in sailing gear and pulling on a waterproof.

'What are you doing?' he asked.

'Getting ready to go.'

'You can't go out in this. Not sailing, anyway.'

'Are you suggesting I'm a fair-weather sailor?'

'I'm suggesting you should be. They won't take you on the water in this, surely?'

'Well, I'm going to go. I don't want to be the only one who doesn't turn up.'

'I think they'd understand if you didn't.'

'Never let it be said that your mother bred a gibber. That's what my mum used to say.'

'Meaning?'

'Don't be such a wimp.'

He looked at her with his head on one side. 'Have you seen the weather out there?'

'Yes.'

'And you're still going?'

'I'll take my stick.' She made the concession grudgingly.

'Well, that won't stop you being blown off the cliff.'

She shrugged.

'Look, give me a minute to get dressed and I'll drive you there. At least I can make sure you arrive in one piece. Then it'll be up to them to *keep* you in one piece.'

He showered quickly, threw on jeans, sweatshirt and

trainers, and met her at the front door with his hair in a damp tangle.

'Ooh, you look hunky,' she said, with a glint in her eye.

Nick frowned. 'Dreadful woman. Come on.' Nick offered her his arm, which she resolutely ignored, so he put it through hers as they walked out into the windy morning.

'Car smells nice,' she said.

'It got a bit damp last night. Caught out by the rain.'

'First rain I've known that smelt of Chanel No. 5.'

Nick said nothing.

'Same as I wear.'

'I know.'

'Did you have a nice time?'

He kept his eyes on the road ahead. 'Yes, thanks.'

'Nice girl. Lovely dark eyes.'

They motored on in silence.

As he pulled down the road that led to the sailing academy she tapped his arm. 'Here will do.'

'But there's another hundred yards to go.'

'Here's fine. I can walk the rest. Need a breath of air, anyway.'

The rain had eased slightly so he let her have her way, remembering how he had hated his father dropping him off outside the school gates in a car that was too showy to be cool.

'Don't get out,' she instructed. 'I can manage.'

He watched her struggle, but resisted the temptation to get out and open her door. It was clearly important to her to do it herself. Instead, he leaned across and pulled at the stiff catch.

Rosie tutted. 'I could have managed.'

'Alex found it too stiff to open last night.'

'Oh.'

She got out and straightened in the stiff breeze. 'Good-bye, then, sweetheart. Be careful.'

'What about tonight?' Nick asked. 'What time shall I pick you up?'

'Oh, don't worry. I'll ring if I need a lift. I'll probably be able to get one of my friends to drop me off.'

She lifted a hand to bid him goodbye, and was turning away when he called, 'Rosie!'

She wheeled round.

'You forgot this.' He was holding her walking-stick. He could see she was about to snap that she didn't need it when a strong gust caught her and propelled her towards the car. Rather than admit she had lost her footing, she tripped forward and took the stick from him. She reminded him of a cat who, having just fallen off a wall, completes the exercise with a jump into the air that implies 'I meant to do that all along.'

'Hmph,' she said, and waved it at him, then walked off to the academy.

He slumped back in his seat and heaved a sigh. He hoped to God they wouldn't take her out on the water on a day like this.

'"I do not attempt to deny," said she, "that I think very highly of him – that I greatly esteem, that I like him."' Marianne here burst forth with indignation – "Esteem him! Like him! Cold-hearted Elinor! Oh! worse than cold-hearted! Ashamed of being otherwise. Use those words again and I will leave the room this moment."' Alex paused and looked out of the window thoughtfully.

'Go on!' pleaded Victoria.

'Mmm?' Alex answered, distracted.

'Carry on with the story.'

Alex turned to her. 'Do you mind if we don't? Could we have a break for a minute?'

'But I want to know what Elinor says. If she really loves Edward or just likes him.'

'Yes.' Alex was already gazing out of the window again.

'Please!'

Alex turned back to the book: '"Excuse me," said she, "and be assured that I meant no offence to you, by speaking in so quiet a way, of my own feelings. I am by no means assured of his regard for me. There are moments when the extent of it seems doubtful; and till his sentiments are fully known, you cannot wonder at my wishing to avoid any encouragement of my own partiality, by believing or calling it more than it is."'

'What's partiality?'

'Mmm?'

'What does partiality mean?'

'It means . . . fondness.'

'You mean she fancies him?'

'Probably. Now, shall we go out and get a breath of air? I think the wind is dropping.'

The man at the bank took the package with little ceremony and assured Nick that he could have it back whenever he wanted. It was a weight off his mind to know that the diamond was somewhere safe, but he still worried about Rosie – not just because she might now be one of those in peril on the sea, but also because of her mental stability. He was not sure that converting money into diamonds was a particularly sensible course of action. From what he had read, the diamond and gold markets were more volatile than bank interest rates, not less so, as Rosie had suggested. But what worried him even more was the possibility that his father was involving his own mother in some kind of scam. If only he would answer his bloody phone. Where the hell was he?

Henry was moving pictures. The last few days had seen quite a run on stock, and he was filling the gaps between the original works with a few signed prints of J-class yachts in full sail, creaming their way across the Solent. He didn't care for them much: when you'd seen one depiction of *Velsheda* edging ahead of *Shamrock* against a pale blue sky and fluffy clouds, or *Endeavour* chasing *Britannia* off the Royal Yacht Squadron, you'd seen them all. But the public had a voracious appetite for them. Thankfully.

He was humming to himself as he positioned the paintings, reminding himself that the only reason he had to do so was because he had had a good week. When the doorbell pinged and Nick walked in he was well disposed enough to offer him a glass of claret.

'God, no! Not at this time of day.'

Henry looked at his watch. 'It's almost lunchtime.'

Nick checked. 'Eleven thirty is not lunchtime.'

'Elevenses, then.'

'A coffee would be good.'

'Suit yourself, dear boy.' Henry shrugged and disappeared into the stock room to put the kettle on.

Nick eyed the walls and saw the preponderance of prints. 'I suppose you'll be wanting some more?'

'Dead right I will,' replied Henry, to the sound of running water.

'Is there any chance of a cheque as well?' enquired Nick, the merest hint of irony in his voice.

'Ah. Will tomorrow do?'

'Henry!'

Henry reappeared. 'Cash-flow.'

'Yours might be difficult but mine's non-existent.' Then he thought of the diamond.

'Why you artists have to eat is beyond me. You can't understand that your work is so much more attractive if you're starving and look emaciated. Couldn't you lose a few pounds and forget to shave for a day or two? I'd get more for your paintings.'

'But nobody who buys them knows what I look like.'

'Don't split hairs.'

The kettle whistled. As Henry went to make the coffee he offered an olive branch. 'How about five hundred? I can give you some more next week.'

'Oh, all right, then. As long as you do.'

'Trouble is, I've got another mouth to feed now.'

'What do you mean?'

'Alex's have sold well. I shall have to ask her to up her output.'

'She'll be pleased.'

'Oh, she is.'

'You've seen her, then?'

'Left just before you arrived. With the kiddie in tow. Sweet little girl. Asked if I'd like her to do some paintings, too. She brought me one as a sample.' He came through from the back room with a sheet of A4 paper on which were stuck shells, sand and feathers. 'To Henry from Victoria,' it said.

'Might become a cult,' said Nick.

'Might win the Turner prize,' countered Henry.

'No,' argued Nick. 'You can see what it's meant to be.'

Henry grinned. 'You're in a good mood, in spite of a lack of funds.' He pulled his cheque book out of his desk drawer and scribbled. 'Here you are. Don't –'

'– spend it all at once.'

Henry went back for the coffee, and Nick shouted after him, trying to sound offhand. 'Alex OK?'

'Well, you should know.' He came back with two mugs.

'What do you mean?'

'You were with her last night, she said.'

'Well . . . yes . . . but I just wondered if she was OK today.'

'Shouldn't she be?'

Henry was winding him up, and Nick knew it.

Henry relented. 'She was fine.' And then, with a glint in his eye, 'If a bit subdued.'

Nick sipped his coffee calmly. 'Probably because of the weather – not good for painting.'

'Very likely.' Then he went in for the kill: 'Are you two . . . er . . . I think the expression is "an item"?'

'Don't be ridiculous! We've only known each other a week.'

'Is that all? God, doesn't time fly when you're selling a lot of paintings?'

'Henry!'

'Sorry. Only a friendly enquiry.' And then, under his breath, 'I've known people to marry quicker than that.'

'Yes, and how long did it last?'

'In my parents' case, it was forty-three years before my dad decided he'd had enough.'

'He ran off?'

'Ran out of breath. Died of a heart-attack.'

'Oh, I'm sorry.'

'No, no. Too long ago for that. My mum married again in her seventies. She's still going strong. Seen off the second husband, though. Reckons that men today have no stamina. Tough, these old birds, aren't they?'

'You can say that again.'

Henry looked reflective. 'Your granny's an amazing old girl.'

'Don't let her hear you say that.'

'Doesn't she like being called an old girl, then?'

'She wouldn't like the "old" bit. I don't think it's a word she includes in her vocabulary.'

'Well, I have to tell you, young Nick, that I reckon she's a bit of a star, and if she was ten years younger I'd be making a play for her.'

'Ten years?' Nick looked at him with incredulity. 'How old do you think she is, then?'

'Getting on for seventy?'

'Ha!'

'Late sixties?'

Nick shook his head. 'Wrong way.'

'Older?'

'Much. Eighty-seven.'

Henry sat down at his desk with a thump. 'You're kidding.'

'Nope. Born in 1917.'

'Well, bugger me.'

Nick grinned. 'I'll take that as an expletive rather than an invitation.'

'She's amazing for her age.'

'I know. Refuses to lie down. Mind you, I do wonder . . . if she had the opportunity . . .' Then he looked serious.

'Look, for goodness' sake, don't tell her I told you her age, will you? She'd skin me alive.'

Henry came out of his reverie. 'Of course not. Well, I'm blowed. Eighty-seven! Old enough to be my mother.' His face bore a look that quite clearly indicated his disappointment. The sort of disappointment that comes when dreams are overtaken by reality.

16
Schoolgirl

In my opinion, rather overrated.

Victoria was unsure of her mother's mood, and when you're trying to persuade a parent to buy you something, you need to be certain that your strategy is going to work. She had decided that she, too, was an artist, but rather than accepting the box of poster paints her mother was prepared to buy her, she had set her heart on a watercolour outfit in a varnished wooden box. She knew that now was not the moment to admit this, and declined what she considered the childish compromise. She settled instead for a guidebook to the Isle of Wight so that she could get to know it better. And, hopefully, find somewhere to live.

Alex, knowing that her daughter's intransigence could be epic when she put her mind to it, bought the modestly priced guidebook without demur and resigned herself to the fact that something was clearly brewing.

'Where are we?' Victoria asked, as she pored over the map of the lozenge-shaped island.

Alex peered over her shoulder. 'Here.' She pointed to the bottom right-hand corner.

'And where is Nick?'

'Here.' Alex indicated the northernmost tip.

'How far away is that?'

'Well, look at the scale. There you are – that line. Five miles is about as long as . . . your finger. How many fingers between here and there?'

Victoria stuck her tongue out of the corner of her mouth, the better to concentrate, and measured the map with her finger. 'Three.'

'Which means we are how many miles away?'

'I'm not stupid, you know.'

'Well?'

'Fifteen miles. Is that close?'

'Fairly.'

'What about you and Nick?' she asked casually, as she folded up the map. 'Are you close?'

Her mother decided attack was the best form of defence. 'Don't be so nosy.'

'I'm not nosy, just curious.'

'I think he's a very nice man, that's all. And I've only just met him.'

Victoria folded her arms. 'Honestly, you're like Elinor Dashwood.'

'Don't be ridiculous. That story was written nearly two hundred years ago and this is the twenty-first century.'

Victoria gave her a quizzical look. 'It's funny how some things don't change, isn't it?'

*

136

The Red Duster was unusually busy, but Henry, having forewarned his friend the landlord of their arrival, had secured a table in the far corner of the bar, albeit with only one chair. He squeezed round it, lowered himself and the bottle of St Émilion into place, then motioned to Nick that he should grab the chair that had just been vacated by a boat-builder.

With a pint of hand-pulled in one fist and a piece of bentwood furniture in the other, Nick elbowed his way through a Gore-Tex clad group of yachties and eased himself opposite his patron.

They had barely begun to converse when a voice cut through the crowd. 'Sorry! Thank you so much. Yes – thank you. Excuse me!' And there she was, standing before them, with a gin and tonic.

Rosie smiled at Henry, who attempted unsuccessfully to stand up. He bowed over the claret and indicated the chair that Nick was putting down. 'Dear lady!' he exclaimed, with a half-excited, half-wistful expression on his face. 'What are you doing here? Afternoon off?'

'Oh, no. Just a lunch-break. Too lumpy out on the water. Bit of a swell. We might capsize. They've brought us to see some special boats that they make here.'

Having given away his seat, Nick had been swept aside by a tide of mariners fresh from a morning's sail and desperate for a pint.

'Everything OK, then?' he asked, temporarily becalmed in the centre of the room.

'Fine, dear. Henry will take care of me, won't you, Henry?'

'Of course. My pleasure.' Henry laid a large hand over hers. 'So, what's it to be? Lamb hot-pot or red snapper?'

'Oh, the snapper, I think. Sounds so much more sparky, doesn't it?'

'A bit like you,' offered Henry, with a roguish tilt of his head.

Nick raised his eyes heavenward and drained his glass.

Nick sat at his mitre block, finishing off a couple of frames for a pair of watercolours he had completed, and listened to Rosie drying the dishes and humming.

She seemed calmer now, almost like the old Rosie. Then she put her head through the doorway of the tiny room and asked, 'Coffee?'

He turned to answer her, and saw that, although she was smiling, her eyes were filled with tears. 'Hey!' He got up, and enfolded her in his arms. 'What's the matter?'

'Oh, nothing. It's just that . . . Oh, I'm so silly . . .' She pulled a tissue from the pocket of the pink sailing trousers she had taken to wearing in the evenings.

Nick released her and stood back to look at her. 'What do you mean?'

'It's just that I don't remember being so happy in a long time.'

'That's not silly, that's lovely.'

'I suppose it is.'

'What do you mean you suppose? Of course it is.' He gave her a squeeze. 'Is it to do with Henry?'

'Oh, no, not really. Well, maybe a bit. He's very attentive.'

Nick grinned. 'Yes.'

'Only he believes I'm younger than I really am.'

'You think so?' Warning bells rang.

'Oh, I know so.'

Nick tried to sound casual. 'How can you be sure?'

Rosie looked away. 'Because I told him I was sixty-nine.'

'What?'

'Oh, I know it was silly of me but . . . he was so nice, and I didn't want him to think I was some senile old woman.'

'But sixty-nine!'

'That would make me only eleven years older than him, and it's not too much of an age gap, is it?'

'Well, no, but . . .'

She seemed anxious now, and met his gaze. 'You won't tell him the truth, will you?'

Nick was cornered. 'Is it important?'

'It is to me.'

'And you think Henry's interested?'

'I know he is. He's asked me out on Friday night.'

'Oh?'

'But I can't go. It's the final evening at the sailing academy. We're all going out for a drink.'

'I see.' Nick was trying to keep a straight face. 'Couldn't you go out for a meal afterwards?'

'Well, yes, I am. But not with Henry.'

Just for a moment, Nick felt like the father of a teenage daughter who was enquiring after her movements. 'Who with, then?'

'There's another man at the sailing academy. He's single, too. In his sixties.'

'And have you told him how old you are?'

'I said I was sixty-six,' Rosie said sheepishly.

At ten o'clock Nick tapped on her bedroom door. 'Can I come in?'

'Of course.'

He opened the door and peeped in. She was tucked up under her duvet, with just her head visible; her hair was encased in a swathe of pink net. 'You're not to laugh at me but it keeps my hair tidy – I haven't been to the hair-dresser's in a week.'

'And you can't let your men down,' teased Nick.

'Of course not.' She pushed herself up a little, and Nick spotted the lace on her nightie. She was elegant even in bed. 'I'm sorry about tonight,' she said.

'Why?'

'For being all those things that I try not to be.'

'Such as?'

'A stupid old woman. Mutton done up as lamb.'

'Don't be silly.' He sat on the edge of her bed. 'And, anyway, they don't sell mutton any more.'

'No. Maybe that's why the market for lamb has increased.' She winked at him.

Nick shook his head. 'You know, I still don't understand you. You're supposed to be out of touch and helpless, and here you are on a sailing course with people half your age . . .'

'Be careful!' she admonished him.

'. . . but you hold your own in conversation with anyone and line up dinner dates like there's no tomorrow.'

'Well, there might not be.' Rosie laughed. 'You are funny.'

'Me?'

'Yes. You. You're thirty-nine and far more staid than I am.'

'I'm not staid, just cautious.'

'There's a difference?'

'Yes.'

'Well, if I were you I'd start to live a bit.'

Nick sighed. 'Am I in for an advice session, then?'

'No. Well . . . maybe just a bit of *friendly* advice.' She looked right at him. 'Get on with it. Don't hang about.'

'Get on with what?'

'Your relationship with Alex.'

'There *is* no relationship.'

'Exactly. But there could be.'

He frowned. 'And what's that to do with you?'

Rosie shrugged. 'Absolutely nothing. But you should be having a bit of fun. She's a lovely girl and she should be having fun, too.'

'What about Victoria?'

'Oh, don't worry about her. She's got her head screwed on. She's older than all of us.'

'You think?'

'Oh, yes. Funny, isn't it? Victoria's ten, but more like forty. You're thirty-nine and more like seventy, and I'm eighty-seven going on thirty! Nobody's the age they seem, are they?'

'You know, there are days when I think you'll live for ever,' Nick said.

'Oh, heaven forbid!'

'But where do you get your energy?'

Rosie nodded at the glass beside her bed. 'Out of a bottle.' Then she became serious. 'Oh, there are days when I have to work hard to get up. Days when I wonder if it's all worth it. But I tell myself it's only natural at my age. Trouble is, you can't let that happen too often. You have to fight it. Don't let it win. Some days my legs don't want to move at all. But I battle on – and it doesn't half hurt. I just grit my teeth and get on with it. Other days I have a good cry, and feel completely done in. Then the sun shines and I feel better, and I'm damned if I'll stay cooped up inside.'

'You're a star.'

'Oh, no. I'm quite scared, if I'm honest.'

'Scared of what?' Nick looked baffled.

'Losing it. I feel a bit funny some days. A bit . . . sort of . . . disconnected. Something happens inside. A voice. It's me, and yet it isn't me, if you see what I mean.'

'Is that what happened at the Russian embassy?' he asked gently.

Rosie nodded. 'I was a bit embarrassing, wasn't I?'

'Just a bit.'

She stared into the middle distance. 'I think it's just that I want a bit more time to . . . understand more. I'd like to be . . . and you mustn't tell me off . . . more at peace with myself before I go.'

Nick raised an eyebrow.

'Oh, don't worry. I'm not going to get religion or anything. Well, no more than I have. I'm content to go to church once a month but I can't be doing with all that happy-clappy stuff – and shaking hands. I always keep this by my bed.' She picked up a small black book. 'The Book of Common Prayer. Lovely language.' She looked up at him and asked evenly, 'Do you say your prayers?'

Nick nodded. 'Sometimes.'

'Good. I say mine every night. Here I am, an old lady – I can refer to myself like that but you can't – saying every night, "Gentle Jesus, meek and mild, look upon a little child; pity my simplicity; give me grace to come to thee – but not yet." I always put that bit in. Hope it makes Him smile.'

He watched as she lay back on the pillow. Calm now. Peaceful.

'He knows, doesn't he?' she said.

'Mmm?'

'Where I came from.'

Nick nodded.

Rosie squeezed his hand. 'Try to find out for me.'

He sighed. 'If you want me to.'

Rosie smiled contentedly. Her eyes were closing. The day's exertions and the sea air were having their effect. 'And I always ask God to bless you all. Derek and Anna, Alice, Sophie and Nick. And Sandy. Do you remember her?'

'Yes.' He half laughed. Sandy had been their first dog. She must have died twenty-five years ago.

And then her conversation was replaced by gentle breathing.

Nick turned out the light, kissed her cheek, and quietly closed the door.

17
Nevada

Of uncertain parentage.

If Nick had been honest with himself he would have realized that the reason he had not arranged another meeting with Alex was that he was too scared. Scared that it might lead somewhere – or that it might not lead anywhere. Or just scared full stop.

He cursed himself for not having had the nerve to ask her out again when they parted. If he had he would have more of an idea now where he stood. As it was he was clueless.

He dropped Rosie off at the sailing academy, with only one warning to be careful. 'Is that all?' she had asked. 'You don't want to walk me in?'

Then he drove on to Newport and the public library. The librarian was one of those polite but contained women who so often preside over books. She listened attentively while he enquired about the best way of tracing one's

144

ancestors, and recommended him to the parish registers in the churches where his parents had grown up, and the National Archive in Kew. 'It's a bit more tricky than that,' confessed Nick. He wanted to ask the question without giving too much away. 'You see, my grandmother came from Russia when she was a baby, and the National Archive doesn't have any record of her real parents.'

'Well, no,' confirmed the librarian, over the top of her rimless glasses. 'That's why it's called the National Archive – it doesn't deal with other countries. The best place to start, I suppose, would be the Russian embassy in London. They could point you in the right direction.'

'Thank you.' He made to leave, feeling dissatisfied. Half of him wanted to tell the librarian the entire story, and watch her eyes widen as she realized who she might be talking to. He turned back and asked the woman another question. 'You know the Russian revolution?'

'I am acquainted with it.'

'After the assassinations . . .'

'Yes?'

'Well, all the immediate royal family were killed, weren't they?'

'Almost certainly.'

'I'd like to find out who is their closest descendant.'

She took off her glasses and asked, just a touch patronizingly, 'Do you have access to the Internet?'

As he switched on the computer he wondered if Rosie had been there before him. Could the quest for her ancestry have been the reason why she had been to computer-skills classes at night school? Why else would she need to be computer literate?

He called up assorted sites with the word 'Romanov' in the title and, after some sifting, found one that looked promising: 'The Romanov Imperial Dynasty in Emigration XX Century by Sergey P. Shishkin, translated from Russian by R. Konnoff.' The typeface and layout of the document had a utilitarian look. Primitive, somehow. East European. He felt a frisson of excitement as he started to read:

The Romanov Dynasty began with the ascension of Tsar Mikhail Fedorovich, to the Russian throne in 1613. Though still a young dynasty, by the 18th century the succession was seriously tested. Although with the accession of Peter III the crisis ended. Peter III was the son of Grand Duchess Anna of Russia and Duke Karl-Frederic of Holstein-Gottorp.

The names were a bit of a mouthful. Not exactly in the Nick Robertson mould. He read on:

His aunt Elizabeth, Tsarina of Russia, adopted Peter and the Romanov Dynasty was saved from extinction. In 1797 at his crowning, Peter's son, the Emperor Paul, wishing to prevent a return to the 'epoch of palace revolutions' issued Succession Laws. The succession was now law and prevented the arbitrariness of the reigning emperor.

Under the 'Pauline Laws' the succession followed a certain sequence, and each member of the Romanov Dynasty's place in that sequence was clearly laid out. The succession was based on seniority. The Emperor as head of the family and after him his eldest son was heir, then son of the eldest son and so on. In the event that the senior line dies out, the throne passes to the next male line closest in relation to the last reigning Emperor.

Nick felt relieved: if his grandmother had been born of a daughter of the Tsar, perhaps it didn't count. Then he scrolled up: 'If the male line dies out completely, then the throne passes to a female closest in relation to the last reigning Emperor.'

Damn. That theory had been shot down in flames. The next statement seemed almost tailor made for Rosie: 'Also, no member could now be denied their succession rights, except those who had voluntarily relinquished them.'

He slumped back in his chair and took a deep breath. So there it was. If she could prove she was of the female line, and should the monarchy be reinstated, Rosie could legitimately claim her position as heir to the Russian throne.

For one brief moment in his life, Nick understood what it was like to be a male Cinderella. At any time in the future he might be whisked away and made to rule his country. He could be only a hair's breadth away from becoming Tsar Nicholas III, after Tsar Derek had taken over from Empress Rosie. No: Empress Alice Marie Xenia. There was no denying it had a certain ring to it. A vision of Alex in a tiara flashed into his mind. He shook his head to clear it of ridiculous thoughts. But what a prospect.

Could a future tsar of Russia continue to live on the Isle of Wight? Would he be allowed to get on with his life, or was there some kind of 'court in exile' that would govern his every move? Perhaps there was a temporary palace that came with the job. No: it was a destiny, not a job. He was destined to rule his people, wisely and responsibly. 'I will be good,' Queen Victoria had said, on her accession to the throne. He remembered that from school. Yes, he would be good.

And then he read the paragraph that followed. It ended his reverie and brought him down to earth with a welcome bump:

The laws were further altered in 1820, and to be considered a member of the Imperial House, members of the family had to marry a person of equal rank; meaning persons from another sovereign house.

It seemed as though the words spoke only to him – to warn him off. He read on: 'Accordingly, the offspring of these marriages were considered dynastic, while children of morganatic (unequal) marriages were not considered members of the Imperial House.'

So there it was. If Rosie had indeed been next in line to the Imperial throne, she had relinquished her claim when she had married his grandfather, who was not, as far as Nick knew, a 'person from another sovereign house'.

For a moment he felt slightly disappointed. He had not become entirely comfortable with the idea, but it had held a certain appeal.

He read the rest of the article, and discovered that the current heir to the Russian throne was Grand Duchess Maria Vladimorovna who was now forty-one and living in Madrid. Well, at least she was older than he was – by a couple of years. She had also had the foresight to marry Prince Franz of Prussia, keeping the marriage dynastic, and they had a son and heir: Grand Duke George Mihailovich 'the present successor to the Russian Throne'.

So that was that. If Rosie had once been heir to the House of Romanov, she was heir no longer. And neither was he. But if Rosie had surfed the Net, how had she not found this particular site, or another offering similar information? After all, he'd turned it up in a matter of minutes. Perhaps that was not her concern. Perhaps it was simply acknowledgement of the truth that was important to her. The confirmation that she was who she thought she was.

He would ask her when she came home. But that night Rosie didn't come home: she went instead to Queen Mary's Hospital in Newport, with a broken hip.

18
Grandmère Jenny

Beautiful when behaving itself.

Nick sat by the hospital bed in which Rosie was sleeping. Occasionally her face would contort in pain, but then it would relax again as the drugs took over.

'She's been sedated,' said the doctor. 'It was a clean break and we've put her back together again. It wasn't the artificial hip, fortunately.'

'And will she be all right?'

'Well, at her age it's difficult to say. It will take her a while to get going and it's likely that she'll be less mobile than she was before. That said, she's fit for her age.'

Nick stroked Rosie's hand, and listened to her breathing.

'We'll need to keep her in for a while, get her on her feet as soon as we can, and then I would suggest a period of convalescence in a home. There are one or two good ones on the island – unless you want her to go back to the mainland so that she can be nearer her friends?'

'I'd rather she was here, but I'll have to check with the rest of the family. My mother's on her way.'

'Yes, of course. We can talk about it later. She's in good hands for now.' The doctor saw the look in Nick's eyes, and answered it: 'The next few days will be the most critical. After that we'll have a better idea of how she's progressing.'

Nick looked back at Rosie. No longer in her lacy nightdress with the pink net over her hair, she was wearing a rough-textured hospital gown that was far too big for her, and her normally neatly curled hair was lopsided and unkempt. Carefully he brushed a wisp off her forehead and into place. Her hands lay on top of the bedcovers, a plastic identity bracelet on her right wrist. She looked like a refugee. Except for her nails: as always they were perfectly manicured, the varnish deep red and unchipped. Even now. It was all he could do to hold back the tears. He gritted his teeth.

The sound of sensible shoes on a hard floor broke in on his thoughts. He looked up. His mother was standing over him.

The grilling took place in the hospital waiting room – *sotto voce*, thanks to the presence of another couple who were waiting for news of their father in the wake of a stroke.

'Well, how did it happen?'

'She slipped.'

'Where?'

'On a boat.'

'Oh, Nick! What was she doing on a boat?'

'I told you, she was on a sailing course.'

'Stupid idea.' Anna Robertson's face was a picture of righteous indignation.

'Well, you were right, weren't you? And I was wrong. I just wanted her to have a bit of fun. And so did she.'

'And this is where it's led. So, what happens now?'

Nick was leaning forward with his elbows resting on his knees. He delivered the information to the floor, rather than to his mother. 'They'll have to keep her in for a while, get her moving. Apparently the next few days are the most critical, in terms of her future mobility, and then they recommend a convalescent home.'

'Of course. Whereabouts?'

'I suggested here, but I thought you'd probably have an opinion on that.'

'It's out of the question. She'll have to come back to Richmond where I can keep an eye on her.'

'Lucky her.'

'Nick!'

He sat up. 'Well, we want her to get better, don't we? And she'll need encouragement for that, not you barking at her all the time, telling her what she can't do.'

'That's not very kind.' She looked hurt.

'No, Mum, but it's accurate,' Nick continued stubbornly.

His mother seemed to be on the verge of saying something, but she failed to articulate it.

'Look, you'll only get cross with her. You know you don't get on, and it would probably be better for both of you if she stayed on the island.'

Anna shrugged.

'Anyway, let's just see how she gets on over the next few days.'

'Does your father know?'

'Not yet. I've tried ringing him but there was no reply. I think he was going abroad.' He avoided meeting her eye.

There was no way he would mention the package, or explain that contacting his father had proved impossible. Every time he thought about it he felt irritable and powerless. He had even called Derek's former secretary, Mavis, who knew everything, but she, too, had drawn a blank – and where the redoubtable Mavis failed, it was unlikely that even Interpol could succeed.

'So what will you do?'

Not 'what will *we* do', he noticed. 'Wait until he gets in touch. That's all I can do, unless I keep ringing him, and there doesn't seem much point in that. Anyway, he's probably changed phones yet again.'

'More than likely.'

'So you don't know what he's up to, then?'

Anna grimaced.

'Silly question.'

'Yes.' She drummed her fingers on her handbag. 'Is she likely to be asleep for long?'

'A few hours. She's only just come out of theatre.'

'I see.' Anna glanced at her watch. 'I've a meeting tonight and I really can't miss it. If you think I should sit by her I will . . .'

'No. You get back. I can keep an eye.'

'Well, if you're sure?'

'I'm sure. You get off.'

Anna got up and smoothed down the front of her black poncho. She laid a hand on his shoulder. 'We'll talk tomorrow, yes? Work out what to do.'

He nodded.

'Don't be angry with me, Nick. I'm only trying to do what's best.'

'I'm not angry. I just . . .' But the words would not come.

He turned to look out of the window as the light faded and the purple haze of dusk settled on the hospital car park.

The doctor had suggested he get some rest and come back the following morning, when Rosie might be more compos mentis. He tossed and turned, willing her to pull through. A phone call to the hospital at nine o'clock confirmed that she had had a comfortable night, and was now sleeping peacefully.

'Peacefully' sounded as if she'd given in, and that wasn't Rosie. He admonished himself for the thought and confirmed that he would visit her at lunchtime when she would be sitting up, they said.

He went into Rosie's bedroom. It was tidy and ordered, the photo of the Tsar, and a smaller one of Granddad, on the bedside table. One of her new boating shirts lay neatly folded on a chair by the chest of drawers. He could see her nightie peeping out from under her pillow. She had only been with him for about a week, and already it seemed like for ever. Her travelling alarm clock ticked loudly, but the house was strangely quiet without her. Life was quiet.

And then he remembered: it was Alex and Victoria's last day on the island. He wanted to tell Alex what had happened, but more than that he wanted to see her. Just to be in the same place as her for a while. He found the scrap of paper on which she had written her address and telephone number. He didn't have a mobile phone but she did, and he was glad of that. He punched in the number and waited for it to ring.

'Welcome to Orange answerphone,' came the reply.

'Damn.'

Maybe she didn't have a signal or her phone was

switched off. He left a message: 'Hi. It's Nick. Just to say hello and . . . hope you're OK. Sorry I've not been in touch. Just had a tricky time, really. Rosie's taken a bit of a tumble. She's OK but she's in hospital. I'll tell you all about it when we can speak. Er . . . that's all, really. Anyway, take care, and I hope I'll speak to you soon. 'Bye.'

He hung up, sat down and thought for a while. He wondered if she wanted to see him or had deliberately switched off her phone so that he couldn't get in touch. Then rationality prevailed: they had parted happily, even if they had not arranged another meeting. She would be out of range, that was all.

He looked out of the window at the pale grey day. At least it was fine. The deck on which Rosie had slipped yesterday would be dry. If only the rain had waited she would have been safe. And what about her dinner date? Had the man discovered her true age? He smiled to himself and grabbed his windcheater. He would talk to Alex later but, right now, he must go to Rosie. He would buy some flowers to take to the hospital. Better still, he would pick some from the clifftop. She'd like that.

The girl on the Isle of Wight ferry looked nothing like Nick. She was short and well rounded, with close-cropped hair and a tanned complexion. The rucksack on her back gave away nothing about her travels, but her brown legs and well-worn boots showed that she had been outdoors for some time. Sophie Robertson was back from South America and saw no point in going to Richmond to spill the beans to her mother. She had headed straight from Heathrow to the ferry at Portsmouth and walked the couple of miles to the Anchorage, only to find that her brother was out. Not to worry, she would wait. She had food and water in her rucksack, and would make herself comfortable in a chair on the veranda until he returned.

She had been sitting there for an hour, reading Paul Theroux, when a woman with a small child walked up the drive. They seemed surprised to see her.

'Hello?'

Sophie got up and leaned over the rail. 'Hi!'

'Is Nick in?'

Sophie glanced at the house. 'If he was I wouldn't be sitting on the veranda.'

'Of course. I just wanted to tell him we're leaving the island today.'

'Oh. Righto. I'll pass on a message, if you like.'

'If you could just say that Alex and Victoria called.'

'Fine. I'll do that.' Sophie never wasted words. It was something she'd inherited from her mother. She sat down in the chair once more and opened her book.

'I tried to ring him on my mobile, but it's bust,' Alex went on.

'Oh dear,' Sophie said, clearly not listening.

'Yes. Right. Well, we'll be going, then.'

'OK.'

'Thanks. Goodbye then.'

'Goodbye. Alex and Victoria. I'll tell him you came.'

As they walked down the drive she heard the child ask, 'Who was that?' and the mother reply, 'I don't know. *I don't know.*'

Sophie had had months of keeping herself to herself, and wondered if, perhaps, she had sounded a little standoffish. She hoped not.

*

156

Alex had seen the rucksack, with the airline luggage label and concluded that Debs had returned.

Rosie was indeed sitting up in bed when he arrived. His relief was unbounded as he bent to kiss her. 'Hello!'

She smiled, with what seemed like an effort, and whispered, 'Hello.'

He sat down on the chair by her bed and lifted the flowers for her to see: red campion and buttercups, stitchwort and cow parsley. He saw her eyes glint, and her mouth force itself into a smile. 'Lovely,' she mouthed.

'I'll find some water for them in a minute. How are you feeling?'

'Sore,' she said.

'I'm not surprised. You had a bit of a tumble.'

Rosie nodded and closed her eyes.

'Are you sleepy?'

She nodded again.

'What am I going to do with you?' he asked gently.

'Don't know.' The voice was resigned, lacked energy, but that was hardly surprising. She lifted a hand and beckoned him closer. He leaned towards her. 'They want to get me on my feet. They like to keep you mobile, I know, but . . . there's no . . . life in me.'

He held her hand and rubbed his thumb on the back. 'Oh, don't you worry, there will be. You're just a bit woozy from the anaesthetic.'

Rosie nodded slowly. 'Woozy.'

'Yes.'

A nurse walked purposefully towards the bed and spoke in a loud voice: 'Hello, Mrs Robertson. We're a bit out of it at the moment, aren't we? A bit dozy?'

'Mmm.' Rosie sounded distant.

The nurse tucked in a wayward length of sheet. 'We'll soon have you back on your feet, though. Would you like a drink? Cup of tea?'

Rosie shook her head and murmured 'No thank you.'

Nick was alarmed. He had prepared himself for her to be angry, frustrated and difficult, but not compliant or world-weary.

'Doctor will be on his rounds soon. Then we'll have a good look at you – sort you out.'

'Mmm.'

She seemed to be drifting off to sleep again – yet she must have slept all night.

The nurse read the concern on his face: 'Still a bit under the weather, but she should pull round over the next day or so, get her bearings. We're just a bit confused, aren't we, Mrs Robertson?'

Nick wanted to explain that, although his grand-mother was of a certain age, she was neither ga-ga nor deaf, and that she was a 'you' not a 'we'. But he thought better of it.

'Shall I put those in water for you?'

'Please.'

The nurse took the flowers. 'You could probably leave it until this evening if you want, Mr Robertson. She should be with us a bit more by then.'

'I'll just sit with her for a while if that's all right.'

'Sure. No problem.'

He stayed by the bed for half an hour, while Rosie slept. Then he kissed her forehead and reluctantly headed for home.

19
Zenith

Useful, underrated and little seen . . .

The sailing to Portsmouth was uncharacteristically quiet. Victoria had her nose buried in the guidebook, and Alex gazed out of the window of the ferry at the grey-green sea, occasionally thumping the buttons on her mobile phone in a vain attempt to prod it into life.

Victoria glanced up furtively from time to time, then returned to her research. Occasionally she wrote something down in a small exercise book, holding the pencil firmly, her head on one side and her tongue pushed between her teeth, the better to form the words.

Eventually the Wight-Link ferry lowered its ramp on to the Portsmouth soil, and they drove off.

It was then that Victoria broke the silence. 'Who do you think it was?'

'I told you, I don't know,' Alex said curtly.

'It might have been his girlfriend,' Victoria persisted.

'He hasn't got a girlfriend,' Alex said firmly.

Victoria gave her mother an old-fashioned look.

'And there's no need to look at me like that. That's what he told me.'

Victoria paused for a moment and then said 'Maybe she was his old girlfriend come back.'

Alex had been doing her best to put that thought out of her mind. 'Look, can we just stop speculating and wait and see? We don't know who it was, and no amount of guessing is going to help us.'

'Are you cross?'

'No, I am not cross, I'm just a bit tired of being asked questions.'

'All right, all right. I'm sorry.' The child folded her arms, pursed her lips and stared out of the window at nothing in particular.

Alex felt mean. 'I'm sorry. It's just that . . . well, it's all very confusing, that's all.'

No reply.

She tried to placate her daughter: 'What have you been doing?'

Still no reply.

'In your book.'

'Writing.' Victoria's lips remained pursed.

'Writing what?' Alex persisted.

'Now who's asking questions.'

Alex sighed. 'I'm only interested.'

'No, you're not. You're just trying to make conversation.'

Alex laughed.

'What? What's the matter?'

'Listen to us.'

'What do you mean?'

'We sound like an old married couple.'

'Yeugh!'

'Exactly. So, you tell me what you were writing and I won't snap your head off if you mention Nick.'

'We-ell,' she hesitated. 'I was writing down good places to live.'

'Ah, I see. And what conclusions did you come to?'

'Shanklin and Sandown are too busy, Newport is too far from the sea, and Cowes is too full of boaty people.'

'So you didn't find anywhere nice?'

'I like Sleepyhead Bay.'

'But there are only about ten houses, and I don't think you'd want to live there in winter. It must be very windy and desolate.'

'I thought of that.'

'And?'

'I thought Godshill was pretty, and it's not too far away.'

'Mmm. A bit chocolate-boxy for me.' Alex wondered why she had instigated this conversation. If her suspicions about Nick's visitor were accurate, the Isle of Wight was the last place she wanted to be.

Victoria continued with her itinerary: 'Seaview's nice, but probably a bit too posh.'

Alex melted a little. 'Don't you do posh, then? It's very select. And Henry's gallery is there.'

Victoria turned to her. 'Are you really interested or are you just patronizing me?'

Her mother studied her. 'Sometimes I wish I'd not taken so much trouble to improve your vocabulary.'

'You didn't tell me you were coming home!' Nick flung his arms round his little sister and lifted her off the ground.

'Didn't know I was until a couple of days ago.'

Nick took a pace back and eyed her up and down. 'God, you look well!'

'All that walking.'

'So where did you get to, and why have you come back?'

'Well, if you let me in I'll tell you.'

Nick sat and listened as Sophie talked of her six months in Costa Rica, of tropical rainforests and coffee plantations, of working among native Central Americans and of transiting the Panama Canal on a banana boat.

'You haven't said why you came home.'

'Dunno. Just felt I needed to for a bit.'

Nick grinned. 'I'm glad you did. Will you go back?'

'Not there. Chile, though, and Peru. Give myself a couple of weeks to get my breath back and then I'm off.'

'What will you do for money?'

'I've got some saved. I worked quite a lot of the time. Didn't earn much, but I don't need much.'

'Well, you might have a bit more than you think.'

'What do you mean?'

Nick filled in his sister on the events of the past few weeks – of Rosie's relocation to the Isle of Wight, her sailing course and the accident, and the diamond legacy that was also Sophie's. He did not mention the Russian royal family. It seemed unnecessary, especially now that he had discovered there was no immediate danger of the Robertsons being called upon to take the throne.

'But why's she doing all this?' asked Sophie.

'For the same reason that you came home, I suppose. It's her time.'

'Wow! What does Mum think?'

'She's furious that I let it all happen. Well, she was at

first. I haven't told her about the diamonds. She knows Rosie's bank account is empty but she doesn't know why. She's probably just putting her head in the sand.'

'Not like Mum.'

'I think she's finally met her match.'

'In Rosie?'

'Yes. She's been trying to keep her under control since Granddad died. You know Mum. She doesn't like loose ends or loose cannons. But I reckon she's realized now she hasn't a cat in hell's chance. She even gave in when I said I wanted Rosie to stay on the island to convalesce.'

'Just wants to get on with her own life, I suppose,' Sophie mused. 'But this diamond you say I'm getting. Where do you think it is?'

'In the bank, I suppose. She told me to put mine there so I don't think she'd be silly enough to keep it in a shoebox under the bed.'

'Well, I'm not really bothered one way or the other. I just want to travel. But I suppose it will make things a bit easier.'

'Are you going to blow the lot on first-class travel, then?'

'Don't be stupid. Do I look like the sort who travels first class?' she scoffed.

'Er, no. A steerage girl if ever I saw one,' Nick told her.

'I tell you what I could do with, though. A bath.'

'I thought you'd never ask. I was just going to open all the windows.'

'Cheeky bugger!' She lunged forward to swipe him with her hand, but he caught it, spun her round and kissed her cheek.

'Nice to have you home,' he said. 'Get yourself cleaned

up and then I'll cook you some dinner before we go and see your granny.'

'Now, there's an offer a girl can't refuse.'

To his relief Rosie was sitting up in bed, and something of her old self had come back. 'Where've you been?' she asked.

'Waiting for you to come round. You were a bit out of it before.'

'Huh. I'm bored stiff, stuck in here,' she grumbled.

'I've brought someone to see you.'

'Oh, not your mother. Tell me you've not brought *her*!'

'Ssssh! Keep your voice down. No, I haven't brought Mum. She came while you were asleep.'

'That was good timing.'

Nick beckoned to the figure hidden behind the door.

'Sophie! Oh, my love, what are you doing here? I thought you were in . . . wherever you were . . . South Africa.'

'South America. Hello, Rosie.' Sophie bent to kiss her grandmother.

Rosie, in a surge of affection, put her arm round Sophie's neck and hugged her. Then she spoke rapidly, through mounting emotion: 'I thought I'd never see you again. This is so lovely. So lovely. I thought you'd be gone for ages but you've come back.' She stroked the back of her granddaughter's head, ruffling the short hair. Then she let Sophie stand up but took her hands. 'Look at you! You're brown as a berry! And so well. But your hair!' She ran her slender fingers through Sophie's golden stubble. 'There's not much left, is there?'

Sophie grinned. 'It's easier if it's short out there. Insects and stuff.'

Rosie frowned slightly. 'I think you're fairer than you were. Aren't you?'

'Sun probably.'

Her grandmother smiled again. 'Now there's only Alice, but I don't expect she'll be home for a while.'

'Not if you behave yourself,' offered Nick. 'And her home *is* in South Africa.'

'Hey!' said Rosie. 'I haven't forgotten – it's just that it's easy to muddle South Africa and South America.'

Nick patted her hand. 'I know.'

'Now, we should be able to get some tea,' said Rosie, 'And you, Sophie, can tell me everything you've been doing.' She called the nurse, organized chairs round the bed, and quizzed Sophie on the details of her trip. Nick could not remember when he had last felt so relieved.

Sophie eased herself into the sleeping-bag on the sofa in Nick's sitting room. 'God, I'm knackered.'

'I'm not surprised,' Nick called from his room next door. Then he laughed. 'What does this remind you of?'

'When we were little,' his sister said.

He laughed again. 'You always wanted to talk, and I always wanted to sleep.'

'Yes. And I usually won.'

'Always.'

'Well, I shan't keep you awake tonight.'

'That's a relief.'

Sophie yawned loudly. 'What are you doing tomorrow?'

'Oh, I've got to get on with a picture of the Needles. And visit Rosie, of course.'

'I'll come with you.'

'That'll be nice.' He thought for a moment. 'And I've

got to make a phone call. Sort out some unfinished business.'

'Oh, that reminds me,' murmured Sophie, as she fought to stay awake. 'I almost forgot. A woman and a little girl were asking for you this afternoon when you were out. Alex and Victoria. Said she'd been trying to get hold of you but that her phone was bust or something. Does that make sense?' And then she fell asleep.

20
Golden Dawn

Its name is rather misleading.

He had wanted to ring her the night before, but by the time he had sorted Sophie out it had been too late. He called her on her home number as soon as it seemed decent to do so – at around eight thirty.

Victoria answered. 'Hello?'

'Victoria? It's Nick Robertson. Is your mum there?'

'No. She's out.' She sounded distracted.

'Oh. When will she be back?'

'I don't know.'

'Could you give her a message?' Nick was flustered. 'Could you just say I rang and that I'm trying to get in touch with her? Maybe she could ring me on my home number when she gets back.'

'Will you be there all the time?'

'I have to go out to do a few things.'

'When would be best to ring, then?'

He tried to think. 'Well, look, if she just tries me, and then I'll try her.'

'But what if we go out?'

She was irritating him now. 'I'll just keep trying.'

'What about this evening? Will you be in then?' she asked.

'Some of the time. I have to go and see Rosie.'

'Isn't she with you any more?'

'No. She's had an accident.' Nick sighed.

There was silence at the other end of the line.

'Don't worry,' he said. 'She's OK, but she's in hospital.'

Silence again.

'Look, if you could pass on the message, and I'm sure we'll manage to speak some time today. OK?'

'OK.'

''Bye then.'

''Bye.' And she hung up.

'Damn,' muttered Nick. He had wanted to tell Alex everything that had happened since they had last seen each other – and he'd wanted to tell her about Rosie himself. Would Victoria remember to give her the message more promptly than Sophie had passed on hers?

Victoria hoped she had given him enough information. He had sounded irritated, but she'd only wanted to make sure he'd be able to talk to her mum, who was agitated – and Victoria knew why. There must be an explanation as to why that strange woman had been on his veranda. She wanted Nick to sort it out. But now she had another worry. Nick had said Rosie was OK, but if she was, why was she in hospital?

'Victoria? Are you there?'

It was the voice of the next-door neighbour, shouting up the stairs.

'Yes,' she said softly.

'Are you all right?'

'Fine.'

The neighbour went back to her ironing, and Victoria tried to concentrate on her homework. To no avail.

Alex had been out to buy a new mobile phone. She had then called in at a bookshop to find something to read after *Sense and Sensibility*, and settled on *Vanity Fair*. She had chosen it partly because her daughter seemed to have a lot in common with Becky Sharp, and partly for its opening sentence, which transported her to the days in which she would have liked to live: 'While the present century was in its teens, and on one sunshiny morning in June, there drove up to the great iron gate of Miss Pinkerton's academy for young ladies, on Chiswick Mall, a large family coach, with two fat horses in blazing harness, driven by a fat coachman in a three-cornered hat and wig, at the rate of four miles an hour.'

Oh yes, that would do very nicely. She walked towards the checkout, but was drawn, for some inexplicable reason, towards a shelf in the second-hand section. It was labelled 'Travel'. She reached up for a guide to the Isle of Wight, not the modern one that Victoria had been devouring but a battered red volume dated 1919. She flipped it open and read:

In the opinion of many this is, in suitable weather, the finest of all the fine walks in the Island. The view embraces at least half the Island, from Cowes on the one hand to St Catherine's on the other, and a considerable portion of the opposite coast. On fair days and foul Tennyson was accustomed to make a daily pilgrimage to this spot, declaring that 'the air on the Downs was worth sixpence a pint'.

She smiled, closed the book and returned it to the shelf.

Nick looked out over the view. Cowes lay beyond the curve of Thorness Bay to his left, and St Catherine's Point jutted out into the Channel on his right, the light-house winking with clockwork precision. The cross on Tennyson Down pointed up to the cloud-filled sky, and he breathed deeply, filling his lungs with clean, cold air. He was glad to be out, and to be alone for a while. For days now voices had echoed in his head asking questions – Rosie's, Sophie's, his father's, Henry's, his mother's. Only Alex's was silent. And hers was the voice he most wanted to hear.

He walked alone from the cross and down towards the Needles, where he set up his easel and painted at speed. He worked all morning until half past twelve when he packed up his brushes and drove to the hospital to meet Sophie at Rosie's bedside.

When he arrived the two were deep in conversation. Sophie was regaling her grandmother with the story of a plantation owner who had asked her to marry him and look after his children.

'And what did you say?'

'I told him to get on his bike.'

'You didn't fancy life on a plantation, then?'

'This isn't *South Pacific*, you know, Rodgers and

Hammerstein. Anyway, I didn't fancy him – or his kids. Spoilt brats. One tried to touch me up.'

'But how did he come to ask you to marry him?'

'Oh, he hardly knew me. He just wanted someone to look after his kids on the cheap.'

'No!' exclaimed Rosie.

'It's true. Better than paying a nanny.'

Nick listened as Sophie warmed to her subject. 'I tell you, you've got to be careful. Some guys are only after one thing.'

'Sex?'

'And an easy life. Just like my brother.'

'That's me,' Nick confirmed. 'Always going for the easy option.'

'And the sex.' Sophie squeezed his arm, then became serious. 'I'm sorry about that message yesterday. Was it important?'

Nick turned to his grandmother. 'How are you today, Duchess?'

'Better in myself, thank you, love, but, ooh, I do ache – and feel so stupid. Fancy slipping! And I had my new deck shoes on. Now I'm stuck in here.'

'Have they started you walking?'

'Have they? I'll say. Up and down the ward like a sentry. Huh! But there's a very nice man who takes me, Joe. There he is – African. He's very nice, calls me Mrs Madam. His English isn't very good, but he's gentle.'

'You want to watch out. He'll be asking you to marry him before the week's out,' Nick observed.

'Ooh, that would be something, wouldn't it?' Rosie's eyes lit up, her old sparkle back.

'Yes. If I were you I'd snap him up.'

Rosie grinned. 'It's probably like Sophie says – he'd only want me for the sex.'

There was a momentary pause, then all three fell about with laughter. Tears of mirth rolled down Rosie's cheeks, and she squealed in pain as she fell back on her pillow.

'Ow!' she exclaimed, still laughing. 'Now look what you've done.'

'Us?' asked Nick. 'It was you who said it.'

Sophie ticked her off: 'Rosie, that was disgusting.'

'Yes, and I'm old enough to know better. Or, as far as you're concerned, I'm old enough to have forgotten how to do it.'

'Too much information!'

Rosie shook her head. 'Shouldn't be allowed. Sex approaching the age of forty.'

'Careful!' warned Nick. 'Sensitive area.'

'Ooh, yes! Sorry, I forgot.' Then her eyes lit up. 'That reminds me.' She turned to Nick. 'Did you tell Sophie . . .' she glanced from side to side, like a spy, '. . . about the legacy thing?'

'Well, I did mention it.'

'Rosie, it's really not necessary,' Sophie told her.

'Yes, it is. I'm not having the Government taking it all. I'd far rather you three had it.'

'Well, it's very kind but—'

'No buts. It's all sorted out. I've given Nick his and he's put it in the bank.' She turned to him. 'You have put it in the bank, haven't you?'

'Yes.'

'Well, I'll give you yours, Sophie, and you can do the same.'

For a moment Nick imagined that she was going to reach

under her pillow, pull out a small bag and dole out a diamond to Sophie. Instead she said, 'As soon as your father comes back.'

Nick was horrified. 'Dad?' he managed weakly.

'Yes. I gave them to him for safe-keeping. I couldn't get to the bank so he said he'd take them for me.'

21
Mary Manners

A little prone to rust.

Sophie knew something was wrong. For the rest of the day Nick was preoccupied, and she assumed it was to do with the woman and child who had come to the house. Open as she was with her brother, she knew that this was not the moment to ask. The relationship, if that was what it was, was clearly at a critical stage, and she kicked herself for having forgotten to give him the message earlier.

During the day Nick called Alex several times but there was no reply. Then, at around five, the phone was picked up. By Alex. 'Hi!'

'Hi!' He felt as though someone had opened a valve in his head, so great was his relief at hearing her voice. 'I'm sorry I missed you. I didn't get the message that you'd called until late.'

'Oh. I see.' She sounded cooler than he had hoped.

'What's this about Rosie? Victoria said she'd had an accident but there was no need to worry.'

'She's broken her hip, messing about in boats, but she's on the mend.'

'Are you sure? It can be tricky.'

'They say that this is the most critical stage. She was a bit dopey at first but she's pulled round now. She's almost back to her old self.'

'Oh, good. We did worry.'

'Yes. Sorry.'

'We called in but you weren't there.'

'I was at the hospital.'

'Of course.'

'Look, I couldn't see you again, could I? Soon.'

'Oh, well . . . it's a bit tricky at the moment . . . Victoria's back at school and . . .'

There was a long silence. He had hoped she would be as glad to hear his voice as he was to hear hers. But she seemed distant. He tried again. 'Perhaps I can ring you tomorrow, then?'

'If you like.'

'Is everything OK?'

'Why shouldn't it be?'

'No reason. It's just that . . . well, OK. I'll call tomorrow.'

' 'Bye, then.'

' 'Bye.'

He put down the phone, hardly able to believe it had happened. Why had she gone so cool on him? Was this the final brush-off? He ambled out on to the veranda and flopped into a chair. Bloody hell! He'd cocked it up again. But this time he had no idea why.

*

'Mavis?'

'Yes?'

'It's Nick again. Any news on Pa?'

Mavis was a sixty-something, amply proportioned spinster who lived with five cats on the edge of Epping Forest. She had devoted the last twenty years of her life to Nick's father – as his secretary-cum-personal assistant – but six months ago Derek had decided that he wanted to be more independent and that Mavis was always too keen to tie him down.

'Very little.' She cleared her throat and took another sip of her sherry. 'But I have put out some feelers.'

'What sort of feelers?'

'International ones.'

'How did you know where to start?'

'Ha!' Mavis laughed. And then wished she hadn't: the smoker's cough took hold and left her incapable of conversation for a good thirty seconds. When she spoke again it was with a bronchial wheeze. 'I've been following up a couple of old contacts. Eastern European ones.'

'That sounds suspicious,' said Nick.

'I think they might bear fruit, but your father doesn't keep me abreast of things like he used to.'

'No. Is there anything I can do?'

Mavis shook her head, and wished she hadn't done that either: the cigarette ash had fallen over her freshly laundered crimson satin blouse. She brushed herself down, holding the telephone receiver between her chin and her shoulder then stubbed out the lipstick-stained cigarette. She picked up the spectacles dangling from the golden chain round her neck, and fumbled on the pad in front of her. 'I've come up with a possible sighting in the Baltic and a new mobile phone number.'

'The Baltic?'

'Yes. On a cruise ship. But it was vague and, to be honest, dear, not from a very good source. On the sherbet, you know. But the phone number might be more reliable.'

'Right.' Nick picked up a pen.

'But I've tried it and there's no reply.'

'Damn. Has he done a bunk?'

Mavis took another restorative sip. 'Oh, I shouldn't think so. He'll just have gone to ground until the deal's done.'

'What sort of deal?'

'Now, you know better than to ask me that. There was a time when I would have known all but couldn't tell you. Now, alas, I cannot tell you because I know bugger-all. Your father no longer tells me what he docs or where he goes. Sad . . . but there we are.'

'But I feel so out on a limb.'

Mavis beamed to herself. 'Join the club, dear. Your father prefers to work as a free agent nowadays.'

'Agent? What sort of agent?'

'Don't be dramatic, dear. He's never done anything on the wrong side of the law and I'm sure he's too old and too wise to start now.'

Nick sighed. 'I do hope you're right.' And then he asked, 'Is there really nothing we can do?'

'No, dear. I'm afraid there isn't. I'll give you the phone number and you can keep trying it, but other than that I've nothing to offer.'

Nick took down the number and thanked Mavis for her trouble.

'That's all right dear. Send me a bottle of sherry at Christmas.'

He would try to remember. And he tried the telephone number. It did not even offer a number unobtainable tone. The line was dead as a doornail. Just like his love-life.

That evening he sat down to supper with Sophie. He was not the best of company.

'Come on, then, what is it?' she asked, spooning up her melon.

'Sorry?' He was preoccupied. Distant.

'What's the matter?'

'Oh, nothing.'

'Yes, there is. You've not said more than half a dozen sentences all day.'

'Oh, just girl trouble.'

'Well, you've got more than most, I suppose.'

'Mmm?'

'Four all told. Alex and Victoria, me and Rosie. Which ones are you especially worried about, as if I didn't know?'

Nick nodded in the direction of the mainland.

Sophie smiled indulgently. 'On your own tonight, then? Only Sis for company.'

Nick poked at the melon on the plate. 'No need to rub it in.'

Sophie looked guilty. 'Maybe I've frightened her off – by being here, I mean.'

'Don't be silly. She's not that feeble.'

'Certainly didn't look feeble.' She popped a piece of melon into her mouth.

'Meaning?'

'Meaning nothing at all. Just that she seemed very . . . capable.'

'She is.' He laid his fork on the table and leaned back in his chair. 'I mean, I said I hadn't got her message until late—'

'Oops, sorry.'

'—but she didn't seem to hear, just asked how Rosie was and said it could be a tricky time.'

'In more ways than one,' muttered Sophie.

Nick leaned forward and put his elbows on the table. 'Was she OK when you saw her?'

Sophie shrugged. 'Suppose so. Didn't really concentrate. I mean, I don't know her so I can't exactly fill you in on her mood.'

Nick slumped back, looking distracted. 'I suppose not.'

'If anything, she looked a bit disapproving,' confessed Sophie. 'Saw her eyeing up my rucksack. Probably thought I was some sort of traveller.'

Nick sat up. 'Did you tell her who you were?'

'Why?'

'Did you say you were my sister?'

Sophie hesitated. 'I . . . don't think so.'

Nick got to his feet and pointed at the rucksack lying in the corner. 'That was on the veranda, with airline labels all over it and you didn't tell her who you were?'

'Well, no. But what have my stickers got to do with it?'

'You – What's the female equivalent of a plonker?'

Sophie looked bewildered. 'Silly bitch?' she offered.

Nick nodded. 'And how.'

'I'm sorry. I still don't see where you're coming from.'

'Alex comes here to tell me she's going, and she sees you sitting on the veranda.'

'So?'

'And she knows I had a girlfriend who ran off to America.'

'Oh.' Sophie sat quite still, and then said, 'Oh, God!'

'Yes. Oh, God. She only thinks that Debs has come back.'

Sophie did her best to keep a straight face, but failed dismally. Her mouth spread into a grin. 'You mean she thinks I'm . . .'

'Yes,' said Nick.

'Debs the Delight?'

'It's not funny.'

Sophie did not agree. In fact, she couldn't speak for laughing.

'Your sister?'

'Yes.'

'Oh.'

There was a pause in the conversation, and Nick wondered if Alex was about to say, 'That's a likely story.' But she didn't. Instead she chuckled and said, 'How silly.'

'Silly of her not to say.'

'And silly of me to jump to conclusions.'

'Typical Sophie. She gets it from our mother. She's a great sister – love her to bits – but she can be a bit short with people she doesn't know.'

Alex brightened and made to brush it aside. 'Yes. Well, never mind.'

'No, but I do mind.'

'Do you?'

There was a pause. Quite a long pause. 'Yes. More than I realized.'

'Oh. That's very nice.'

'Look, can I see you again – soon?'

'How soon?'

'Tomorrow night?'

'Well, I . . . yes . . . I suppose so.'

'Shall I come over to you? I mean, you've been over here a lot lately.'

'No. No. I'll come to you. I'll just have to find a sitter, that's all. Oh, and I have a new mobile. Same number, but it works now.'

'Right. See you tomorrow, then.'

'Yes.'

'And . . . er . . .' He fumbled for the right words.

'Yes?'

'It will be lovely to see you.'

'Oh, and you.'

He put the phone down. In spite of the other 'local difficulties', he felt strangely empowered.

A few moments later Nick's mother rang. She was unusually compliant. She had been giving some thought to Rosie's convalescence, and had decided, she said, that perhaps it would be best if Rosie stayed on the island. Rather than risk moving her. There was a calm finality about her tone. Nick wondered, for a moment, whether he was imagining it. She said little, but her resigned manner spoke volumes.

He hung up. It was a defining moment. To all intents and purposes, his grandmother's future care was in his hands. It would not surprise him if his mother never mentioned her again.

He wondered if he was being dramatic. Perhaps it was just something about the day.

*

'I don't really want to go out, you know,' grumbled Sophie, the following evening.

'I know, but you owe it to me, don't you?'

'Mmm. I suppose so.' She was changing in the bathroom and talked to him through the half-open door. 'What time will it be safe for me to come back?'

'Will you stop talking as though there's some kind of furtive liaison going on?'

'OK, OK – I just don't want to barge in and interrupt anything, that's all.'

'Neither do I.'

'I'll be back about ten, then.'

'What?'

Sophie grinned. 'Only teasing. I don't want to cramp your style. I've booked a room at the Royal London – I'm meeting up with a few old drinking mates.'

Nick back-pedalled: 'Look, you can come back here. Nothing's going to happen. I just want us to have a bit of time on our own.'

'Of course. And who'd want their sister hanging around?'

'It's not that—'

'Even if she has only been home a couple of days.'

'Soph!'

She came out of the bathroom wearing a T-shirt and jeans. 'You're *so* easy to wind up.'

'And you're so good at it.'

'Years of practice.' She reached up and ruffled his hair. 'Better clean yourself up a bit, though. Don't want to put her off.'

'I will – now I can get into the bathroom.'

'You are *so* selfish. It's just me, me, me with you, isn't it?' she teased, and they burst out laughing.

'Well, you might meet some rich yachtie at the club who'll sweep you off your feet,' Nick said eventually.

'Oh, yeah? Who says I want to be swept off my feet?' Sophie smiled ruefully. 'Too scared.'

Nick looked reflective. 'Family trait.'

'Come on! Time you had a bit of fun. Debs isn't the only woman in the world.'

'I know that.' Then he added softly, as he walked into the bathroom, 'Now.'

He met her at the ferry terminal at Fishbourne, in the MG with the hood down.

'Is this wise?' she asked. 'Having the hood down?'

He leaned across and kissed her cheek. 'No rain forecast.'

'Where are we going?'

'I thought we'd eat in. Try to do a bit better than last time.'

Alex grinned. 'That's nice. No need to worry about anyone else.'

He looked at her meaningfully. 'No.'

They didn't speak much on the journey, just sat back, happy to be in each other's company. She watched his feet on the pedals as he drove over the bridge at Wootton Creek; looked at the way the hair curled on the back of his neck as they sat on the chain ferry between East and West Cowes, and smiled as he opened the door for her to get out once they had reached the Anchorage.

'There you are,' he said. 'Dry as a bone.'

She smiled. 'In more ways than one.'

'Oh, don't worry. The Cloudy Bay is on ice.'

'Cloudy Bay? Are we celebrating or something?'

'Yes,' he said. 'The end of a misunderstanding.'

He ushered her up the steps and on to the veranda where a small table was laid for two, with a bowl of wild flowers.

Alex sat down beside the table and Nick disappeared into the cottage. The evening was unseasonably warm. Away to the west, the sun was setting over the Dorset coastline, staining the sky with copper light. She had to work hard to tell herself this was no dream. This was where someone could live. Where someone could stay.

He returned with a bottle of the New Zealand wine and two glasses. He poured, they drank, and looked out over the sea as the sun sank below the horizon.

'Do you ever take this view for granted?' she asked.

'No. It's never the same twice.'

'A bit different from my view in Portsmouth,' she said. 'You're so lucky.'

He smiled at her. 'I know.'

Over supper – lobster, bought from the fisherman at Sleepyhead Bay – he told her about Rosie's accident. Then, feeling the need to unburden himself, he explained about Rosie's preoccupation with her Russian ancestry and his researches into the royal family. It no longer sounded ridiculous. He found himself talking easily and she was attentive, absorbed, and asked questions in all of the right places.

Finally he said, 'Unbelievable, isn't it?'

Alex shook her head. 'No. Unusual, but not unbelievable.' And then, 'Oh, my God!'

'What?' He stared at her, worried that something had happened.

'Our names.'

He sighed with relief. 'I know. Silly, isn't it?'

She grinned. 'I think it's rather sweet. Did Rosie notice?'

'Immediately.'

'I'm not surprised.' Alex looked more serious. 'And you still don't know for certain who her parents were?'

'No, and I don't really know where to start. The librarian in Newport suggested the Russian embassy, but I'm not sure how tactful that would be.'

'Could I have a go?'

'Mmm?'

'Maybe I could do a bit of reading. Research. It might be easier for me – not being related.' She hesitated, not sure if she'd overstepped the mark.

'If you like. That would be great!' Nick said enthusiastically.

'You jot down the facts and the names you know, and I'll have a dig around, if you're sure you don't mind.'

'I'm pleased you want to bother – that you think it's worth it.'

'Of course! It's fascinating. Not sure what we'll find, but it'll be a bit of an adventure.'

'As long as you want one.'

Alex looked across the table at him, and then laid her hand on his. 'Oh, I think so.'

He led her into the bedroom, then turned to face her. His heart was pounding. 'Are you sure?' he asked.

She nodded.

Nick put his arms round her and kissed her forehead, cheeks, and lips. Her skin was soft and fragrant, her body lithe and supple. He caressed her back and waist, then unfastened the tortoiseshell clip that held back her sleek brown hair and let it fall round her shoulders. He stroked it as she nuzzled his neck, and kissed him, running her fingers across his shoulders.

Then she pulled away a little and gazed at him. Her eyes were shining, lips parted. She held up her hand and he took it, then pulled her towards him and kissed her again, his hands moving down her back. She sighed softly, before lowering her own hands towards his belt. She undid the buckle, and he raised his hands to her shirt and peeled it upwards. Soon she stood before him in her underwear – lacy and white.

Gently he ran the back of his hand across her flat stomach and up towards her breasts. He circled them with his fingers, then undid the bra and let it fall to the floor.

She looked vulnerable now, and he could hear her breathing, almost as though she was frightened. She reached down, and slid her hand inside his trousers. He put his arms around her and pulled her towards him.

They sank on to the bed, and within moments were naked and entwined.

Later, they lay silently in each other's arms, as the evening breeze rustled the muslin curtains at the window.

Then he asked, 'Do you have to go?'

Alex stroked the hair back from his forehead. 'I should really say yes.'

'But?'

'Victoria's with friends – I couldn't get a sitter.'

'Stay, then?'

'Yes, please.'

22
Max Graf

Seldom sets any fruit.

He watched her as she woke. The early-morning light caught her dark hair and made it shine like polished jet. It can be difficult for those who have never been in love to think poetically, but Nick was an artist and it seemed as natural as breathing. He could not remember ever feeling so calm as he did at that moment. Lying next to her in his bed. Feeling her warm and naked body next to his.

She stirred, and opened her eyes, squinting at the rays of dawn. For a moment he thought she might not remember where she was. Might suddenly regret the impulse of the night before, jump out of his bed and throw on her clothes, but she didn't. Instead, she smiled at him and snuggled closer. 'Hello, you,' she murmured.

'Hello, you,' he echoed.

They lay still for a few moments, silent except for their

soft breathing. Then they made love again, and lay in each other's arms, silently.

Soon, Alex rose from the bed and went to the bathroom. He watched her go, captivated by the sight of her. When she came back, she slid in beside him and laid her arm across his chest. 'What are you thinking?' she asked.

'About you.'

She raised herself up on one elbow and looked him in the eye. 'You don't think I was . . . well . . . a bit fast.'

He nodded. 'Like lightning.'

'Oh, God! I didn't mean to be. I'm not usually, only . . .'

'Hey!' He squeezed her shoulders. 'Just kidding.'

'Oh. Well, that's all right.' She relaxed. 'I wish I could stay.'

'Can't you?' He looked at her, his eyes hopeful.

'No. The neighbours will take Victoria to school – with their little girl – but I've got to get back. There's shopping to do.'

'What?' Nick sat up and looked at her incredulously.

'We have to eat,' she said, and giggled.

'You're lying in bed with me and all you can think of is doing the shopping?'

'It's all right for you! You have no responsibilities but I have another mouth to feed.' She got out of bed to search for her clothes.

Nick frowned at her. 'So do I.'

'Yes, but yours is being taken care of by the health service at the moment.' She kissed him lightly on the forehead, slid out of bed and asked, 'Can I have a shower?'

'Only if I can join you.'

Henry sat by Rosie's bed while the nurse arranged a large

bunch of red roses in a vase on the bedside cabinet. 'They're beautiful,' said Rosie, her eyes shining.

'Cut them myself this morning,' said Henry, with a wink.

'Dreadful man. They must have cost a fortune.'

'Worth it to see your face, dear lady. I've been a bit worried about you. Glad to see you're on the mend.'

'Slowly. Very slowly.'

'So, what happens now?' he asked.

'Another week or so in here, and then I've got to go into a nursing home.' She grimaced.

'What?' He looked horrified.

'Oh, not permanently, just to convalesce. Nick's going to arrange it. They'll keep me until I'm back on my feet. It'll be fine, I suppose.'

'Here or on the north island?' Henry still looked worried.

'Here. I don't want to go back there just yet.'

'Oh, good.' He reached out his hand and held hers. 'I wouldn't want to think you were going away.'

Rosie smiled. 'You're very kind, Henry.'

'Not kind at all. Just, well . . .'

'Whatever it is, I'm grateful.'

Henry gazed at her, sitting there. Somehow Rosie didn't fit here. She was a doer, and doers are always up and about, not lying in bed. She caught his eye. 'Not much fun is it?' she asked. 'Getting old, I mean.'

'No,' Henry agreed ruefully.

'We're no different, really, are we? No different from the way we've always been.'

'Except that some bits don't work as well as they used to,' Henry said wistfully.

'I just wish younger people would understand.'

'Understand what?'

'That you never stop being you. That you still have feelings just as much as you did when you were younger.' Rosie sighed.

'Yes. Except that somehow . . .'

'I know. They're not quite so . . .' She sought a word.

'Raw?'

'Yes. That's it. Raw. I mean, I'm every bit as passionate, every bit as interested, it's just that somehow it all gets . . . blunted.'

'Is that how you feel now?' he asked gently.

'When I'm a bit down, yes. I just wish I could feel the joy in life that I felt when I was younger. It all seemed so straightforward then.' She looked distant, distracted.

'I think you should rest for a while. Try to get some sleep.' Henry patted her hand.

'What happened to pride, Henry?'

'I'm sorry?'

'When I was younger we were all so proud. So confident. Not arrogant, just . . . sure. We were bombed by the Germans and there was no money, and not much food, but we still had our pride. We stuck up for ourselves. Believed in ourselves. Knew we had to. It wasn't blindness, was it? Were we fooling ourselves?'

'No. No, we weren't fooling ourselves. It was just different then.'

Rosie looked as though she was searching for the right words. Then she asked, 'Is it wrong to feel proud of what you are?'

'Of course not.'

'Well, why aren't we allowed to any more? I get so down, reading all this stuff in the papers, everyone at each other's throats.'

Henry nodded understandingly. 'There's not much optimism, is there?'

'Maybe I'm better off out of it. I just don't seem to belong anywhere any more.'

'Oh, I think that's enough of that.'

'Well, it makes me cross, Henry. So desperate. I look around and see a world I don't recognize any more. I can cope with technology – some of it – but I can't understand the attitudes. I stand in the middle of the pavement sometimes, quite still, while people mill around me, and I feel invisible. No – more than that, I feel non-existent. It's as if I'm in a different world. I'm not . . . what does Nick call it? . . . attention-seeking, just trying to understand it. Trying to see how it works and I can't. It's as if everything I've ever lived for has begun to evaporate and leave me behind. I don't want to be left behind. I want to keep up – to be a part of it. But somebody or something won't let me.'

She stopped talking and gazed out of the window, eyes glistening with tears. Then she said softly, 'I never used to cry, you know. Not much anyway. But now I seem to do it all the time.'

Henry touched her cheek with his finger, worried that her fighting spirit had been dented. It must be the medication. He convinced himself that was the case. Anything else was . . . well . . . just not worth thinking about. He stroked back a stray wisp of hair, and Rosie turned to look at him.

'It's only natural,' he said. 'Probably something to do with the anaesthetic. At the moment, I mean. It's still wearing off. You'll feel better soon, and the world will seem a nicer place.'

She leaned back on the plumped-up pillows. 'I hope so.

I'm sorry to be a pain – I didn't mean to burden you with all this.' She reached for a tissue, and wiped her eyes. 'Bless you, Henry,' she said.

'Well, we've got to get you back on your feet as soon as we can and out of this place. Then, perhaps, you'll let me take you out to dinner.'

Rosie looked anxious. 'Henry, there's something you should know.'

'Mmm?'

'Well, you remember when we were talking in the pub?'

'Mmm?'

'I was less than honest with you.'

'Ah.'

'I didn't want you to think that I was a feeble old lady so . . .'

Henry cleared his throat. 'If you're about to say some-thing about your age, then I should mention something before you do.'

Rosie looked apprehensive. 'You know, don't you?'

'Yes. I do know. I know that I'm not really fifty-eight.'

'I'm sorry?'

'I lied to you about my age. I'm actually sixty-three.'

For a moment Rosie's face bore a look of surprise. Then she grinned at him. 'Are you really?'

'Yes. Will you forgive me?'

She looked at him with mock admonishment, then melted. 'Of course I will.'

'You're very kind. Very generous.'

Rosie squeezed his hand. 'You know what that means, don't you?'

Henry raised an eyebrow.

'It means that you're only six years younger than me.'

*

It was eight thirty that evening before Nick had a moment to phone Alex. After the mundanities of life – doing his own shopping, taking the car for an oil change, repairing a window at the Anchorage – and visiting Rosie in hospital, he dialled the number.

'Hello?'

'You got back, then? Shopping successful?' he asked sarcastically.

'Yes, thank you!' She was stifling a laugh. 'And thank you for last night. It was very . . . special.'

'Yes.' He paused. 'Yes, it was. I'm glad you stayed.'

'Me too.'

'And how's Victoria? You weren't in trouble?' he enquired.

'Not exactly. I got a few what you might call "old-fashioned" looks. You know – about staying out all night.'

'Did she know who you were with?'

'No. I'm afraid that when it came to the crunch I couldn't tell her. I said I had to go and see someone about work and that I'd be back the following day.'

'And she accepted that?' he asked, nervously.

'Rather too easily,' she admitted. 'She probably knew exactly where I was.'

Then a note of anxiety crept into her voice. 'I'm a bit concerned.' She hesitated. 'I don't want to give her too much to take in at one go. And I suppose . . . if I'm honest . . . I don't want her sitting in judgement.'

'It's going to be tricky, isn't it?'

'I suppose so,' she said forlornly. 'But don't worry – I'll handle it. It's my problem.'

He tried to say the right things. Make the right noises.

Let her know that he knew how difficult it must be, and that he wanted to help her find a solution. Then she said, 'Just give me a couple of days to sort myself out.'

They said goodbye fondly, but he felt uneasy. He told himself to give her time. To give them both time. This was something not to be rushed and, for him, there were few complications. True, he felt apprehensive and a little guilty at launching into a relationship so soon after the last one, but compared with what he felt for Alex, his relationship with Debs now seemed hardly like a relationship at all.

He got up and walked outside on to the veranda. Dusk was falling. Way below he could hear the sound of breakers on the pebble shore. In the far distance, through the rising mist, the green light of a container ship floated across the water. Another day, another night. He was alone with his thoughts – of Rosie, his father, wherever he was, and Alex. She had been here just twenty-four hours ago, and now she was on the other side of this stretch of water, seemingly as far away from him as it was possible to be.

He sat down and watched the sea until it was no longer visible. Then he went indoors and dreamed of her until morning.

23
Gloire des Rosomanes

*. . . was important in the early breeding of the
Bourbons.*

Victoria gazed out of the window as her mother read
aloud: ' "By the side of the tall and bouncing young
ladies in the establishment, Rebecca Sharp looked like a
child. But she had the dismal precocity of poverty. Many a
dun had she talked to, and turned away from her father's
door; many a tradesman had she coaxed and wheedled into
good humour, and into the granting of one meal more. She
sate commonly with her father, who was very proud of her
wit, and heard the talk of many of his wild companions –
often but ill suited for a girl to hear. But she never had been
a girl, she said; she had been a woman since she was eight
years old." ' Alex looked up. 'Are you listening?'

'Mmm?'

'I said are you listening?'

'A bit.'

'Well, if you're only listening a bit I'll stop.' She closed the book.

'I don't like her very much.'

'Who?'

'Becky Sharp.'

'Well, you don't really know her yet. We've only just started.'

'She sounds a bit scary. And anyway I don't like this as much as Jane Austen.'

'Why?'

'Because of what it says at the top of the first page.'

Alex opened the book again and read, 'A novel without a hero'.

'Ah, I see. No Mr Darcy.'

'No. And no Edward Ferrars.'

'So you liked Edward Ferrars?'

'Not at first, but in the end.'

'Why?'

'Because he was nice.'

'I thought you preferred Mr Willoughby. He was much more dashing. You said Edward Ferrars was a wimp.'

'Well, he was, but he got better. And by the end I could see why Elinor loved him.'

'And you think he was worth it?'

Victoria shrugged. 'Who knows?'

Alex turned away and murmured to herself. 'Who indeed?' Alex thought.

Whatever else Nick expected to happen the following morning it was not Henry's arrival on his doorstep. 'Are you feeling all right?' he asked. 'Normally you never venture this far without your passport and immunization.'

'There's no need for that. I'm on an errand of mercy.'

'That sounds ominous. Do you want some coffee? Even you can't drink claret at this time of day.'

Henry glared at him.

'Sorry.' Nick felt he might have overstepped the mark. 'What's the errand, then?'

'I went to see Rosie yesterday.'

'That's kind of you.' Nick was busy with the coffee and didn't look up.

'She was talking about what will happen when she comes out of hospital.'

'It won't be for a couple of weeks yet.'

'Three days, actually.'

'What?'

'I asked the nurse. The consultant had just done his rounds. They can get her a physio in her rest home and they reckon she'll be fit to go there by the end of the week.'

Nick put down the kettle. 'They didn't tell me that. I haven't sorted anything out yet. Barely had time.'

'I thought that might be the case. Anyway, she'll probably be happy to get out of the place.'

'But she's hardly mobile yet,' Nick was worried.

'Pressure on beds, apparently. Too many old folk falling over obviously, and they want to move out those who are likely to cope.'

'And they reckon Rosie can?'

'She's probably done her best to persuade them.'

'But it will be difficult to find somewhere at such short notice.' He could hear the panic in his voice as he spoke.

'I'd thought of that. I might be able to help.'

Nick sighed. 'I'm not sure you can. I'd better get my skates on and scout round for somewhere. Damn! I should have thought of this before. I just thought I'd have more time. Are there any convalescent homes on this side of the island?'

Henry fished into his inside pocket. 'My card.'

Nick took the small rectangular business card from Henry. It was a little crumpled at the edges. 'Henry J. Kinross, MCSP, SRP', it said, in minute copperplate.

'Henry, why do I need this? I know where you live.'

Henry pointed to the letters after his name. 'There.'

'MCSP, SRP. What's that? Some art-dealers' organization?'

'No. It stands for Member of the Chartered Society of Physiotherapists. And SRP means State Registered Physiotherapist.'

Nick looked at him open-mouthed. 'You're a physiotherapist?'

'Correct.'

'State registered?'

'Yes.'

'But you're an art dealer.'

'The two are not mutually exclusive. And I wasn't always an art dealer.'

'But . . . how long is it since you practised?'

'Ooh, about half an hour.'

'What?'

'Why do you think I open the gallery late every morning? It's not because I have a hangover. I have a few private patients. Not many, just a handful who are prepared to pay well. It keeps the old skill going and it takes my mind off temperamental artists. I spoke to the consultant, and he agreed that Rosie could stay with me. I have a niece on the mainland who can come over and keep an eye on the gallery while I'm not there, and Rosie will recover more quickly than she would in some impersonal nursing home.'

Nick was stunned. The kettle whistled, and he took it off the hob. 'You never said anything.'

'Dear boy, if there is one thing in life that I've learned it's that it doesn't do for people to know everything about you until they need to.'

Nick handed him a mug of coffee. 'You dark horse,' he said.

'Well . . .' Henry grinned, '. . . it gives me an air of mystery.'

'You know,' said Nick, with a twinkle in his eye, 'I'm not sure I should trust you with my grandmother.'

'Dear boy. I never mix business with pleasure.'

'Good.' Nick laughed.

'But in the case of your grandmother I'm prepared to make an exception.'

Alex felt guilty at being a little cooler with Nick on the phone than she should have been. To make amends she had decided to do a bit of research – see if she couldn't come up with some information about Rosie's past that might reassure him that she cared.

She rang the Russian embassy, but they insisted they could offer no help over the phone, and probably not even if she came in. There were many millions of Russian subjects and they did not have the staff to attend to such requests. Did she realize how complicated this might be, and how much paperwork it would entail?

So, disheartened but not discouraged, and armed with her shorthand book and the snippets of information she had written down, she spent the afternoon in Portsmouth library. What she found there surprised her and gave her reasonable cause for celebration. It was nothing definite, but it had to be more than a coincidence.

Having checked with the hospital that Rosie was indeed being released in three days' time on account of (a) Henry's kind offer, (b) Henry's acquaintance with the consultant and (c) Rosie's insistence that she would be better off out of hospital, Nick drove back to the Anchorage determined to do the sort of things that a man does when his grandmother is about to be released into the care of someone like Henry. But as he had not the faintest idea what these things were, and as there was little point in packing her bags just yet (it seemed disrespectfully premature), he faffed about for an hour or so, said, 'Damn it,' a few times, then slung his painting bag over his shoulder and left the house.

He drove to Newport, then on through Blackwater and Godshill, took a right turn towards Wroxall and finally arrived at Appuldurcombe House. It had been a stunning Palladian mansion, but now it was just a ruin, though from a distance it still looked handsome and imposing, set in rolling folds of downland.

The sky was pale pewter grey, which offered a less than flattering light to the stately pile, but he made a start, and added a touch of Payne's Grey to the clouds to make a greater contrast between sky and stonework. He tried to think of nothing but the Worsleys who'd owned Appuldurcombe for hundreds of years; several had been governors of the island. It had no governor now, just an MP, a lord lieutenant and a high sheriff. Maybe it no longer warranted the grandeur – last provided by Lord Mountbatten; it seemed to have died with him when that bomb exploded in Ireland.

He remembered how incensed Rosie had been. His grandfather, who had served with Mountbatten on HMS *Kelly*, had been silent. 'Surely now they'll do something about it,' Rosie had said. She had never been able to come to terms with the fact that the atrocities continued. All her life Rosie had believed there was a solution for everything, if only the effort could be made to find it. The sentiment, he had to admit, had rubbed off on himself. There had to be a solution to his problem. He just had to find it.

He tried to concentrate on the ruined house, but Alex's face kept drifting into his mind. He sat, motionless, brush poised above the paper, as if frozen in time. Was he imagining all these emotions? Was he just carried away in the heat of the moment? Perhaps it was just lust, pure and simple. Every time he thought of her naked it gave him deep pleasure. Maybe it was just the sex.

He found himself shaking his head. No. It was more than that – he was sure of it. And why had he never felt like this with Debs? It was a question to which there would never be an answer, however hard he strove for it. He had been prepared to settle for a comfortable relationship – but the relationship on which he had just embarked was anything but comfortable. It had complications – if Victoria could be called a complication. Yet it was somehow so straight-forward. He had no option but to love Alex. It was easy, natural – and disturbing.

Once he had been able to concentrate on his painting, and had wanted little from life, except an easy ride. Now, none of that seemed enough. He was restless, discontented. Half of him was irritated by it. Could he not just call a halt and go back to the way things were?

Clearly not in the case of Debs – and he didn't want to go back there. But couldn't he regain his equilibrium, his comfortable state of mind? He could finish with Alex. It was not as if anything had really started. They had slept together, but that hardly constituted a relationship. Did Victoria like him? Did it matter? His relationship was with Alex, not her – so there *was* a relationship. He groaned, and washed his brush in the jam-jar of purple-grey water, then got up, stretched his legs and thrust his hands deep into his pockets. He strode up and down for a few minutes, then threw back his head and closed his eyes, breathing deeply. He was in this thing now, for better or worse, and the truth of the matter was, that he wanted to be with Alex more than he had wanted to be with anyone else he had ever met. Scary or not, he'd better buck up or back out. A blob of rain fell upon his face.

Alex had just got home from her trip to the library when there was a knock at her door. Whoever else she had expected to find when she opened it, it was not her husband.

24
Baronne Prevost

. . . coarse in growth and rather thorny . . .

'What are you doing here? I thought you'd gone.'
Alex's surprise was mixed with irritation. She had
almost managed to get Paul out of her mind. It had been a
struggle, not least because Victoria had kept asking about
him, but she told herself that she needed to move on – that
she was allowed to. Some days were better than others. But
when pangs of guilt at being a single parent assailed her, she
assuaged them by convincing herself that Paul had gone
anyway. It seemed she had been fooling herself.

'Not till tomorrow. I was delayed. I came to say goodbye
to Vicks.'

'She's at school. She'll be home any minute.'

'Can I come in and wait?'

'No. No you can't. Look, we've been through all this.
We've said all we had to say.'

'I just want to say goodbye to her, that's all.'

A woman walking down the street turned in their direction. 'Look . . . oh, come in – but just for a minute.'

She closed the door behind him, then backed away to stand behind an armchair. She needed to distance herself from him, physically as well as mentally. 'This really isn't fair, you know.'

Paul nodded. 'I'm sorry, but they delayed me for a couple of weeks and I didn't want to leave without seeing her.'

'But you know it will only upset her. Last time you saw her it was supposed to be for the last time. She had nightmares for days afterwards, Paul.'

'Don't exaggerate.'

'I'm not. It's not that she doesn't love you, it's just that . . .'

'What? What is it then?'

'She's frightened of you.'

'But that's ridiculous. I've never touched her.'

Alex tried to sound sympathetic. 'I know that, but she needs stability. She can't cope with this whirlwind who descends on the house, rows with her mother, then takes off again. Can't you see that?'

'So it's all my fault, is it?'

'Of course not. But try to see it from her point of view. It's taken me ages to get her settled. She's only ten.'

'Going on eighteen.'

'That doesn't mean she feels things like an adult. Just because she's old for her age doesn't mean that she's emotionally equipped to handle it. It doesn't mean that you can dump on her.'

'I'm not dumping on her. I know she'll understand that I need to say goodbye properly.'

'*You* need to?' His arrogance made her fume. She looked

at him, standing there with his hands in the pockets of his well-cut suit. He was six feet three, darkly good looking and immaculately dressed. His self-assurance had once attracted her but now she found it repellent. Ridiculous, even. It wasn't simply the old excuse that they had 'grown apart'. They had grown to realize that they were, fundamentally, different in outlook, always had been, but they had put it to one side and allowed the physical attraction to carry them along. Now she could not imagine why she had thought it a good basis for marriage, but at the time she had been overwhelmed by it. More fool her. The similarity between her original physical attraction to Paul and now to Nick crossed her mind. But only fleetingly. There was no comparison between them. Not in the slightest. Where Paul was brutish, Nick was gentle. Where Nick was considerate, Paul was oblivious. She wasn't imagining it, was she?

She shook her head and blurted, 'No, I'm sorry, you'll have to go. It's really not fair on either of us.'

'Can't we be grown-up about this? Try to be reasonable.'

'I'm trying to be both. But I don't see why you should play around with our emotions – mine and Victoria's.'

'Oh, so it's you as well now is it? Not sure that we're doing the right thing?'

'Oh, please! You really are the limit. Of course we're doing the right thing. It's over, you know it is. Don't start those games again.'

Paul shrugged. 'What games?'

Alex moved towards the door. 'No. I'm sorry. I'm just not going to do this, Paul. It's all been said and sorted. You're going and we're staying.'

'Yes, but—'

'No. There are no buts. I need a fresh start. You know you can see Victoria – we'll arrange all that, she's your daughter as well as mine – but right now she just needs to get her mind round the fact that her mother and father don't live together any more. Just give her a bit of time.'

Paul leaned against the wall. 'So that's that, then?'

'Yes. That was that three months ago – three years ago.'

'Oh, don't bring all that up again. She's not coming with me.'

'Only because someone else is.'

'Who told you that?'

Alex shook her head. 'You're so obvious, Paul. And you should have known better than to tell your friends and think it wouldn't get back to me. I wish you wouldn't treat me as though I was stupid as well as unimportant.'

Paul looked away.

'Go on. Go and bury your head in the sand. Go to America. You can see Victoria when you come back.'

He turned to face her. 'It didn't have to be like this, you know.'

Alex sighed. 'Oh, it did.'

He walked away without a backward glance. Alex closed the door behind him, then burst into tears.

Rosie was sitting up in bed, her lipstick freshly applied, holding out her hand as a manicurist varnished her nails.

'I thought this was a hospital, not a beauty clinic,' Nick said, as he arrived beside her.

Rosie looked up at him and beamed. 'Hello, love! I'm just having my nails done.'

'So I see.'

'They come once a week. Useful, isn't it?' She nodded

towards the girl in the pink nylon overall who was bent over her right hand. 'This is Clare. She's come to get me ready for my trip.'

'Trip?'

'To Henry's.'

'Ah, yes.' He nodded at Clare and smiled.

Clare, evidently aware that a family heart-to-heart was about to ensue, packed away her varnishes and emery boards then bustled off with a nervous smile.

Nick sat on the edge of the bed.

'Don't do that. They'll tell you off. You're not meant to sit on the bed.'

He moved to a chair, then asked earnestly, 'Are you sure about this?'

'Certain. I heard the nurse tell someone off yesterday when they perched on the bed.'

Nick laughed. 'No. I mean, are you sure about moving in with Henry?'

'Oh, I'm not moving in with him like *that*! We're not – what do they call it? Co-something.'

'Cohabiting.'

'Yes. I'm not doing that.'

'Well, you'll be under the same roof.'

'Not in the same bed, though.'

Nick spluttered. 'I should hope not.'

Rosie looked at him with a serious expression on her face. 'Would it be so terrible if we were?'

'Rosie!'

She shook her head. 'You're all the same.'

'Who are?'

'People your age. Always imagining that sex is something for the under-fifties.'

Nick glanced around apprehensively. 'Will you keep your voice down?'

Rosie grinned. 'You don't suddenly stop, you know, when you've had your children.'

'I don't want to think about this.'

'No, but I do.'

He shot her a warning look.

'Only joking,' she said. And then, rather wistfully, 'Chance would be a fine thing.'

Nick leaned back in his chair. 'Are you trying to shock me?'

She looked him in the eye. 'Maybe.'

'Mmm. Well, it worked.'

Rosie smoothed down the bedcovers and patted her hair into place. 'Trouble is, when you're in here you have too much time to think. If only I hadn't slipped on that deck I wouldn't be in this pickle.'

'No,' he agreed. 'And I didn't have much choice about letting you go, did I?'

'No,' she agreed ruefully.

'Well, thanks for being honest, at least.'

Rosie leaned back on the pillow and closed her eyes. 'I'm tired.'

'I'm not surprised.'

She opened her eyes. 'But I'm happier. I've got something to look forward to now.'

Nick paused, more serious now. 'Look, don't you think you'd be better off where they can look after you properly?'

'Henry can look after me properly,' Rosie insisted.

'But he has a gallery to run.' Nick took her hand.

Rosie looked indignant. 'Are you saying I'll get in the way?'

'All I'm saying is that I don't think Henry knows what he's letting himself in for.'

Rosie squeezed his hand. 'Shall I tell you something? I know he doesn't.'

'You're a wicked old lady!'

'I know. But it's more fun that way!' She grinned.

Nick sighed. 'How do you do it?'

'Bloody-mindedness, love. Sheer bloody-mindedness. Don't let them grind you down.'

Nick laughed, relieved that her old spirit was back.

'I'm going to stay with Henry,' Rosie continued. 'I mean, what's the worst thing that can happen? He'll find me too much for him and decide after a few days that I'd be better off in a home. He likes the prospect of looking after me, but it will wear off. I'm ready for it, though, so I'll take the chance.'

'Do you take more chances now?'

'Heavens, yes. Some don't – I've watched them. They get in a rut. Look at Mr and Mrs Stevens next door to us in Cheltenham. Same routine every day. Same piece of fish on a Friday. Bed at the same time every night. It would drive me mad.'

She saw his face and smiled. 'I know I'm odd, and your granddad found it wearing – he was happy to do the same things every day, bless him. But I can't. Too many things I've not done, and not much time left to do them. If you can do something every day that you've never done before you can remember every day and it's special.' Then she said, pointedly, 'It's in my blood.' Then came the expected question: 'Have you found anything out?' she asked. 'About my parents?'

'A tiny bit,' he said, 'but nothing very helpful.'

Rosie pushed herself up in the bed a little. 'Well?' She was wide-eyed, like a child expecting a bedtime story.

Nick explained the difference between marriages with members of sovereign houses, and morganatic marriages, and told Rosie about the true heir to the Russian throne.

'So we're not in line, then?' she asked evenly.

'No.' He paused. 'But you knew that, didn't you?'

Rosie was silent for a moment. 'Yes.'

'Why didn't you tell me?'

'Because I wanted you to find out for yourself. I wanted you to be curious about your family history.'

'Is there anything else you know that you haven't told me?'

'That's all. I still don't know who my parents were. The Internet couldn't help me there.' She smiled guiltily.

Nick said nothing, just looked at her lying back on her pillow, eyes a clear forget-me-not blue, skin soft and smooth, lips perfectly made up. She was, he had to admit, the eighth wonder of the world.

'And what about you?' she asked.

'What about me?'

'Alex. Is it going well?'

'I think so.'

'Don't want to rush it? Is that why you're not seeing more of each other?'

He nodded, looking preoccupied.

'Mmm. Well, don't wait too long,' she said sharply.

'It's not as simple as that.'

'Why not?'

'Well, she's still married – separated, but not divorced – and there's Victoria to think about.'

'Oh, those things will sort themselves out.' Rosie was dismissive.

'You seem very sure.'

'Stands to reason. If she wants you as much as you want her then the first one needn't be a problem, and Victoria – well, she's nobody's fool, and I think she knows a good man when she sees one.'

He sighed. 'Oh, it's all so complicated. I mean, how fast to take it. Where do we live? What happens—'

'Stop! Why all the questions?'

'They've got to be answered.'

'Yes, but not all at once. Take things a day at a time. You know where you're going but you can't get there in one big step. Just . . . well . . . you know . . . chill out.'

'What?'

'Chill out.'

Nick laughed.

Rosie looked concerned. 'What's so funny?'

'You are.'

'Why?' She was indignant now.

'Nothing. It's nothing.'

'Some days I worry about you,' Rosie told him.

'Yes,' he replied. 'And some days I worry about you. Though for the life of me I can't imagine why.'

He sat with her for another hour, and when he left he felt strangely confident. As though a weight had been lifted from him, as though he could do anything, conquer any situation. He knew it wouldn't last, but for the moment he would enjoy it.

The rain that had been threatening all day was now falling, that fine rain that soaks you to the skin. He had already put up the hood on the MG, and drove home with the inefficient wipers doing their best to clear the windscreen.

He made a dash for the veranda, and as he slipped his key into the lock he heard the telephone. When he answered it, it took him a moment to recognize the voice at the other end of the line.

And then he identified the caller who was gasping out seemingly disconnected phrases between the sobs: 'Paul . . . goodbye . . . Victoria . . . school . . . missing.'

25
Country Living

. . . fading to almost white.

When he could finally make sense of what Alex had said, the seriousness of it sank in. Paul had been to see her. He had asked if he could say goodbye to Victoria. She had refused. Victoria had not come home from school. She thought it likely that he had taken the child with him.

Nick ran through the other possibilities. Could Victoria have gone home with a friend? Alex had thought of that and contacted them all. She was not with any of them.

Could Victoria have gone into town on her own? It was unlikely. She always told Alex if she was going to be late home.

Would Paul really have taken the child? Alex said she didn't know. She'd rung him but there had been no answer. He had never done anything like this before but, then, they had never been in this situation until now.

'Has she taken anything with her?' asked Nick, hardly

knowing why that should be important but clutching at straws.

'What sort of things?' asked Alex, her desperation audible.

'I don't know. Clothes, washbag, that sort of thing.'

'No. Only the clothes she was wearing. And her school bag, with her books and pens and stuff.'

'And she didn't say anything this morning?'

'No.'

'Was she OK?'

'She's been a bit distant lately, not really concentrating. Her mind's been elsewhere. She always has her head buried in that Isle of Wight guidebook she made me buy her.' And then, 'Oh, God! You don't think she's gone to the island, do you?'

'I don't know. It's possible. She didn't *say* anything about coming here?'

'Nothing.'

'I think she's most likely to be with Paul if you want my honest opinion, but I could go and look.'

'But where? Where will you start? I mean I know it's a small island but it's not that small. She could be anywhere.'

'Have you told the police?'

'No. Not yet.'

'Well, I think you should.'

'Oh, God!'

Nick could hear the rising panic in her voice. It was so unlike her. Alex the level-headed one; Alex the sensible mother with the sensible child. He could hardly believe this was happening.

'I'll go and look in all the obvious places. The places she knew. Sleepyhead Bay and the place where you stayed.

Sophie will wait here in case she shows up. Try not to worry.'

'I'll do my best, but how can I get in touch with you?' she asked.

'Ring the Anchorage and let Sophie know if anything happens. I'll give her your number so that she can call you.'

'Right.'

He knew she was biting back the tears. 'She'll be fine, I'm sure of it. I know there'll be some explanation for it and it will be OK. I'm sure. Paul will probably bring her back soon.'

'Yes.' She was quieter now, but clearly desolate. 'I just wish I'd seen it coming.'

'Don't blame yourself – OK? We'll sort it out.'

After a few more placatory phrases he put down the phone and went to the yacht club to find Sophie.

'She's what?'

'Gone missing.'

'Oh, hell! Any clues?'

'Well, her father came round an hour or so before she disappeared, and Alex wouldn't let him see her.'

'Was that wise?'

'Victoria's always in a state when he's been. I think Alex was just trying to keep her on an even keel. Anyway, she thinks he might have taken her, and it does seem likely. The only other thing is that she was welded to an Isle of Wight guidebook. I think she's fallen for the place.'

'Oh, God, poor Alex.' Then the organizer in Sophie came to the fore. 'I'll get back to the house. You go and look wherever you think she might be. Have you rung the ferry company to see if she was spotted coming over? I'll do that.

Take this.' She handed him a mobile phone. 'It's new. I've stuck the number on it so I don't forget. I'll ring Alex and give her the number, then she can ring you – or me at the Anchorage – if she hears anything. Now get off and look.' Sophie strode off up the lane in the direction of the Anchorage.

'Thanks!' he yelled after her. She waved without turning round. He thanked God that she had come to stay.

The sun was sinking below the horizon as he walked down the steps to Sleepyhead Bay. The rain had stopped, but the rough wooden planks were wet and slippery, as were the rocks in the cove. He hopped from one to another, looking for a small girl he hoped might be fishing for shrimps, as she had been when he had first met her. He did not want to think of her in any other way. Occasionally the prospect of the worst sight of all insinuated itself into his mind, but he banished it. They would find her alive and well, wondering what all the fuss was about.

He knocked on the doors of the small cottages, but with no luck. Nobody had seen a small girl on her own. Nobody had noticed anything out of the ordinary.

He tried the hotel where Alex and Victoria had stayed. They remembered mother and daughter, but had seen neither of them since. They promised to call if she came, and wished him luck in his search. They were sure she would come home. She had seemed such a sensible child.

On he drove, to places where he knew Alex had taken Victoria, but his enquiries yielded nothing and it was getting dark.

He drove slowly along the main street of Godshill,

looking to left and right. He even asked at the pub, just in case. But as everywhere else he drew a blank.

At half past eight he rang Sophie in desperation. 'Have you heard anything?' he asked.

'No.'

'What about the ferry?'

'Yes – but they had a school party on board.'

'Don't they check people on? For safety and all that?'

'Yes, they do. But they said it's just possible she could have slipped on without them seeing. They were very apologetic.'

'Damn.' He tried to think straight. 'Oh, God, Soph, what do I do now?'

'Ring Alex and tell her you've no news – bad or good.'

He did as Sophie suggested, and told Alex exactly where he had been. Could she think of anywhere else he should try?

She said there had been so many places – St Catherine's Point, Tennyson Down – most of which he couldn't visit in the dark.

'What did the police say?' he asked.

'They're talking to the Newport station. They say that if Victoria doesn't turn up in the next couple of hours they'll launch a full-scale search, here and on the island. I don't know what to do, Nick – I just don't know what to *do*.' She sounded at her wit's end.

'Listen . . .' He tried to sound positive, but it was hard. He hardly knew Victoria, but he liked her. And she'd seemed to like him. *And* she was Alex's daughter, which was all that mattered. 'We'll find her – you *must* believe that.'

'I feel such a failure, such a bad mother. Why didn't I let him see her? Then all this wouldn't have happened.'

He felt so desperate that he wasn't with her. How he hated mobile phones! Why did she have to be at the end of one now instead of right next to him where he could hold her and tell her it would be all right? 'You're not a failure. You're a great mum. Victoria knows that.'

'So why has she gone?'

He tried to find an answer, but could only find questions. 'Is there still no sign of Paul?'

'No. They've alerted the airports, and the ferry terminals, but I can't believe he'd run off with her.'

'Have you rung him?'

'Still no reply.'

'I know someone else like that.' In spite of his undistinguished relationship with his father, Nick wished Derek was here now. Perhaps he would have some cunning means of tracking her down. But his father's schemes were mostly doomed to failure. What Nick needed now was sound, reasoned advice. 'Look, I'm not giving up. And you mustn't – you mustn't think the worst.'

'But I can't help it.'

'I know – but it will be fine, I'm sure of it.' He surprised himself with his confidence. Maybe it was just bloody-mindedness, a refusal to accept things you didn't want to believe. Perhaps he got it from his grandmother.

'I'm so glad you're there,' whispered Alex. 'I don't know what I'd do without you.'

He pocketed the mobile phone and set off again on his search.

It was almost completely dark now. Patchy cloud gave way to small expanses of sky, studded with stars, and the moon ducked in and out. Victoria was out there somewhere. But

218

where? Here or on the mainland? On her own or with her father?

Bugger. Why couldn't he sort this out? Why couldn't he think straight? If Paul had taken her with him there was nothing he could do. But if she had wandered off on her own it should be possible to work out where she had gone.

Where would a child go if she was disturbed by her parents splitting up and looking for some kind of escape?

She'd look for somewhere comforting. Somewhere that gave her a kind of stability. Somewhere she felt at home.

It all pointed to the island. He remembered the conversation she had had with Alex the day they met on the beach. 'I prefer this side,' she'd said, meaning the south of the island. 'Why's that?' Alex had asked. 'Because there's more sea,' had been Victoria's response.

He remembered asking her if she liked the sea, and she said that it was not so much the sea as that it took longer to get home from there. It was the furthest place from home she could think of.

She had been poring over the guidebook, Alex had said. Deciding where she would like to live. But he had tried Sleepyhead Bay, and Godshill, all the places she had mentioned to Alex.

His reverie was broken by the shrill ring of the mobile phone in his pocket.

'Nick?'

'Soph?'

'I think I've seen her.'

'What?'

'I know this sounds stupid but I was making some tea

about five minutes ago and I glanced up at the window and I'm sure I saw a face.'

'What?'

'Honestly. I know I did.'

'Did you go and look?'

'I ran out as fast as I could but I couldn't find her. I'm sure I didn't imagine it, though.'

'And you think it was Victoria?'

'Well, I only met her once and I wasn't taking that much notice, but I'm as sure as I can be that it was. Do you want to phone Alex?'

'Not until we're certain. Damn! Where did she run off to?'

'Beats me. I'll go now and keep looking. If I have any more news I'll ring you, OK?'

He slipped the phone back into his pocket and leaned against the car, gazing up at the moon in the hope that it would offer inspiration. But the moon wasn't playing. It slid tantalizingly behind a cloud and the night was dark as ink.

26
Golden Moss

. . . it detests wet weather and can be rather shy.

Rain began to fall, gently at first, then heavily, slanting across the sky in the light of the street lamp. Nick had pulled over at the side of the road in Seaview, to take a rest from driving. Seaview. Alex had said Victoria thought it was posh. It was certainly the island's smartest resort, the houses neatly painted, the gardens smart and well tended. This was where cabinet ministers and actors had their weekend cottages. Henry fitted in rather well at Seaview, which provided him with a good number of well-heeled clients, who were interested, as Nick now realized, in muscle manipulation as well as art.

His mind did not stay on Henry for long. He had come here only because he wanted to explore every town and village that Victoria had mentioned. Stupid, really – he could give them no more than a cursory search, driving up and down the main streets, looking to right and left. And what chance was there of seeing her? Would she really be walking down the high street looking in shop windows? But what else could he do? When someone was missing and you wanted to find them, you had to start somewhere, however futile the attempt might seem.

He watched the rain running in rivulets along the pavement and into the gutter.

The phone in his pocket rang. It was Alex, sounding desolate and drained.

'The police say they can't do anything until morning now. Have you found anything?'

He was unable to keep from her the glimmer of hope. It seemed unkind. 'Sophie thinks she saw a face at the window, and that it was Victoria's.'

'Oh, God!'

'Now, stay calm. I'm looking absolutely everywhere. I've been to all the places you mentioned, and there was no sign of her at the moment. But the weather's foul. I reckon if she's here she's probably sheltering from the rain and there's no way we're going to find her until morning.'

'No,' she said flatly. Trying to hold on to her emotions.

'Do you want me to come over there?' he asked.

'No. Stay on the island. If she's there it's pointless you being over here.'

'I'm doing my best,' Nick said. 'I'm going everywhere I think she may go. Why don't you try to get some sleep? The police will let us know if they come up with anything – if there are any sightings, I mean.'

'I can't.' She let out a sob.

How he wished he could be with her. 'Well, try. At least go to bed,' he said gently.

'Will you keep looking?' she asked. 'But don't drive. You must be too tired to drive now. It's not safe.'

'I'll take the car home and look round the coast there.'

'Be careful.'

'And you.'

The phone clicked off. He could only imagine what she was going through, the scenarios playing in her mind. It was every parent's lot to fear the worst. He knew that without having been one.

He drove back to the Anchorage, and found Sophie asleep in an armchair. She started up when he walked in, eyes wide, then asked, 'Any news?'

Nick flopped on to the sofa. 'Nothing. Nothing at all. I'm beginning to wonder if it was your imagination. Maybe it was just rain on the window.'

Sophie shook her head. 'No, it wasn't. Unless rain wears a woolly hat.' She held up a lavender blue knitted hat. 'Found it in the rosebush outside the window. It was hanging from one of the thorns.'

'Why didn't you ring me?' he asked angrily.

'I did. You had no signal.'

'Bloody mobile phones!'

'You'd have been in a bit of a state without one today, though, wouldn't you?'

'I'm going to phone Alex. I don't think she'll be asleep.' He walked over to the phone and dialled the number.

She answered almost immediately. 'Hello.'

'Alex, it's me. Does Victoria have a blue woolly hat?'

'Yes.'

'Did she have it on today?'

'She wears it to school, even when it's sunny. In case it rains.'

'Thank heavens! We've found it outside the house. On a rosebush. She must be over here.'

'Oh, God! I'll come over.'

'You won't be able to. The ferries have stopped now. And if she rings home, you should be there. I'll keep looking here, and I'll tell the police.'

Within the hour the police had turned up at the Anchorage, and searched the house and garden. They sat down with Nick and Sophie and questioned them in detail about their knowledge of and relationship with Victoria. Their manner was cold at first, unfriendly even, but as the interview proceeded it became clear that they had accepted what they were told.

When they finally departed, dawn was breaking, and a pale, watery sky replaced the inky black and pouring rain of the night before.

'You look terrible,' said Sophie.

'You don't look so good yourself.'

'I'm not surprised. I haven't slept for three days.'

'Three?'

'Had a bit of a rave the night before last. Doing the pubs with a couple of old mates. Didn't get to bed.'

'You are making up for lost time, aren't you?'

Sophie pushed herself out of the chair. 'Better have a shower. No. Come to think of it, you look worse than I do. You have one.'

'No. I can't. I need to start looking again.'

With the bossiness reserved for sisters, she ushered him to the bathroom, then cooked him breakfast.

'How do you feel now?' she asked, as he slumped down at the table.

'Better than I should,' he replied, rubbing his face.

'Nervous energy.'

'Probably.'

Sophie nibbled reluctantly on a slice of dry toast while she waited for the kettle to boil. 'Where will you go first?' she asked.

'St Catherine's Point.'

'Why there?'

'It's the most southerly part of the island, and I know she liked the south coast better than the north.' The moment he had said it he was aware that he had spoken in the past tense. 'Likes. She likes the south coast better than the north.'

Sophie put her hand on his. 'She'll be fine. You'll see. You'll find her today. She'll be cold, fed up and hungry by now. When you're cold and hungry two things become irresistible.'

Nick looked at her questioningly. 'Warmth and food?'

'Exactly.'

'I wish I shared your confidence.'

'You're too close to it, that's all.' Sophie came to the table and sat down opposite him. 'What's Victoria like? Do you get on?'

'I think so, but it must be a bit hard, seeing your dad and mum break up, then having your mum find a new friend so soon.'

'I guess so.'

'But it just sort of happened. I don't think either of us was looking to start a relationship. It just . . . well . . . crept up on us.'

'Love on the rebound?'

'No. I don't think so. I could have walked away, had

nothing to do with her, but she's fun, good company . . . No. It's more than that . . .'

'Hey! There's no need to defend yourself. I'm not sitting in judgement . . . you know what I think?'

Nick shook his head.

'I think you're in love. You're a changed man – you're cheerful, fun to be with. Not like you were with Debs.'

Nick raised an eyebrow.

'Sorry, but it's true. She did put a bit of a damper on you, you know.'

He nodded. Seeing it clearly for the first time.

'Well, I hate to say it, because it really goes against the grain, but if that's what love is, it gets my vote.'

'Thank you.' He smiled ruefully.

'Are you sure you can take on a ready-made family, though?'

'I think that depends on whether or not she's prepared to take on me . . . It was Victoria who introduced me to her mum. On the beach at Sleepyhead Bay, she saw me painting and asked me to give her mum some advice.'

'She was quite bold, then?'

'Yes. It's since then that she's got quieter. More thoughtful. Not that I saw a lot of her. She came round one evening with Alex. She was talking to Rosie. They seemed to be getting on really well, then Rosie started talking about the Russian royal family thing.'

'What?'

Nick realized he'd put his foot in it. 'I forgot to tell you – well, I didn't actually. I was waiting for the right moment.'

'For what?'

'This isn't the right moment either, but, in a nutshell, you know Rosie was born in Russia?'

'Ye-es?'

'And she never knew who her real parents were?'

'Ye-es.'

'Well, she's got this bee in her bonnet that she's related to the Tsar.'

'*What?*'

'Exactly.' Nick got up from the table. 'I haven't really got the time to tell you now – I need to get out and start looking again – but the long and the short of it is that Rosie thinks her mother was Grand Duchess Tatiana who was assassinated with the rest of the Russian royal family in 1918, but she doesn't know who her father was. In spite of making enquiries at the local library and searching the Internet I'm no nearer to finding out. Alex has promised she'll do some research, too.'

Sophie cleared her throat. 'This is all a dream. I'm hallucinating.'

'No, you're not.' Nick was pulling on his coat and making for the door. 'You're just part of a family with some colourful history.' He opened the door. 'Wish me luck.'

'Good luck,' she said, as he closed the door behind him. 'I hope you find her. I'm sure you will.' Then she slumped back in the chair and tried to work out whether she was really conscious, or slipping into a state of sleep-deprived delirium.

27
Prospero

Needs extra special care to thrive.

He shuddered when he looked down over the rocks at St Catherine's Point. Normally he would have found it a majestic sight, irresistible to paint – trying to catch the light on the spume as it was flung high into the air. Today it only reminded him of what might have happened to Victoria. If she had lost her footing and slipped, who would ever find her?

He shook his head, to clear it of unwanted thoughts, and climbed wearily into the MG for the umpteenth time over the last twenty-four hours. He drove through the tiny village of Niton, then through Rookley and Blackwater where the villagers were emerging and going about their business.

He drove to Carisbrooke. Maybe the castle ruins had captured her imagination. Victoria loved Jane Austen, Alex had said, and Jane Austen had loved the Isle of

Wight. Maybe there was some connection, but he was a pale shadow of Sherlock Holmes, and life was seldom as complicated as Conan Doyle made out.

Leaving the car outside the towering walls, he circumnavigated the castle. It was so large, so impregnable; the vast hill on which it stood must have been capable of withstanding the most determined army.

As he looked up at the solid stonework, it struck him how small Victoria was, compared with all this. They were on a tiny island, yet they were still dwarfed by everything around them. How could he find her among all this? And yet he felt that there was no threat in the air. The castle was protective, benign. Its bloody history was behind it now, the imprisoned King Charles long gone, and it sat, like some battle-scarred leviathan, on its hill, ready to offer shelter to all who needed it. He chided himself for his sentimentality. But he wanted to believe that this island, *his* island – and its people – would protect the waif who was wandering through its valleys and along its lanes.

Perhaps he had simply become an incurable romantic – but he wanted to believe that the islanders were good people, that the world was not filled with perverts and cranks but in the main with ordinary, decent folk who, on seeing a lost ten-year-old, would take her in, find out where she was from and get her safely home to her mother.

Then he remembered what Rosie had said when he had taken her to tea at Brown's. It seemed like years ago now, but it was barely a couple of weeks. 'People think what the newspapers and television tell them to think.'

Of course there were more good people in the world than bad. It was just that you never heard about them.

Rosie. He had put her out of his mind – there had barely been room for her during the events of the night. She had got on so well with Victoria and would be desperate when she heard the news. Unless . . . He slipped back into the car and drove to the hospital.

He walked down the long corridor, then turned the corner that led into Rosie's ward. She lay in her bed, sipping her morning tea. 'Hello, love!' she said. 'Guess who's come to visit me?'

At first he could see nobody. Maybe she was imagining things. But then, as he approached the bed, he saw, at Rosie's shoulder, a small figure sitting on a chair. She looked bedraggled and tired, and her face bore a worried frown. 'Have you been looking for me?' she asked.

The phone calls were the first thing. Alex burst into tears at the news, said, 'Thank you, thank you . . . oh, thank you,' then hung up to rush for the ferry. He called the police, and then Sophie, who agreed to meet Alex at the ferry terminal. Then he sat down in the hospital waiting room and talked to Victoria, trying to understand.

'I just wanted to see if Rosie was all right,' she said.

'I thought you knew she was?'

'I wanted to see for myself. I wanted to talk to her.' She looked up at him now, suddenly shy. 'And I wanted to see you.'

Nick felt stunned. 'Why?'

'To try to understand what was going on.'

Nick put his arm round her. 'Is it very confusing?'

Victoria looked at the floor and nodded.

'I'm sorry. I didn't mean to make things hard for you.'

'I know.'

'It's just that . . . well . . . things happen sometimes and you don't have much control over them,' he said.

She looked up. 'Like you and Mum?'

'Yes.'

'I just wanted to know if you love her as much as she loves you?'

Her candour took his breath away. 'Do you think she loves me?'

Victoria nodded. 'Oh, yes. I just think she's a bit scared.'

Nick cleared his throat. 'I think we're all a bit scared. What do you think?'

She managed a weak smile. 'That you're very nice.'

Nick gave her a hug. 'And I think you're nice, too. But why on earth did you run away?' He frowned.

'Because of Dad. When I was going home from school I saw him going into the house. I didn't want to go back there, so I walked into town and got on to the ferry to come here. I didn't mean to stay away. I didn't want to make Mum worry. I was going to go back when I'd seen Rosie and you. But you weren't there and it took longer than I thought. When I got there I looked through the window and that lady was there, the one we saw when you were out.'

'My sister?'

'I think so. She saw me, so I went and hid, in case she stopped me finding Rosie.'

'Where did you hide?'

'Under the veranda, by the little boat. When she'd gone, and I knew you weren't there, I walked into Newport.'

'Following the signs?'

'Yes.' She looked concerned. 'Was Mum cross?'

'She was very worried.'

'What about Dad?' She looked frightened now. 'Is he coming?'

'No. He's gone. We thought you might have gone with him.'

She shook her head violently.

Nick wondered whether he should ask the question, but found it impossible not to. 'You don't seem to get on with your dad.'

Victoria shook her head again.

Nick sat and waited. He didn't like to probe.

Eventually she said, 'He's all right with me, but he's not nice to Mum. He doesn't make her happy.'

'I see.'

Then she looked up at him. 'Not like you do. You make her happy.' She had a quizzical look on her face. 'Are you a good man?'

Nick was taken aback. 'I'm sorry?'

'Are you a good man?'

'Well . . . I try to be.'

'Because I think she deserves a good man.'

The power of speech temporarily deserted him – such old-fashioned, adult conversation from a ten-year-old!

'So do I,' he stammered eventually.

'I hope you're not wasting her time.'

There was no possible answer to this, so Nick said, 'We'd better get you cleaned up. Do you want to come back to the Anchorage and wait for your mum?'

'If it's not too much trouble.'

'Oh, it's no trouble. No trouble at all.'

*

'This place is beginning to seem like a seaside hotel.'

They were sitting round the small table at the Anchorage – Alex and Victoria, Nick and Sophie.

'Not for long. I'm off next week,' said Sophie.

'It wasn't a hint,' said Nick, 'just an observation. It's quite fun, really.'

Alex had been waiting for Nick and Victoria on their return from the hospital. Nick had left them to talk while he and Sophie had gone food shopping in Cowes, the better to cope with the sudden influx of guests.

When they returned, they found them curled up together on the sofa, Victoria lying against Alex, who was stroking her hair and whispering to her. They got up when Nick and Sophie came in, and then they had all set about preparing lunch. Nothing more had been said about Victoria's adventure. Until now.

'I'm sorry for all this,' said Alex, 'but I think we've cleared it up now.'

Nick noticed that they had both been crying, and yet there was a calmness about them.

Alex stood up, clearly wanting to change the subject. 'How's Rosie?' she asked.

'She comes out of hospital in a couple of days.' He told them about the plan for her to stay with Henry.

'Well, bugger me! Oops! Sorry!' said Sophie, evidently remembering that Victoria was with them.

'Henry? A physiotherapist?' asked Alex.

'I've tried to tell him that he'll have bitten off more than he can chew,' Nick said, 'but he's insistent. As soon as the consultant gives the nod, Rosie's going back to *chez* Henry for rest and recuperation.'

'He's mad!' opined Sophie. 'She'll drive him bonkers.'

'No, she won't,' Victoria chipped in. 'She has lots of good stories.'

'Well, I just hope he's appreciative,' said Sophie.

Alex asked softly, 'Is this wise?'

'Probably not,' said Nick. 'But if you can stand in the way of those two when they've set their minds on something, you're a lot braver than I am.'

'You talk about them as if they were a couple.'

'Well, they seem to be, in a funny sort of way. Rosie's old enough to be his mother but they've taken a shine to each other.'

Victoria, who was eating ice-cream, said, 'I don't think age matters.'

'Victoria!' exclaimed her mother.

'It's whether or not people are suited that matters, not how old they are.'

Without thinking, Sophie said, 'And you're an expert on this, are you?'

Victoria nodded. 'A bit. Mummy and Daddy were the same age and they didn't get on. But Nick is much older than Mummy and they do.'

'Excuse me!' protested Nick. 'I'm only–'

'Ahem.' Alex coughed.

'–slightly older,' he murmured.

'So, what happens now?' asked Sophie, and began to clear away the plates.

'I think we'll head home,' said Alex, looking at her watch. 'I'd like to get Victoria back to school this afternoon.' She ruffled her hair.

'Can't we stay here?' asked Victoria, turning her attention fully to her mother and putting down her spoon.

'No, sweetheart. We ought to get back to normal.'

'But you can come back soon,' offered Nick.

'How soon?'

'We'll see,' said Alex. 'We'll see.'

Through the open bedroom door Nick and Sophie held their nightly conversation.

'Are you as knackered as I am?' she asked.

'No. I'm more knackered. Stop talking and go to sleep.'

'Victoria's wonderfully old-fashioned, isn't she?' she said thoughtfully.

'Comes of reading too much Jane Austen.'

Sophie heard a rustle of bedclothes and then he was standing in the open doorway. 'Do you think she's just old-fashioned or a bit scary?' He looked worried.

She sat up in bed. 'She's not scary, just scared.'

'Scared of her mum getting it wrong again?'

'Yes.'

Nick sat on the edge of the bed. 'With me?'

'Oh, no. Quite the reverse. I think she's worried her mum will let you go.'

Nick looked stunned. 'Are you sure?'

'Yes. And Victoria's pretty astute, too. She's got a great mum in Alex but it's not enough. She needs a dad, too. Look at me, I should know. Never had one . . . for more than five minutes anyway.'

Nick looked bewildered. 'You didn't say anything . . .'

'Of course I didn't. I wasn't going to admit it. But it was grim. Oh, there were other girls at school who were worse off than I was – mums and dads at each other's throats all the time, mums covered in bruises, dads falling down drunk in the gutter, but it doesn't have to be extreme to be bloody. It can be as subtle as you like. The thing is, you know it's not right. For me Mum was always so right and proper and beautifully turned out, and Dad was just . . . never there.'

'But you . . .'

'Oh, I always jollied myself along. No point in getting depressed about it. But I got out as soon as I could. That's what makes me keep on travelling. Stupid, really. One day I'll have to stop and face up to it.'

'Face up to what?'

'Life. Relationships.'

Nick ruffled her short-cropped hair. 'Do I have to worry about you?'

'No more than usual. I'm just buggered if I'll take on a heap of shit. Someone like you, that's what I want. Someone pleasant and malleable who'll be good to me.'

Nick pushed her shoulder so she fell back against the pillow. 'Pleasant and malleable? Is that how you see me?'

'It was meant as a compliment,' she said seriously.

'I'll take it as one.' He laughed. Then he became serious. 'It's a big step, isn't it?'

She sat up again and looked him in the eye. 'Oh, yes. Just make up your mind whether you're ready to become a dad as well as a lover.'

'You think it's that serious?'

'I know it is. And so do you. That kid is not the sort to watch her mum having loads of boyfriends. She wants to believe that all relationships turn out well in the end, like in her Jane Austen novels – that's why she's hooked on them. They're her escape into a world she'd like to live in. She has to believe it can happen. What she needs more than anything is stability. I know you're not a social worker, and you've got to get something out of it yourself, and it's all happened so suddenly, but if you're not serious about Alex – and about Victoria – then get out of this thing right now. Or I'll never forgive you. And I'm your sister.'

28

Mermaid

*The rewards from the flowers, however, give ample
compensation for scratches received while
pruning . . .*

Sisters! Doncha love 'em? thought Nick. Just when you think you've got enough on your plate, what with intimate relationships, grannies, fathers and other local difficulties, they can't resist slinging in their own two-pennyworth and giving the whole lot a stir.

Then he wondered if he could get out of going to the hospital to see Rosie, go off on his own for a few hours. But his conscience got the better of him: he picked up his keys from the table and closed the door quietly behind him. Having delivered her keynote speech, Sophie was still asleep.

For a moment he stood on the veranda, leaned on the rail, and breathed in the fresh morning air. The sea was unusually calm, like a polished pewter plate, and a pair of seagulls wheeled over the cliff edge, splitting the morning air with their shrill call. 'Kee-kee!' Or was it 'tee-hee'? he wondered.

A fortnight ago his life had been simple and straightforward. Undemanding. Now he had an old lady to look after, a woman he was in love with and a child he *could* love but for whom he was already expected to assume responsibility. His own mother had all but washed her hands of him, his father was on the loose, wreaking goodness knows what kind of havoc with the family inheritance, and his sister was breathing down his neck. No wonder he felt beleaguered.

His thoughts were interrupted by the postman. 'You look as if you've lost a shilling and found sixpence.'

Nick came to with a start. 'Mmm? Sorry?'

'It can't be that bad.'

'No, it's not. Morning!'

'Getting a bit complicated, is it?' The postman gestured towards the house.

'You could say that, yes.'

'And there's me thinking you had the perfect life.'

Nick looked surprised. 'What?'

'Well . . . wonderful bachelor pad, nice job – painting – no ties. Not like me.' He shuffled the letters in his hand, muttering as he did so. 'Five kids, no money, a missus with expensive tastes and a credit card in meltdown.' He grinned. 'Fun having responsibilities, isn't it?'

'Yes,' said Nick.

'Anyway, I'm glad I caught you. I've got a special for you. Can you sign?'

He offered Nick the small padded envelope, and indicated on the card in his hand where Nick was to make his mark.

'Cheer up!' he shouted, as he walked back down the path. 'Worse things happen at sea!'

'Yes,' muttered Nick. 'But, then, I am at sea.' He looked down at the package. It was addressed in his father's handwriting.

He pulled in the car on a small, rough track that looked out over the bay. He did not want to open the packet in the house. Sophie might appear and be curious, and he had no idea what he would find.

He ripped off the sellotape, prised apart the staples and slid out the contents. A small white linen bag landed in his hand. It was tied at the top. He loosened the knot, opened the mouth of the bag and tipped out the contents. The feeling that he had first experienced on discovering the contents of the packet his father had left for him to hand over to the two heavies returned. He felt slightly sick. In his palm were four large diamonds. From memory they were not the ones he had handed over, but they were of a similar size and clarity. They dazzled him in the clear light of morning. He dreaded to think what they were worth.

He tipped them back into the bag and drew the string tight. Then he fished inside the envelope and pulled out a folded sheet of hotel writing-paper, headed 'Pobedonostsev Hotel, Dzhunkovsky Square, Moscow'. There was no date.

Dear Nick,
Sorry I had to ask you to do that bit of business for me, but it all seems to have turned out OK. As I said, there was no need for you to worry, but thanks all the same. I appreciate it.

I'd have done the job myself but I had rather pressing

business here, and sometimes things are safest done at arm's length. I'm sorry about the two heavies who turned up. They were just sent to collect the packet – I hope they didn't put the wind up you too much. Not very tactful sometimes. Occasionally they have to be tough, and I'm not sure their boss was convinced I would come up with the goods. Alright now though.

The enclosed were given to me by Rosie to take care of. Well, their friends were. I'm sending them back now in the safest way I know. I think it would be a good idea if you put them in the bank.

Have fun and don't worry, old lad. It's all quite above board.

Yours ever,
Dad

He turned the paper over. The reverse side was blank. There was no indication of when his father would return, or anything else for that matter. The note was, in his father's usual style, short and sweet. And what did he mean by 'well, their friends were'? If these were not Rosie's diamonds, had he substituted fakes? Or were they similar to but different from those she had given him? Oh, God! He would get them valued as soon as possible, but for now he had to put them somewhere safe.

Nick folded the note and slipped it back into the padded envelope with the linen bag. Then he drove straight to the bank and deposited the contents with the diamond Rosie had given him.

He felt unreal when he came out. He found himself looking right and left to see if he was being watched. He presumed the diamonds were not stolen. No. He didn't even want to go there. His father had never fallen foul of the law, so why should he start now?

But supposing he had just never been found out? No. His dad was sharp, but not dishonest. 'Opportunist' was the word. But what did he mean when he said, 'their friends were'? Whose friends? He shook his head. He had never understood his father's way of working, so what chance was there of him starting now?

By the time he arrived at the hospital his head was swimming, but Rosie was on cracking form.

'I think I've sorted them out.'

'Sorted who out?'

'The nurses here. One of them has boyfriend trouble, and the other one's husband has just run off.'

'Oh.'

'In a bit of a state, both of them.'

'So you sorted them out.' There was irony in his tone.

'Are you going to be unpleasant?' Rosie asked, her brow furrowed.

Nick felt suitably chastened. 'Sorry. It's been a bit of a morning, that's all.'

She was sitting up in bed, fresh as a daisy, her hair neatly coiffed, her lipstick freshly applied and her cheeks rouged. She looked like a duchess about to receive visitors at a morning audience. How appropriate, he thought, and smiled.

'Victoria's all right now?' she asked.

'Yes, thank God.'

'And Alex?'

'As far as I know.' He looked distracted.

'Oh. That sounds ominous.' He didn't reply, so she took his hand. 'Sorry. I expect everybody's putting their oar in, aren't they?' she said gently. 'I suppose Sophie gave you the female point of view?'

'Yes,' he admitted.

'She's good at that.' Rosie chuckled. 'Headstrong we used to call it. It sounds old-fashioned now, what with all this feminism stuff.'

'Are you not a feminist, then?'

'Oh, yes. A different kind, though. Wily.'

Nick grinned. 'You? Wily?'

'Oh, yes.'

'In what way?'

'Well, I look at all these women moaning on about men. Using a sledgehammer to crack a nut. You don't have to do that. You can get where you want to go much more quickly if you gentle them along – flatter them, flutter your eyelashes, instead of all this bra-burning business.'

'But wasn't that liberating?'

'Only for breasts. Damned uncomfortable for everything else.' She was warming to her subject now, eyes glowing. It was good to see her back on form, bright as a button, trying to shock.

'Look at that Germaine What's-her-name? Where's all that bra-burning got her? She still hasn't got a man.'

'Er . . . maybe she doesn't want one.'

'Well, she's gone the right way about not getting one, hasn't she? All this business about men not being the superior sex. Good heavens! We know that and they know that, so why keep banging on about it?'

Nick laughed. 'Go for 'em, Rosie!'

'And another thing.'

'Yes?'

'Breast enlargements.'

Nick choked. 'What?'

'Why do they make them so big?'

'Keep your voice down!'

'Is there no control over the size of them? Most women would be happy with a thirty-six B, but they end up with a thirty-six double F. What sort of man is going to want to go out with a woman with a pair of footballs fastened to her chest?'

'Stop it!'

'I mean, she only has to turn round sharpish and she'll knock you over. Heaven knows what the weight of them will do to her back.'

'Ssh!'

'Oh, I'm telling you, in a few years' time the papers will be full of it – "New Survey: Large Breasts Lead to Back Trouble. Fifty-six per cent of housewives with big boobs have trouble bending over. Or standing up again."'

She paused. Nick was squeezing in the sides of his mouth to stifle the laughter. 'Stop, stop!' he said.

'And then there'll be the lawsuits. Silicone companies sued for being overgenerous with implants.'

Nick waved an arm in the hope of flagging her down.

Rosie lay back on her pillow. 'Better now?'

He nodded. 'Much better.' And then, with feeling, 'Thank you.'

'Don't mention it, love. And you just keep your end up. In a manner of speaking.'

'Rosie!'

'Oh, I know. It's a difficult time, and lots of people's emotions are involved, but don't underestimate your own. It's hard deciding how serious you are in a relationship when there are complications. Just remember that there are three people involved. You're one of them, and your feelings are as important as anybody else's. The danger is that you'll put everyone else before yourself. That's not always a good thing. It just makes you embittered.'

'Are you speaking from experience?'

Rosie was silent for a moment. 'Perhaps.'

'So what do I do now? Wait and see how they are?'

'Oh, I just wanted you to know that I understand the problem. It'll all come good in the end. You're a good man, and she'll see that.'

'Victoria asked me if I was a good man.'

Rosie shook her head. 'Funny child. Astute.'

'And scared? Sophie thinks she's scared.'

'Oh, yes. But all children of that age are. They just have different ways of dealing with it. Some lash out. Others turn bad. Those like Victoria go into their imagination. Who's to sit in judgement?'

'So how do you solve the problem, apart from just giving it time?'

'If I knew that, love, I'd be sitting in the House of Lords.' She smiled.

'Now, there's a thought. You'd look good in ermine.'

Rosie looked at him hard. 'And I might have been, mightn't I, if things had turned out differently?'

He watched her expression change. There was something of that earlier wistfulness about her now, the look he'd seen when he'd picked her up from the police station.

She leaned back on the pillow and turned her head towards him. Suddenly she was looking tired. It was as if the energy she had needed to jolly him out of his woes had sapped her strength. 'We will find out, won't we? About my mother?' she asked.

'Of course.' He stroked her hand.

'Only I would like to know before . . . Well, soon.'

She closed her eyes. He held her hand until her breathing was soft and steady, then slipped away, determined to sort himself out. Clever Rosie. She always knew what he was thinking. How did she manage to play every moment so that it brought out the best in people? At least, that was how it seemed. Except, of course, when she misbehaved. Then she was a liability. But right now it seemed churlish to harbour such a thought, and he had to face facts: those days were probably over.

29
Perle des Jardins

Probably better under glass in cold, wet districts.

They had not spoken for thirty-six hours. He did not know how she was feeling or what she was doing. He wanted to ask if she and Victoria would like to come over and stay for the weekend, though he was fearful of putting the question; afraid of being turned down.

'I'm not sure,' she said. She sounded preoccupied, hesitant. It was as if the passion and conviction they had shared only a few days previously had evaporated.

'Do you want to meet first? To talk?' he asked.

'Yes. Yes, that might be best.'

'Shall I come to you?' He knew at once what the answer would be. She seemed anxious to keep him out of her world. He hoped it was because she wanted to leave it behind, and thought of him as her new life.

'No. I'll come to you. I'll get the seven o'clock ferry.'

'Fine. I'll pick you up.'

And she was gone, with no talk of love, just a brief goodbye. But it was enough to make him want to fight for her. As for his chance of success, that was anybody's guess.

Filling the day would be the main thing. He needed something to take his mind off her. Well, not her so much as the likely outcome of their meeting. Something he could concentrate on. Like diamonds. He drove into Newport and looked in the windows of the jewellers' shops, but there seemed little point in going inside to ask questions: the rings in the windows were priced in hundreds, and the stones were barely visible in their settings.

Eventually, while he was taking a short-cut between the two main streets down a narrow alleyway, he passed a small shop with an ornamental metal grille on the inside. Several bright spotlights shone on assorted rings and necklaces that pirouetted on deep blue velvet turntables, the gemstones shimmering in the light.

The sign on the shop front read, 'Elliott Williams, Jeweller', in ornate, gilded script. He pushed at the navy blue door, but it refused to open. Then he saw the printed notice: 'Please Ring For Attention'. He pressed the button on the wall and the door buzzed. He pushed it open, and went into the lavishly appointed shop.

As the door closed behind him, the outside world receded. The gems dazzled him.

'Can I help?' The voice was soft, well spoken and civil. At first he could not see where it was coming from. Then a figure appeared from behind one of the display cabinets. It was a man, tall and slim, in his sixties, with grey hair, slightly too long, brushed back from his face. He wore a pinstriped dark blue suit with a striped shirt, white collar and too much cuff showing. The broad-striped tie was held in place by a diamond pin.

'Well, I hope so. It's just an enquiry, really.' Nick did his best not to look nervous.

'Fine,' the man said. 'Fire away.'

'I just wondered if you could tell me anything about diamonds.' The moment he had said it, he realized the idiocy of the question.

The man laughed. 'I'll do my best. It's my name on the sign outside so I should be able to hazard a guess at most things.'

'Of course. Sorry.'

'Look, it's rather quiet at the moment. Would you like some coffee? Miranda's making some.'

'Thank you.'

Elliott Williams put his head round the door that led to a room behind the shop. 'Can you make that three, Miranda? We have a guest.'

Nick heard a compliant murmur, and tried to take in the contents of the display counter immediately in front of him. There were gems of all colours and sizes – rubies, emeralds, diamonds and sapphires, in brooches, on rings and even tiaras. He wondered how much call there was for diamond tiaras on the Isle of Wight. 'How do you get them to shine so much?' he asked. 'I suppose it's the lighting.'

'Partly, but mostly it's down to the cut . . . So, what do you want to know?'

Nick pulled himself out of his reverie. 'Well, I've been given some diamonds. Well, a diamond. And I just want to know a bit about them, really.'

'Do you have it with you?'

'No, but I could bring it in.'

'That might be an idea. They come in all sorts of sizes and the quality varies. You know about the four Cs, I presume?'

'The four Cs?'

'Yes. A diamond is graded according to four character-istics – cut, carat, which is its weight, clarity and colour.'

'Right.'

'Is your diamond particularly large?'

'Well, I suppose it's about as big as my little fingernail.'

Elliott Williams paused. Then he said, 'Hmm. I think you *had* better bring it in. You do have it somewhere safe, I hope?'

'The bank.'

'Good. A lot will depend on the other three Cs, as I've said. Is it cut or uncut?'

'Oh, it's cut.'

'Shape?'

'Roundish, I suppose.'

'In which case it will probably have fifty-eight facets. The better proportioned the facets, the better the light reflection and the more the diamond will sparkle.'

Miranda, a rather superior-looking girl with long blonde hair and a tight black mini dress, brought in two cups of coffee on a silver tray. She looked, and walked, like a model.

'Thank you,' said Nick, as he took the proffered cup. She smiled absently but did not meet his eye. Nick found himself musing on her relationship with Mr Williams. Daughter? Girlfriend? Then he came back to the matter in hand. 'Are they all cut the same?'

'There are recognized cuts. The most usual is the AGS Ideal Cut, sometimes known as the American Ideal Cut.'

'Always American!' said Nick, making polite conversation.

'Except that it was first published in England by a man called Towkowsky who worked for a Belgian firm of cutters.'

'Ah.'

Elliott Williams was warming to his subject. 'There are slight variations on the theme, but we usually call them Ideal Cuts. Then we come to weight, measured in carats. There are a hundred points to a carat, so a fifty-point diamond weighs?'

'Half a carat?' suggested Nick.

'Correct.' Elliott sipped his coffee, then took a key from his jacket pocket and opened the back of the display case. He slid out a flat, square cushion on which rested a single stone with no setting. He laid it on the counter. 'Here you are. Take a look.' He handed Nick a small lens with which to examine the stone under the light.

'Wow!'

'Beautiful, isn't it? But it's not flawless. If you look very closely you'll see one or two very slight imperfections. It's what we call a VS1, which means it has very small inclusions. A VVS1 has very, very small inclusions – imperfections. Flawless is the best, down to I3, which has inclusions visible to the naked eye.'

'I see.'

'Yes, even you would,' retorted Elliott, amused by his own witticism.

Nick smiled politely. 'So the clarity of my diamond is very important?'

'Oh, yes. It will affect the value tremendously. A one-carat diamond could vary in price between a hundred pounds and twenty-five thousand, depending on its quality.'

Nick recapped, to make sure he had all the facts. 'So that's cut, carat and clarity. What about colour?'

'Anything from D to X.'

'Sorry?'

'From white to yellow, though you can also get blue, pink, red, green and even brown diamonds. But they will usually have been irradiated.'

'Aren't white ones the best?'

'Well, there's a lot of call for yellow at the moment. Fashionable, you know.'

Nick sipped at his coffee. 'And where do they come from? South Africa?'

'Oh, not always. They may come from Australia, Namibia, Botswana . . .'

'What about Russia?'

'Oh, yes. Increasingly. Around twenty-five per cent of the world's diamonds come from Russia.'

'And are they good quality?'

'Undoubtedly. They didn't discover them until the nineteen fifties and until recently there was a strict export quota. But that changed in 2002.'

'So there are more of them about now?'

'Certainly.'

Elliott drained his coffee cup and looked at his watch. 'Well, if that's all you need to know, I have an appointment to get to.'

Nick realized that he had probably trespassed on Elliott Williams's time rather more than he should have. 'Of course. Sorry.'

'Not at all. If you want an appraisal I should charge you,

but why don't you pop back with the diamond and I'll give you a rough idea of its likely value for nothing?'

'Thank you. I will.'

Nick said goodbye and thanked his educator. He wondered if he dared take in all the diamonds, or whether that would make Elliott Williams suspicious of how he had come by them.

In this, and in other matters, he would need to come to a firm decision over the next couple of days.

When he got back to the Anchorage Sophie was packing her bag.

'I thought you weren't going until the weekend?'

'Been here long enough. Given you enough grief. Thought I'd better move out.'

'Don't be stupid!'

'No, it's all right. You need your space. Especially now.'

'But you can stay. I don't mind.'

Sophie stopped folding a shirt. 'What I said last night. Sorry if I got carried away. Too much wine.'

'Don't worry – you were quite right. I was talking to Rosie today and she was telling me her side of the story.'

'Poor Nick. You're getting it from all sides, aren't you?'

'Oh, I can cope. I'm made of tough stuff.'

Sophie put her head on one side. 'Do you know? I think you are!'

'You sound surprised.'

'I am. Always thought you were the gentle one.'

'It's a common misconception. That just because somebody is quiet and doesn't make a fuss, they're ineffectual.' He smiled at her.

Sophie zipped up her bag and picked up her jacket.

'You'll cope. I'm sure that whatever happens will be for the best.'

'Yes. Of course.' And then, under his breath, 'I just wish I shared your conviction.'

He was waiting for her in the MG at half past six, in case the ferry was early. They never were, but tonight he wanted to be sure. He wondered what she had said to Victoria, and what Victoria had said to her. He fretted and tried to imagine their conversation over and over again, but paranoia made it come out all wrong.

'Do you have to go?' Victoria would have asked.

'Just one last time,' would have been Alex's answer. 'Then I'll be back here for good.'

He must be more positive. He knew Victoria liked him. She'd told him so, hadn't she? She'd said her mother loved him. But how could she know?

He tried to stop speculating, knowing it was counter-productive, but when the human mind discovers a weakness it gnaws away at it like a dog with a bone.

Eventually he got out of the car, leaned on the bonnet and looked out across the water. He could see the ferry rounding the headland. It would be here in five or ten minutes, and then he would know his fate.

He brushed down his trousers. He had decided on the navy chinos and the dark blue shirt in the hope that they made him look irresistible. He grimaced at the thought. Him? Irresistible? That was a laugh. He had looked at himself naked in the mirror that morning, doing a kind of stock-take of himself at nearly forty. He was still in passable shape, still staving off the advent of middle-age spread, still upright, reasonably muscular, not too pale. And then he had shaken his head at his own vanity, and pulled on jeans and a sweat shirt for his trip into Newport. But now he was clean shaven and smartened up.

The ferry shimmied up to the slipway and the ramp descended. Cars flooded off, and to either side of them came foot passengers: teenagers with rucksacks, parents with children, old men and women, some with sticks. There were a couple of dogs and half a dozen cyclists, but no sign of Alex.

Perhaps she was holding back. Waiting until all the traffic had disembarked. Yes, that must be it. But after ten minutes, when the last car and pedestrian had walked up the slipway, and the cars for the return crossing were being driven down to the water's edge and up the ramp of the ferry, he realized she was not there – that she had not come.

30

Blush Damask

. . . the decayed flowers are very reluctant to fall.

'Do you think you could move your car, sir? It's causing an obstruction.'

He didn't answer. He was miles away.

'Sir? Excuse me!'

'What?'

'Your car. It's in the way. Could you move it or get on board?'

'Yes. Yes, of course. Just a minute.' He got out of the car, ran across to the booking office, bought a ticket, then drove on to the ferry. If she wouldn't come to him, he'd go to her. Even if she didn't want to see him, at least he could clear things up, tell her that if she ever changed her mind he would be there whenever she needed him. She and Victoria.

He had her address but was not familiar with that part of Portsmouth. The ferry seemed to take an age, waltzing around the Solent as though it were on a dance floor. Just as he thought they were making headway, the vessel seemed to slow down. What was the problem? Why weren't they going faster? Then he realized that they couldn't dock at Portsmouth until the other ferry vacated the berth. Damn! He looked at his watch. A quarter to eight. With any luck he'd be there within fifteen minutes. Thirty at the outside.

What would he say? What *should* he say? Right now, no words would come. His mind was blank. He tried to think clearly. Tried to imagine why she hadn't come. Perhaps she had decided to catch a later ferry – the one that was only now leaving the berth. He scrutinized the row of passengers leaning over the rail. She was not there. But he might have missed her. Perhaps she was inside. He tapped the steering-wheel impatiently.

When he drove off, a lady walking a dog offered directions, and soon he was driving in a smart street on the edge of the city, looking for number twenty-nine.

As he pulled up outside the modern terraced house, he saw Victoria's face at the window. As soon as she saw him she turned away, clearly talking to someone. Then she looked out again. Alex appeared at her shoulder. He got out of the car and waved. She waved back. But she did not smile.

He found it difficult to talk in front of Victoria, and so did Alex. 'Why don't you pop up to your room, sweetheart?' she said.

Victoria looked from one to the other. 'Do I have to?' she asked.

'Yes,' Alex told her.

'OK.' She paused in the doorway and said, 'Goodbye, Nick.'

He raised a hand, then turned back to Alex, who was filling the kettle. 'Why did you say you would come?'

'Because I didn't want to disappoint you.' She looked agonized. 'I'm sorry, I really am.' She motioned him to sit at the kitchen table.

'What is it?' he asked. 'It seemed to be going so well. Even when Victoria went missing we found her together.'

'I know. It's just that . . .' She seemed reluctant to meet his eye. She looked embarrassed, almost ashamed. 'I just think we'd better stop seeing each other for a while.' She said it with little enthusiasm.

'But why?'

'Because I have to think of Victoria.'

'Why does that mean we have to stop seeing each other?'

'Because I don't want to upset her any more. She's been through a lot lately, what with her dad leaving, and then going missing . . .'

'But she only went missing because she wanted to see Rosie and find out if she was all right.'

'No. She went missing because she was upset, unsettled and frightened.'

'Is that what she said? She told me it was because she wanted to see Rosie.' He hesitated. 'And me.'

Alex studied him carefully, then came and sat down. 'I can't risk anything going wrong between her and me. I just can't. She's all I've got.'

Nick sat back. 'She's not. You've got me, you know you have.'

Alex shook her head. 'No, I don't. I know we've had a good time, but I don't really know you. And you don't

258

really know me. It might be fun for a few more weeks, months even, but what if it all ended then? Where would that leave Victoria?'

Nick bridled. 'How can you say that? How can you say that we simply "had a good time"? You know it was more than that.'

'Do I?'

He was angry now. 'Yes, you do. And if you're trying to claim otherwise, then you're fooling yourself. If you can say that when we were together – properly together – you didn't really know me, then I don't believe you. You felt the same way as I did. Even if you didn't say so.'

She spoke quickly now. 'You just can't see, can you?'

'See what?'

'Why I have to do this?'

'No, I can't.'

'But then you've never had a child.'

He was stung, knowing how things could have been so very different. He hesitated a moment before he spoke. 'It doesn't mean I can't see how important Victoria is, and why it's important that she's happy – but that shouldn't mean that *you* have to be unhappy. You can't simply live your life for her.'

'Why not? I brought her into the world. She's my responsibility. I can't mess up.'

He was exasperated now. 'Why this obsession with "messing up"? It can't be right to shut yourself away and not have any relationships of your own.'

'But I had a relationship of my own and it didn't work.'

'So what? That doesn't make you a failure. Doesn't mean you'll never have a good relationship. But you have to give yourself a chance.'

'It's a chance I can't take.'

Nick stood up. 'Rubbish! It might be a chance you're not *prepared* to take, but only if you're a coward.'

'I'm not a coward!' There was a catch in her voice.

'Well, why are you trying to break up with me? What's the point in that?'

'The point is that Victoria's life—'

'Victoria, Victoria, always Victoria! What about Alex?'

'I can't think about me right now.'

'Well, you should. What sort of life is it going to be for Victoria, knowing that she has a mother at her beck and call the whole time, but only because her mother daren't have a relationship in case it upsets her?'

'That's ridiculous!'

'Is it? You have a bright child up there,' he pointed in the direction of Victoria's room, 'and she'll know it makes no sense for her mother to be alone.'

'She's only ten—'

'Yes, and she's sharper than many fifteen-year-olds. But she's not emotionally equipped yet, and treating her like some china doll isn't going to help her in that department.'

'And neither is a string of boyfriends.'

'Oh, I see.' He was angry now. 'You reckon I'm the first in a long line, do you?'

'No. But that's what might happen.'

'It might. But that's not my intention. I came here because I love you and I want to be with you. And I've thought about Victoria, too. I know how important she is to you, and I like her a lot. She'll become important to me, if you give me a chance. But if you just shut yourself away because of what *might* happen, then you'll never know joy. The sort of joy that we knew the other night. Passion, yes, but more than that. Pleasure in each other's company. And love, too. Deep love. It wasn't just lust. Or am I the one who's fooling myself?'

'No,' she said quietly. 'You're not.'

'Then don't break up with me. Please! Give me a chance to show you that I care – for you both. That's all I ask. A chance to prove myself.'

'But you can't promise that it will turn out all right.'

'No, I can't. But I can promise you I'll try – with every fibre in my body. If it doesn't work out in the end I'll have done everything I possibly can to make it work, and that must count for something.'

The kettle's shrill whistle brought a halt to the conversation. Alex got up and turned off the gas. 'I'm sorry. It's just that with Paul coming back and Victoria going off the rails . . .'

'She didn't go off the rails.' He spoke softly now, his tone conciliatory. 'She just got a bit . . . lost inside herself. Needed to find something to cling on to.'

'And I wasn't there.'

'You were. It's just that Paul was there, too, and that threw her.'

Alex turned to face him. 'I'm sorry.'

'No, *I'm* sorry – sorry you feel it's all your fault. It really isn't, you know. You're a wonderful person. The very fact that you're having this conversation proves it. But don't give up on your own happiness because you think it's the only way to ensure Victoria's. I can't believe that's true. It doesn't make sense.'

Alex lowered her head, and he could see tears flowing down her cheeks. She wiped her face with the back of her hand.

He got up and walked across to comfort her, but she turned away from him and stared out of the window. 'You'd better go now. It would be for the best. I'm so sorry.'

He stood for a moment, one hand outstretched as if it was frozen. He lowered it. 'What a lot of sorries,' he said. And then, quietly, 'Goodbye.'

She did not reply.

As he left he did not turn back. If he had done, he would have seen the face of a small girl standing in the upstairs window, her body gently rocking from side to side.

31
Nymphenberg

. . . colour varies with soil and weather conditions.

Only three days before they had all been sitting round the table, he and Alex, Victoria and Sophie, enjoying being together and teasing each other. Now it seemed that it was all over. That it would never happen again. He could hear the echoes of their laughter, the ticking of the clock. He cursed himself for not having fought harder. He'd thought he'd given it his best shot. Well, if he had, it had clearly been wide of the mark.

So that was that, then. Maybe in a year or two's time Alex would realize that the days they had spent together had not constituted a casual relationship. It had been special, out of the ordinary – to him, at least. But maybe not to her.

He would get on with his life. Perhaps he had been right all along: there was no such thing as *that* sort of love. Not if it lasted so short a time. He had always expected that it would be so. A heightened passion. Nothing more. But he knew his old prejudice no longer held good. There was, indeed, such a thing as deep, all-consuming love. It had shown itself to him so clearly – then slipped through his fingers and disappeared.

He poured himself a large Scotch and went to the sink for some water. Every sound seemed heightened. The tap gushed loudly. The glass clinked against the edge of the sink.

He flopped into a chair and took a large gulp. The liquid burned the back of his throat.

Trying to make sense of it all set his head spinning. How could Alex think that the only way to Victoria's happiness was to give up on her own? It was so short-sighted, so . . . unreasonable.

Suddenly he saw Victoria as a little demon. 'No!' he said aloud. He wouldn't take it out on her. After all, he had hardly been given a chance to know her. She was old-fashioned in some ways, and yet an innocent child in others. But she was companionable, refreshing – he knew they would get on, that she would come to appreciate his sense of humour. He almost smiled. Then he remembered that awful day. Debs had only been three months into her pregnancy. There was always a reason for these things, the doctor had said, but it had been a bitter blow. They thought they might try again. But somehow they never did. They never told anybody. Just kept it to themselves, as usual.

He remembered the rawness of it all. The bitter disappointment. He recalled the long walks he had taken afterwards, alone across the downs, trying to stay positive. How much did that have to do with their splitting up?

Could he have been a better partner, offered more support? But it was a pointless exercise. Debs had gone. It had not worked. For whatever reason.

Maybe that was why he had been so happy to get to know Victoria, why he hadn't minded the prospect of taking on a ready-made family. Others might have seen it as a burden, but for him it would have been the fulfilment of a dream. A dream not dreamed for fear that it could never become reality. Now he had to put it out of his mind again. This *was* reality. Bitter and plain.

Now he would never know Victoria properly, and she would never know him. In trying to ensure that her daughter was not exposed to life's sadnesses, Alex would also be shielding her from potential joys. It was all so unfair – unfair on Victoria, unfair on Alex and, yes, unfair on him.

He drained the glass and went to bed.

It was Saturday, and the beginning of June. Cowes would be seething. The prospect of fighting through the crowds did not appeal. He showered, pulled on a pair of jeans and a T-shirt, then had a bowl of cereal and a mug of tea.

Normally he would talk to himself from time to time. It seemed quite natural. But not this morning. He was silent. His jaw ached from being clenched. The newspaper was full of party politics and the sexual indiscretions of people he had never heard of. He made a mental note to cancel it. It was a waste of money. How did all these things ever affect his life?

He walked out on to the veranda. It was a grey day, and the wind was from the east, cold and bullying. Not like June should be. He shivered, went back inside and made his bed.

Then he sat. And sat. And felt sadder than he could ever remember having felt before.

Henry was beside Rosie's bed as soon as the hospital doors opened.

'You're amazing!' he said.

'Why's that?' she asked.

'Look at you! It's barely eight thirty and you're all done up and ready to go!'

'Well, they wake us up so early, and I've never been one to hang around. Not that I've got much choice on that front.'

'How's the walking coming along?'

'Slowly. And it's a bit painful.'

'More than a bit, I should think.'

'We won't go there. Anyway, I've been thinking.'

'That sounds dangerous.'

'Be serious, Henry. If I do come and stay with you . . . well, there are one or two things I want to sort out.'

'Yes?'

She was clearly trying to measure her words. 'Well . . . I will have my own bedroom, won't I?'

Henry threw back his head and roared with laughter. 'Of course you will! Good heavens! The very idea! I'd be struck off.'

Rosie brightened. 'Well, I knew I would, really. It's just that we've never talked about . . . arrangements, and I thought we should.'

'Quite so.' Henry tried to suppress a smile, not altogether successfully.

'And then there's the problem of getting dressed. I'm very self-sufficient – I'm not a helpless old lady – but at the moment it's a bit difficult to . . .'

Henry patted her hand. 'I've thought of all that. The niece who's coming over to help me in the gallery is a sweet girl, and she can do all the bits you wouldn't want me doing.'

'I see.' She looked thoughtful.

'It's one of the reasons they're allowing you to come out early – because I can arrange for you to be looked after properly.'

'Why are you going to all this trouble? I'm no catch, you know.'

Henry laughed again. 'On that subject, madam, I beg to differ.'

Rosie frowned. 'Oh, come on, Henry. You know as well as I do how old I am.'

Henry assumed an expression of wide-eyed innocence. 'I don't know what you're talking about.'

'Oh, yes, you do.'

'Well, let's say we've both been economical with the truth and leave it at that.' He winked.

'You've still not answered my question.'

'Well, you're not Mount Everest, if that's what you think.'

'I beg your pardon?' Rosie looked baffled.

'I'm not doing it just because you're there.' He smiled at her, his eyes twinkling. 'Do you really want to know? Honestly?'

Rosie nodded. 'Yes. Honestly.'

'There are two reasons.' Henry shuffled about in his chair, then pushed his hands into his pockets and spoke to the floor. 'One is because when my mother grew older I saw what an amazing lady she was. I saw what she'd been through, and how she'd survived. I never managed to tell her that, and I was too late to help her at the end.'

'I see. So you're salving your conscience by looking after me?'

He looked up. 'A bit,' he admitted. Then he looked directly at her. 'The second reason is that I don't think I've ever met anyone quite like you in my entire life.'

'Oh, Henry!' She smiled, then looked down coyly, and smoothed the bedcover.

'It's true! You make me laugh, you exasperate me, you make me question things but, above all, you make me glad to be alive.'

'Well . . .' Rosie glanced away. 'I don't know what to say.'

Through the dampness in his own eyes, he saw the tears in Rosie's. 'Don't say anything, then.' He cleared his throat. 'Don't they serve coffee in this place? I'm dry as a bone.'

'Not until nine o'clock, but if you turn on the charm with that nurse over there I'm sure she'll oblige. In a manner of speaking.'

Alex would happily have stayed in bed. She had woken early, but couldn't muster the will to get up. She stared into the middle distance and thought of him. Endlessly. But this wouldn't do, she thought. She had to get on. She had a child to sort out. On Saturday mornings Victoria went to a swimming class. She had to be showered and fed before being driven to the leisure centre.

Alex looked at the clock on the bedside table. It was a quarter to eight. They had to be there by nine thirty. Plenty of time yet. Plenty of time to . . . what? Brood? Mope?

She threw back the covers, got out of bed, stretched, then caught sight of herself in the mirror, standing there with her dark hair tumbling over her shoulders, her body encased in a baggy white T-shirt. God, she looked old and weary. She hadn't felt like this for ages. She'd managed to buoy herself up when Paul was with the new woman in his life – she knew she didn't want him, so what did it matter who he was with? But the emptiness she felt now had nothing to do with him. She was suddenly overwhelmed with sadness. Wearily she crossed the landing.

She tapped on Victoria's door, then opened it. The child was sitting up in bed with a book.

'Don't you ever stop reading?' asked Alex, teasingly.

Victoria shook her head, still concentrating.

'What is it today?' She pushed back her hair.

Victoria held up *Sense and Sensibility*.

'Again?'

Victoria shrugged. 'I like the stories.'

'Do you know how many other ten-year-olds read those books?'

'No.'

'Very few.'

'It's not wrong, is it?' Victoria asked anxiously.

'Of course not.' Her mother ruffled her hair.

'Read a bit to me?'

'Oh, love, I don't think I can focus at this time in the morning.'

'Please!' There was insistence in her voice, but not of the sort that foretold a tantrum. Not the sort of insistence that says 'if you don't I'll make your life hell for the rest of the day'. Just a positive note that made Alex sit on the edge of the bed and take up the book.

'From there,' instructed Victoria, pointing to a passage near the end of the book.

'Budge up, then.' Alex slipped into bed beside her daughter, who rested her head on her shoulder as she read.

'"Marianne Dashwood was born to an extraordinary fate. She was born to discover the falsehood of her own opinions, and to counteract, by her conduct, her most favourite maxims. She was born to overcome an affection formed so late in life as at seventeen, and with no sentiment superior to strong esteem and lively friendship, voluntarily to give her hand to another!"' Alex stopped.

'Go on! Go on!'

Alex spoke more softly now. '". . . and *that* other, a man who had suffered no less than herself under the event of a former attachment . . ."'

She closed the book. 'Oh,' she murmured.

32
Madame Berkeley

Somewhat muddled . . .

It was midway through the afternoon when the hospital called. Nick was cleaning a wooden garden bench with wire wool. It was a mindless task, but the only thing he could settle to. When the phone rang he dropped what he was doing and ran inside, hoping it might be Alex. When he discovered it was a nurse, his heart sank.

'Mr Robertson? It's Sister Bettany from the hospital.'

'Is everything all right?' he asked, knowing she wouldn't have called if it had been.

'It's Mrs Robertson. She's a little under the weather and we wondered if you could come in.'

'Of course. I'll be there as soon as I can. Is she . . .?'

'She's comfortable at the moment, but I think she'd like to see you.'

'Yes, of course.'

His mind raced as he made the short drive to the

hospital. The sun had come out now, but it didn't seem to matter.

As he walked down the corridor to the ward, Sister Bettany put her head out of her office and beckoned him in.

'Is it serious?' he asked.

'It's difficult to say,' she said. 'She has a urinary infection. It sometimes happens and it does cause the patient to be a little confused. She was fine earlier, but she's declined over the day. She's a bit disorientated, too, I'm afraid.'

'But will she recover?'

'Oh, we hope so. She's strong for an old lady, but we must take account of her age.'

Nick was more worried than ever now. It was the one thing he had never expected to hear. Nobody took account of Rosie's age, because she took no account of it herself.

He walked along to her bed. Her eyes were closed. He sat down and took her hand. It felt warm and soft. He squeezed it gently and she opened her eyes. When she saw him she smiled. 'Hello, my love. How are you?' she whispered.

He was appalled to see her so weak – she had been making such good progress that he had come to believe she was invincible.

'I'm fine, but what about you?'

She tried to say something, failed, and drifted off again. Her eyes closed and flickered.

He sat with her for the better part of an hour as she slept fitfully. Then he walked down to the office and waited for Sister Bettany to return from her rounds.

'We'll keep a close eye on her for the next day or so,' she said. 'Pop in whenever you want. I'll make sure the nurse on duty knows.'

'Thank you.' It was all so sudden. Things seemed to have been going so well. He asked the obvious question. 'Does this mean she won't be coming out quite so quickly?'

'Yes, I'm afraid so. We'll just have to play it by ear now.'

'Yes, of course.' He hesitated. Then he asked, 'How serious is it?'

'Serious but not critical,' she said. She smiled kindly. But he thought he saw worry too.

'Thank you,' he said, walked slowly out of the hospital and drove home.

Henry was incredulous. 'But I was with her first thing this morning and she was in fine fettle.'

'I know. Apparently it happened quite suddenly.'

Henry plonked himself down on a wooden captain's chair, which creaked under his weight. 'Well, I'll be . . . I'd no idea. Well, you wouldn't have. I mean, she was so . . .'

Nick nodded. 'I know.'

'So I suppose I can stand my niece down.'

'Yes. I'm afraid they don't know when she'll be coming out now. It all depends on how quickly she recovers.'

Henry looked at him. 'And are you all right?'

'Yes. Yes, I'm fine,' he said distractedly.

'Well, you don't look it. You look exhausted. It's the shock. Let me make you some coffee with something stronger in it.' Henry pushed himself out of the chair with an effort.

'Thanks.' Nick wandered through to the back room in the wake of his burly patron.

Henry switched on the kettle. 'And that's not all, is it?'

'Mmm?' Nick was distant. Preoccupied.

'There's something else, isn't there?' And then, seeing he was not getting through, 'Woman trouble, is it?'

'What?' Nick came to. 'What do you mean?'

'You know, Nicholas and Alexandra.'

Nick was defensive. 'What about Nicholas and Alexandra?'

'Look, dear boy, I've not asked any questions – I've been very circumspect, and after all, it's none of my business, but if two of my *protégés* are at a tricky stage in their relationship I'd just like to know so that I don't put my foot in it. They're not very big feet, but they do have quite a lot of weight above them.'

Nick hesitated, then tried to speak but settled instead for a sigh.

Henry busied himself with cups, sugar and coffee, and spoke over his shoulder. His tone was gentle, his language considered. 'Look. It was never going to be easy, was it? There's a lot of history there. A lot of – what is it they say nowadays? – a lot of issues. God! I hate that phrase.'

Nick was staring at the floor.

Henry warmed to his subject: 'Life is full of these expressions, isn't it? "I have issues", "Your family is dysfunctional", "They have trouble parenting". Load of cock, if you ask me. What happened before those neat little boxes were invented? I'm not sure that the circumstances existed until the vocabulary came along. In the good old days, instead of "having issues", somebody was "temperamental". Dysfunctional families were "not people like us" and "parenting" was something that happened, coincidentally, while you tried to bring up your family as best you could.'

'It's all so confusing,' murmured Nick.

'Oh. Right. Well, if we're going there you'll need quite a large tot.' He tipped a generous measure of Famous Grouse into the coffee, and handed the cup to Nick. 'She did talk to me, you know,' Henry went on. 'Alex.'

Nick took a sip of the brew and gasped at its strength.

'Nothing intimate. Not about you,' Henry assured him, 'but about . . . what was his name? Paul. Nothing physical, no violence, but quite a lot of mental cruelty. And *that* phrase has been around for a long time, more's the pity.'

Nick said nothing.

Henry continued. 'He wasn't the most faithful of husbands, you see, and it wasn't just the odd affair. He was a serial adulterer, by the sound of it. Travelled a lot, woman in every port – that sort of thing. She never found out until about three years ago, when he started living a double life, half in the States and half over here. Came across some letters in his dirty washing. And not just from one woman. Careless, eh? But maybe he wanted her to find out. Anyway, she tried to patch it up for the sake of the child.'

Nick was shocked. 'She didn't tell me about the women.'

'No? Well, you wouldn't, would you? It's not something to boast about. Eventually she realized she was on a hiding to nothing and told him she'd had enough. He agreed to go – there was yet another woman. Now she just wants to give her daughter a fresh start.'

'I know. That's the trouble.' Nick paused. 'She doesn't seem to set much store by her own happiness. Doesn't want to risk another relationship. She'd rather stay on her own so that Victoria has a stable upbringing.'

'Shame,' said Henry.

'That's what I think.' Nick drained his cup. 'I'd better be off.'

'What are you going to do now?'

'Who knows? I'll go back and see Rosie this evening. Nothing else to do except,' he pointed to the walls of the gallery, 'fill these, I suppose. But I can't get into the mood.'

'Look,' said Henry, 'there's no pressure. I have enough to keep me going for a week or so. Don't feel you've got to knuckle down. You'll need time to sort Rosie out, and yourself. Really there's no rush. Concentrate on the important things for now.' As Nick closed the door, he shouted after him, 'Both of them.'

'Why did you want me to read you that bit?' Alex had avoided the subject all day. Now it was late afternoon, and having taken Victoria swimming, and then shopping for clothes – a girly bonding session to try to obliterate the memory of the last couple of days – she found herself facing up to the inevitable.

Victoria was staring out of the window, as she had been for the past ten minutes. Alex had noticed that she had been more introspective than usual all day. It was time to get to the bottom of things.

'Victoria?'

The child did not move.

'Are you cross with me?'

Victoria shook her head but did not turn round.

'What, then?' Alex realized she was crying. 'What is it?' She walked over and put her arms round her daughter, rocking her.

Victoria sobbed silently as Alex stroked the back of her head. 'Hey, come on! It can't be that bad, can it?'

The child nodded.

'What, then?'

No reply.

'Come on. Come and sit with me.' She shepherded Victoria to the sofa, and sat with her as she sniffed back the tears.

'It's just . . . things,' she choked out.

'What sort of things?'

'I don't . . . know.' There were more sobs between the words.

'Are you unhappy?'

Victoria nodded again.

'Why, then? What is it?'

'I try to be happy, but I can't be. Not here.'

'Oh, poppet, I know. But what can I do?'

Victoria's cheeks were red and puffy. 'Can't we go back?'

'To the island?'

Another nod.

'Not really, sweetheart. Not now.' Alex stroked her daughter's hair.

'But why?' The child sniffed loudly. 'I thought you liked it there.'

'Well, I do, but it's just that life is a bit complicated at the moment.'

'But it wouldn't be. Not there,' Victoria said pleadingly.

'Oh, angel, if only you knew . . .' Alex gave her daughter a squeeze.

'I know he loves you.'

'What?'

'Nick. He loves you.'

'Well, it's up to me to decide what I'm going to do about that, isn't it?'

Victoria eased away from her. 'I don't understand.'

'What don't you understand?'

'Well, you weren't happy with Daddy, were you, but you kept on being with him?'

'Yes. Because – because you do. You can't give up on someone just like that. Someone you've had a baby with. You have to try to make it work.'

'But in the end you couldn't make it work?'

'No.'

'So if that happens, are you ever allowed to try again?'

'Well, yes, of course you are. But you might need a bit of time to get over it.'

'How much time?'

'I don't know, sweetheart. I really don't know,' Alex sighed.

'Marianne Dashwood didn't need much time – not when she saw how kind and nice Colonel Brandon was after Mr Willoughby had run off with that other woman for her fortune.'

'Oh, I see. That's what it is.' Alex put her arm round Victoria's shoulders and drew her close. 'The trouble is, poppet, things don't always work out the way they do in stories. Sometimes they're a bit more complicated.'

'Why?' Victoria persisted.

'I don't know, they just are. I suppose people's emotions are not always so straightforward in real life.'

'But I thought you said Jane Austen was the best writer that ever lived?'

'Well, yes, she is, but—'

'And that she was very good with emotions?'

'Well, yes – but she was writing almost two hundred years ago. Society was different then.'

'Oh. I see.'

Alex stroked her daughter's arm.

Victoria spoke again: 'Colonel Brandon loved Marianne, didn't he?'

'Yes, he did. Very much.'

'But although he was . . . very nice . . . she wasn't sure she loved him?'

'No.'

'But she still agreed to marry him, because she thought that being nice was important.'

'Well, she had great respect for him.'

'Was she wise, do you think?'

'She probably had her own reasons for doing what she did.'

'If she had loved Colonel Brandon as much as he had loved her, would it have been more straightforward?'

'Oh, yes. Much more straightforward. I don't suppose she'd have hesitated at all then.'

'I see.' Victoria looked up into her mother's eyes. 'Do you love Nick?' she asked.

At first Alex found herself unable to answer. Then she looked away, swallowed hard, took a deep breath, and said, 'Yes. I do.'

33
Semi-Plena

. . . deserving more attention . . .

By evening Rosie seemed to have rallied a little. Nick sat with her, holding her hand, for the better part of two hours. Sometimes she drifted off to sleep, sometimes she woke and lay with her eyes open but said nothing. Occasionally, she asked him about the car, or the wild flowers on the cliff. Then her eyes would close again.

He worried about her long-term prospects. She couldn't die! She was never ill! Watching her now made him anxious, and irritable. He needed her to get better and listen to him. Then he was ashamed of his selfishness.

Someone touched his shoulder and he looked up.

Alex was standing over him. 'Hello,' she said.

He slipped his hand out of Rosie's and got up. 'Hello,' he said uncertainly.

They looked at each other, then Alex put her arms round him and laid her head on his chest. 'I'm sorry.'

At first he thought she was talking about Rosie. 'They think she'll be all right, but they can't be certain yet,' he said stiffly.

Alex nodded. 'I do hope so.' She stepped away from him.

'Thank you for coming,' he said, hoping that she'd leave soon and not prolong the agony.

'I had to come. Too many things to say.'

Nick looked at her quizzically.

'Sometimes it's difficult to think straight,' she said, 'and to see the wood for the trees.'

He wasn't sure he had heard her correctly, and didn't want to pre-empt the situation by saying anything.

'I was a bit hasty,' she went on. 'Like you said, if I shut myself away in case of what might happen, I'll never know joy . . .' There was a catch in her voice. 'And I'd quite like to know joy. So, if it's all right with you . . .'

Nick held out his arms and said, 'Come here.'

Alex saw the tears welling up, and wrapped her arms round him again.

'I'm so glad you're back,' he whispered. 'So glad.'

At ten o'clock he took her to the ferry, kissed her tenderly, then watched the lights of the vessel recede into the distance until they were swallowed up by the night. She had gone again, but this time he knew she would return.

Tomorrow was Sunday, and she had said she would bring Victoria over for the day. His pleasure at the prospect was tempered by concern for Rosie. He looked up at the star-filled sky and hoped with all his heart that both of the women he loved would make tomorrow a day to remember.

*

'I have a surprise for you,' said Alex.

They were sitting in a café at Seaview, breakfasting outdoors in the early-morning sun, before they drove to Newport to see Rosie.

'I've had enough of those,' said Nick.

'This is a nice one,' Victoria told him.

'Mmm?' Nick was less than convinced.

'Mummy's been researching.'

'That sounds very official.'

'Very unofficial, actually,' confessed Alex.

'Oh?'

'Well, I promised I'd do some digging around to see if I could discover anything about Rosie's parents. And I'm not making any outrageous claims, but I do have one or two suggestions.'

Nick dipped a piece of croissant into his coffee and popped it into his mouth. 'Well?'

'I've been at the library in Portsmouth.' Alex dug deep into her rucksack. 'You know you said that Rosie's mother's name – I mean her real mother – was given as Matilda Kitching?'

Nick nodded as he chewed.

'And her father's name . . .' Alex flipped through her shorthand pad until she found the page she wanted. '. . . was George Michaels.'

'Yes.' He took another sip of coffee.

'Well, as Rosie said, there was no mention of either in the National Archive at Kew. Not with the right dates, anyway. You can call things up from there on the Internet now so the research wasn't too difficult.'

'No joy, then?'

'Well, not until I started to look at the names of other

people involved, who might have been around at the time.'

'And?'

'George Michaels was supposed to be part of a British delegation, wasn't he? I tracked down that particular visit. It was pure luck, but I suppose all researchers need luck as well as intelligence. Anyway, it struck me that I'd often seen pictures of the two of them – George the Fifth and the Tsar – in naval uniform, and Portsmouth has been the home of the Royal Navy since God knows when. I found a naval archive in Portsmouth library that dealt with diplomatic relations between the British and Russian navies during the late nineteenth and early twentieth centuries. In 1917, the British sent a secret delegation over there. It was during the First World War, remember, so it must have been difficult.'

'They didn't give the names of all the people involved, did they?' asked Nick excitedly.

Alex paused, the better to build the tension. 'Oh, yes, they did. Right down to the last button polisher. The junior naval attaché at the Admiralty was called . . . George Carmichael.'

'You clever thing!' Nick made to take the pad from Alex's hand.

'Not so fast. I've not finished yet.'

Victoria beamed. 'She's very clever, isn't she?'

'Brilliant!' he agreed.

'That was too much of a coincidence to pass over. But what it didn't do, of course, was give me any information about the mother. It also failed to show any meeting between the grand duchesses and the delegation. In fact, they had been in two different places – the delegation was sent to Murmansk, right up north on the Barents Sea. It had only been linked to St Petersburg by rail in 1916 and was just about to become an important port because it remained ice-free all the year round. Anyway, when the delegation was in Murmansk, most of the royal family were in St Petersburg, more than five hundred miles away, and there is no record of the delegation going there. They sailed from Portsmouth, up round the Norwegian coast and the North Cape, direct to Murmansk where they met the Tsar. They did not go via the Baltic to St Petersburg and take the train north.'

'Which knocks Rosie's theory on the head,' said Nick, despondent.

'Well, it does seem to rule out the grand duchesses.'

'I feel a but coming on,' said Nick.

'And there is one. Before he was married the Tsar had a mistress. Now I can only guess at this, and I may be wrong, and there are a lot of ifs.'

'Go on.'

'If the Tsar had not relinquished the love of his life, and they still occasionally had liaisons, and one happened to be in Murmansk during the time of the naval delegation . . . and if the mistress did not confine her attentions to the Tsar . . .'

'You're right – there are a lot of ifs.'

'It would hardly stand up in court. Pure conjecture, that's all.'

'But what was the mistress's name?'

Alex spun the book round and showed him. 'Mathilde Kschessinska.'

He was stunned. 'Matilda Kitching?' he wondered aloud.

'It's possible.' She smiled tentatively.

'What happened to her?'

'She eventually married one of the Tsar's cousins, Grand Duke Andrei, in Cannes in 1921.'

'They escaped the revolution, then?'

'Yes, although Mathilde's mansion was ransacked. She eventually ran a ballet studio in Paris – even taught Margot Fonteyn.'

'But she's dead now?'

'Oh, yes.'

'So I don't suppose we'll ever know for certain?'

Alex shook her head. 'It seems unlikely.'

Nick reached out and squeezed her hand. 'Thank you for going to all the trouble.'

'It was a pleasure. But I've probably just uncovered a lot of coincidences.'

Nick leaned back in his chair. 'It's a lot to take in, isn't it?'

'Interesting, though,' piped up Victoria.

'Yes. Very.'

'Are you going to tell Rosie?'

'That depends on how she is.' Nick's face bore a distracted look.

The three walked down the long corridor towards Rosie's bed, Victoria in the middle, holding Nick and Alex's hands.

As they rounded the corner, they saw Rosie lying in bed, propped up on a mountain of pillows. She raised both hands in greeting, and Victoria rushed across to plant a kiss on her cheek.

'Hello, sweetheart!' Rosie murmured. 'How lovely to see you.'

Nick and Alex bent down and kissed her too, then Nick

darted off to find three chairs. When he came back he asked, 'How are you?'

'Oh, you know.' She looked and sounded weak. She wore little makeup, and her hair had not been combed. Each time he came he hoped to observe some sign of increased strength, but so far he had not.

'Need to get you back on your feet,' he offered.

Rosie nodded. 'A bit feak and weeble,' she said to Victoria, who grinned at the little joke.

'Mummy's been finding things out,' volunteered Victoria. 'About your mummy and daddy.'

Rosie's face brightened and a light shone in her eye. 'Have you?'

Nick cut in: 'She's been working very hard, but I think we should tell you later when you can take it all in.'

Rosie did not demur. She half closed her eyes. 'Weary. Sorry.'

Nick glanced at Alex, who read his mind. 'Come on, Victoria. We'll let Rosie rest for a while. We'll come back later.' And then, softly, to Nick, 'We'll wait for you by the car.'

He nodded in agreement, and they left with a wave. Then he swapped chairs so that he was closer to Rosie's head.

'Sorry, love,' she whispered. 'I'm done in.'

'Ssh! You get some rest. It's too early, really.' It was a quarter to ten. 'We should have let you sleep.'

Rosie shook her head. 'Plenty of time for that later. It was lovely to see them both.'

'Yes.'

'Lucky boy.' She nodded in the direction Alex and Victoria had gone. 'Special. Very special.'

'I know.'

'Lucky girl, me. Very lucky girl.'

He stroked her cheek lightly. 'You sleep now,' he said. 'We all need you better.'

She smiled weakly and closed her eyes.

'Would you come with me to the jeweller's to have them valued?' he asked.

'But isn't it a bit personal? I mean, do you really want me to know?'

They were sitting on the veranda at the Anchorage, sipping coffee after an early dinner. They had walked the old path from Yarmouth to Freshwater in the afternoon, alongside the river Yar, past the old mill, between the reed beds, as far as Freshwater church, where Victoria had found it impossible to believe that the large stone tomb in the graveyard should contain Alfred, Lord Tennyson's widow but not Tennyson himself.

'I think it's awful.'

'But he's in Westminster Abbey. In Poet's Corner.'

'Well, he should be here. He shouldn't have left her alone.'

Alex and Nick had shot each other a sympathetic glance. It had occurred to them both that their current proximity was due in no small measure to Victoria's romantic leanings.

'Quite right,' they said in unison, then laughed.

Right now, Victoria was sitting in the dinghy, pulled out from beneath the veranda and beached on the rough grass in front of the house. Her head was buried in a book, and she absentmindedly curled a strand of hair around her index finger as she read.

'I don't want to have any secrets from you. Not even financial ones.' Nick was adamant.

'Well, if you're sure.'

'Positive.'

'Could you bear to come over again tomorrow?'

Alex smiled resignedly. 'I'm turning into a commuter. But I'll have to be back for Victoria coming out of school. If I catch the nine o'clock ferry over, I could take the two o'clock back. Would that be OK?'

'Fine. I shall miss you, though, when you go. I always miss you.' Nick stood up, lifted her off her chair and sat down with her on his lap.

'Hey!' she said. 'I'm far too heavy for this. You'll regret it.'

'Never.' He put his arms round her waist, and they watched Victoria in the boat until the sun sank behind the Dorset hills and it was time for the mainlanders to go home.

34
Fortune's Double Yellow

. . . best grown with support.

Nick was nervous. He had the entire contents of the bank safety-deposit box in the inside pocket of his jacket and he had no idea what Elliott Williams would say either about their value or that they were in Nick's possession.

Before they made their way to the jeweller's he opened the bag in the car to show Alex.

'Oh, my God, they're huge!' she said. 'Are you sure they're real?'

'Well, no, I'm not – apart from the one Rosie gave me, which she said was real.'

Alex pushed at them with her finger, the better to make them sparkle. 'I've never seen anything like them. Not even in a jeweller's window.'

'It's a bit scary, isn't it?'

'And you don't know where they came from?'

'Not exactly. Rosie said she converted her savings into diamonds – bought in London presumably – then handed them to Dad for safekeeping, but she kept mine back to give me on my birthday. That's this one.' He indicated the smallest of the five stones. 'Rosie reckoned this was worth twenty-five grand. I don't know what the others are worth, or why there are five altogether. There was supposed to be one each for Alice, Sophie and me.'

'And you think these came from Russia?'

'That's what the hotel writing-paper said.' Nick had already explained about the visit from his father and the two heavies who had come to collect the packet.

'So these ones just turned up out of the blue? In the post?'

'Yes. Recorded delivery.'

'And the note said nothing about where they were from?'

'Here it is.' Nick pulled the note from the small linen bag and handed it to Alex. 'See what you make of it.'

Alex read it. Then she repeated: '"The enclosed were given to me by Rosie to take care of. Well, their friends were."'

'What do you make of that?'

'It's obvious, isn't it? These aren't the diamonds Rosie gave him.'

'Yes. But are they better ones or fakes?'

Alex looked thoughtful. 'Well, he wouldn't have sent fake diamonds by recorded delivery, would he?'

'Unless he wanted me to believe they were real.'

'Would your dad really do that?'

Nick shook his head. 'No. At least, I don't want to believe he would.' He tipped the stones back into the bag. 'But there's only one way to find out, isn't there?'

*

Elliott Williams was as welcoming and urbane as he had been on their first meeting, and especially solicitous to Alex. Coffee was made promptly on their arrival by another bright young thing (Elliott clearly had a private supply), and then he said, 'Right. Let's have a look at the stones.'

He reached under the counter and took out a roll of dark blue velvet, which he smoothed out across the glass surface.

Nick handed him the small linen bag and watched as he undid the top and tipped the stones out on to the fabric. They fell silently, and then picked up the light from the overhead spotlights and he suppressed a gasp.

At first Elliott Williams said nothing. He put the magnifying loupe into his eye and held up each stone to it for what seemed an age. As he finished with each one he laid it down on a different part of the velvet.

As he lowered the last of the five stones, he removed the glass from his eye and cleared his throat. 'Yes, well . . .'

Nick and Alex hung on those words. All sounds, except the ticking of the long-case clock in the corner of the shop, had subsided.

'We have here three different grades of diamond.' He gently pushed the one Rosie had given Nick towards the front of the cloth with his little finger. 'This one is pretty good. A VVS1, if you remember what that is?'

'Very, very small inclusions?' offered Nick. Alex looked impressed.

'Precisely. Not flawless, but very fine nevertheless. Value? Around the twenty to twenty-five thousand mark.'

'That's what I thought,' said Nick, involuntarily.

Elliott Williams shot him a look. 'Oh, only because

that's what my gran – that's what I was told it was worth when it was given to me.' And then, to reassure the jeweller that he was not wasting his time, 'That's the only one I was given a value for. I haven't a clue about the others.'

'Right. These three here . . .' he pushed a matching trio forward '. . . are internally flawless and worth probably around seventy-five thousand apiece.'

'Gosh!' Nick tried to hide his surprise.

'And this one,' Elliott pushed forward a diamond the size of his fingernail, 'is flawless. Quite beautiful and very well cut. It will be worth between seven hundred and seven hundred and fifty thousand pounds.'

Alex gasped. Nick said, 'Good God!' and Elliott Williams said, 'You're a very lucky man.'

'Yes. I suppose I am.' And then, 'Are you sure I don't owe you anything for the valuation?'

'Absolutely not. It was my pleasure to see them. And if you need them set – in a ring or a pendant – I'll be happy to do the job for you.'

'Thank you. Yes. Thank you very much.'

Nothing very sensible seemed to be coming out of Nick's mouth. Nothing at all was coming out of Alex's, which hung slightly open.

Then Nick saw the questioning look on Elliott Williams's face. He felt obliged to give some explanation. 'I suppose it all looks rather suspicious . . .'

'Oh, I never ask questions, sir.'

'They were left to me by my grandmother. Well, she's still alive but . . . and she wanted . . .'

'Really, sir, it's a private matter and I quite understand.'

Nick realized that anything he said would sound even

more unlikely although it was truth, so decided to quit before he dug himself into an even deeper hole.

The jeweller scooped up the diamonds, tipped them back into the bag, pulled the drawstring tight and handed it back over the counter. 'I'd get to the bank as soon as you can, sir,' he said.

'Yes. Thank you. We will. And thank you again.' Nick and Alex left the shop, doing their best not to look like the Lavender Hill Mob. When the diamonds were safely back in the custody of Lloyds TSB, they treated themselves to lunch in a wine bar, with a particularly fine bottle of sauvignon blanc.

Once Alex was safely on the ferry to Portsmouth, Nick drove to the hospital, and was delighted to find Rosie sitting up in bed, hair and makeup in apple-pie order. 'Look at you!' he said.

'I did. In the mirror. Much better,' she retorted.

'Are you back to your old self?' he asked.

'Getting there. Oh, I did feel ropy, and I'm still not a hundred per cent, but I'm on the mend, I think.'

He bent to kiss her, and was relieved to smell Chanel No. 5 once more, instead of the sanitized aroma of hospital. 'You really had us worried,' he said, patting the back of her hand as it lay on the covers.

'Oh, I'm a tough old bird,' she said, but he noticed that her voice did not hold its usual conviction. 'What have you been up to?' she asked.

'I found a girl, and she found me.' He sat down, and tried not to sound too pleased.

'Anyone I know?' she asked.

'Oh, yes.' He beamed.

'Two girls, then? That's nice.' Evidently she was happy for him.

'Are you sure you're OK?' he asked. Something about her seemed not quite right.

'Yes, of course,' she said. 'Anyway, I'm glad about you.' She smoothed the blanket. 'You said yesterday that you had some news for me, didn't you, about my mother? Or was I dreaming?'

Nick hesitated. 'Yes. But only when you're ready.'

'I'm ready. Go on. Tell me.'

The prospect of disappointing her filled him with dread, but he told her of Alex's researches, the delegation and George Carmichael. Then he mentioned Mathilde Kschessinska. He stumbled over the pronunciation. 'MK, the same initials.'

'Well I never. So instead of using my real mother's name, Tatiana, they used one belonging to the Tsar's previous mistress to avoid suspicion?'

Nick found it impossible to contradict her: she thought the naval attaché had had an affair with Grand Duchess Tatiana and that the Tsar's former mistress had been brought in as a smokescreen. What was the point? What good would it do? And he wanted her to get better, not to brood on a distant past that had no bearing now on her life.

He shrugged. 'That's as much as we've been able to find out,' he said.

Rosie's eyes were shining now. 'So they did exist. This man, George Carmichael, did go there. And it's true.'

Nick could only smile, he hoped not deceitfully.

'Oh, what a relief.' Rosie flopped back on the pillow and closed her eyes.

After a few moments she opened them. Her face was

relaxed now. The pinched look had gone. She put out her hand and took his. 'I knew you'd come through for me.'

'Not me. Alex.'

Rosie nodded. 'Good girl. I knew she would, too.' She looked at him pleadingly. 'Do something for me?'

'Of course.'

'When you next hear from your dad . . .'

'Yes?'

She beckoned him closer. 'Thank him for sorting out the diamonds.'

'What?' He was astonished.

Rosie pointed to her bedside cabinet. 'There's a letter from him in there.'

Nick opened the door, and among the cotton wool, tissues, Lucozade and wet wipes, he found a letter on identical stationery to the one he had received from his father.

'How did he know where you were?' he asked.

'Oh, your father seems to know everything. I've never dared ask him how. Open it.'

Nick did so, and unfolded the letter. The writing-paper bore the name and address of the same Moscow hotel.

Dear Rosie,

I hope this finds you well. I took care of the little stones as you asked, but I had an opportunity to make them grow a bit. Don't ask how. I know you always worried about my schemes, but if I learned one thing from you (and you probably thought I learned nothing at all) it was never to leave until tomorrow what you could do today. *Carpe diem* and all that.

There was nothing underhand about the deal (and I

know you worry about that, too!), but I've been doing a bit of business over here – Russian capitalists are grateful for all the help they can get from wide-boy westerners like me, and they have interesting ways of showing their gratitude.

I've sent the stones back to Nick – the slightly better versions of them – and told him to put them in a bank for safe-keeping. He'll probably wonder what they're all for, but I'll leave you to tell him that.

See you soon. And don't worry.

Your boy Derek xxx

'So, does Dad keep in touch with you then, when nobody else knows where he is?'

'Sometimes. When he feels like it.'

'But the diamonds . . .'

'Mmm?'

'I had them valued today.'

'Did you? Well, don't tell me,' said Rosie. 'I don't want to know.'

'As well as the one you gave to me, there are four, one large one and three smaller ones.'

'That's right.'

'Are you going to tell me what to do with them?' he asked, exasperated.

Rosie frowned. 'If you'll give me a chance to get a word in edgeways.'

'Sorry.'

Rosie grinned. 'You look just like you did when you were a little boy and I told you off.' Then her face became serious. 'Now, the diamonds. Can you make sure that, of the three smaller ones, one each goes to Sophie and Alice

– wherever they happen to be. I know Sophie's gone off on the toot again because she came and told me. And Alice is in South . . . well, you know.'

'I'll make sure they get them,' he assured her.

'And you've got yours, haven't you?'

Nick nodded.

'But it was a bit smaller than the ones your dad sent back, or so he said.'

'Oh, that doesn't matter,' he said, dismissively.

'Well, hopefully it doesn't. You see, the third one is for Alex.'

At first he thought he had misheard her. He wanted to ask, 'Alex who?' Instead he blurted out, 'What do you mean?'

'Well, I could see that you two were made for each other, even if *you* couldn't.'

'But . . .'

'And it wasn't just that you were called Nicholas and Alexandra. I'm not that stupid.' She looked reflective for a moment. 'Odd, yes, but stupid, no.'

'You can't . . .'

'Oh, I'm afraid I can. Old lady's prerogative. You can't stop me.'

'I suppose not.'

'And the last one . . .'

Nick had barely had time to keep up with the last bombshell, when Rosie said, quite calmly, 'The last one is to be sold and the proceeds are to be put into a trust fund. I don't know what it will amount to, but it should make sure that the brightest little girl I've ever encountered gets a decent education.' She looked hard at Nick. 'I take it you're managing to keep up?'

'Victoria?' he asked.

Rosie nodded. 'Yes. Something tells me that she's going to be very special.'

'But this is so sudden! How do you know—'

'How do I know that you'll stick together?'

Nick nodded.

'I don't. I just have a feeling. And it's such a strong feeling that I see no reason to question it. Sometimes you have to rely on your instincts. I've always done that. You're a good man and she's a good woman. You're also crazy about each other, and the child. Anyone with half a brain can see that. You've got your heads screwed on. You'll manage.'

Nick's face bore the expression of someone with concussion.

Rosie leaned back on her pillow mountain and smiled. 'Go on,' she said. 'Say it for me.'

'Say what?'

'Oh, I think you know.'

For a moment he looked bewildered, and then he smiled. And as he smiled, so the tears welled up in his eyes. 'You know,' he said, 'you really crack me up.'

35

Reine des Violettes

*If I had to choose just one Hybrid Perpetual, it
would have to be this one.*

Just three days later Rosie Robertson died peacefully in her sleep. Nick was with her, holding her hand. There were no last words, just a sigh, and a great calm. He eased his hand out of hers, and kissed her forehead. Unable to stop the tears cascading down his face, he sat with his head in his hands for a while and wept, remembering nothing but the good times.

Death was due to delayed shock, said the doctor. It happened quite often in people of advanced age when they had suffered a broken hip.

At first Nick found it impossible to believe she had gone. The loss of Rosie's company, her influence and her wise counsel had left him bereft. He would also miss her unpredictability, his exasperation with her, and the laughs they had shared. Yes. He would miss those more than anything.

Victoria, too, took it hard. It was her first experience of death.

Alex was a rock to them both, and a comforting shoulder to cry on. There were lots of tears, but Rosie had left many happy memories – and quite a lot of money. It was some time before Alex could come to terms with her bequest, and her daughter's legacy. 'For now,' she said, 'do you mind if I just leave it in the bank?'

The day of the funeral was warm and sunny. There were few people at the Newport crematorium. Nick's parents made it, and stood next to each other silently. There were half a dozen friends from Cheltenham, who had seen the announcement in *The Times*, Sophie and Nick, Alex and Victoria. Henry spent most of his time blowing his nose into a large red and white spotted handkerchief, and blaming the pollen from the flowers. Rosie would have liked that.

There were no hymns, just prayers of thanksgiving. Rosie had always believed in God, but had not been a regular churchgoer and thought it would be hypocritical to have an overly religious ceremony. She had said as much in a letter she had lodged with her solicitor. She also asked that Nick read something for her. It took all his willpower to get through it, but get through it he did. With clarity and with great feeling he spoke the words of a poem that Rosie had loved:

> Do not stand at my grave and weep;
> I am not there. I do not sleep.
> I am a thousand winds that blow.
> I am the diamond glints on snow.
> I am the sunlight on ripened grain.

I am the gentle autumn rain.
When you awaken in the morning's hush
I am the swift uplifting rush
Of quiet birds in circled flight.
I am the soft stars that shine at night.
Do not stand at my grave and cry:
I am not there. I did not die.

Sniffs and a fumbling for tissues followed, and then came the only piece of music in the short ceremony, which generated both smiles and tears as it rang out from the speakers at the front of the chapel. Rosie's coffin disappeared to the strains of 'Lara's Theme' from *Dr Zhivago*. Whether or not she had come into the world as a Russian princess she certainly went out as one.

As they emerged into the sunlight, Nick's parents came over to where he, Alex and Victoria stood. There were the usual family pleasantries – a little strained – and compliments on Nick's having managed to get through the poem. Anna greeted Alex as some dowager might a visitor to her home, and Derek, in smart suit and camel coat with astrakhan collar, gave her a peck on both cheeks. He winked at Victoria, who smiled nervously.

As they got into their cars and drove away, Nick noticed that his mother was tidying her hair and that his father was already on his mobile.

Then there were the goodbyes and thanks to the friends who had taken the trouble to come from Cheltenham, and afterwards Nick, Alex, Victoria, Henry and Sophie gathered together to go off for lunch at the Red Duster.

It was only then that Nick noticed the solitary figure laying a wreath of lilies under the card that bore Rosie's name, where the family flowers had been placed. He was an old gentleman in a dark coat, tall, a little stooping, with iron-grey hair.

Nick walked over and introduced himself. 'Hello. I'm Nick Robertson. Thank you for coming.'

'My pleasure,' said the old man, with a neat bow. He had a thick accent.

'I'm afraid I don't know who you are,' Nick confessed.

The man bowed once more. 'I am sorry. I should have introduced myself. I am Oleg Vassilievsky.'

'Ah.' Nick hesitated. 'Have we met before?'

'I don't think so.'

'You must have known my grandmother.' He was curious now.

'Not exactly. But I was aware of her.'

The confused expression on Nick's face elicited more of an explanation.

'Your grandmother was from Russia.'

'I know.'

'She was a Romanov.'

'Ah, yes. Well, she thought she might have been, but we've discovered that it was very unlikely.'

The old man shook his head. 'She was a Romanov. Not a legitimate one, but a Romanov nevertheless.'

Nick was incredulous. 'How do you know?'

The man smiled kindly. 'We know all the members of the family. We try to keep track of them.'

'That sounds a bit sinister.'

Oleg Vassilievsky shrugged. 'It is not intended to be. We like to think of it as loyal support.'

'I don't understand . . .' Nick looked over his shoulder at Alex and Victoria, who were deep in conversation with Sophie. Then he asked, 'Why have you never appeared before?'

'We had rather lost track of Mrs Robertson until our attention was drawn to her.' He nodded at Alex. Then he continued, 'We endeavour to show our respects on occasions such as this.'

Nick began to feel as though he were having a bad dream. 'So who were her parents?'

'Her father was an English naval officer.'

'We'd worked that out. But what about her mother? It wasn't really Grand Duchess Tatiana, was it?'

'No, it was not.'

'Thank God for that.'

'It was her sister, Grand Duchess Olga.'

Nick looked for something on which to steady himself. He found nothing. After several seconds he managed to speak. 'How can you be sure?'

'We are sure,' he said firmly.

'But . . . what does this mean?'

Oleg shook his head. 'Very little now. Your grandmother is dead. We came to say goodbye. That is all.' He offered his hand. Nick shook it and asked, 'Who is "we"?'

'You will not have heard of us. We are a small group of people loyal to the Russian royal family. We do not think that they should be forgotten.'

'Is that all?'

Oleg bowed once more. 'That is all. Please accept our condolences. A very good day to you.'

He turned and walked towards a black car, whose engine was already running. He got into the rear seat, and as the car moved off he turned, waved, then disappeared from view.

'You're not saying much?'

'Sorry?' He jumped, startled.

'You're very quiet,' said Alex, patting his leg as they sat at the table in the Red Duster.

'No. Just thinking.' He smiled, giving her his full attention.

'Well, it's been quite a day, but I think she'd have been happy with her send-off.'

'I hope so.'

Casually she asked, 'Who was that man you were talking to?'

'Just an old acquaintance of Rosie's,' Nick said.

'He looked a bit scary.'

'No. Not really. Just wanted to pay his last respects.'

'That's nice.'

One day he would tell her about the man. And about Rosie. But not now. For now he just wanted to take the two of them home, and try to start a new life. A normal life. A life as a husband, and as a father. When he felt the moment was right to ask them.

He watched as the two of them smiled and chatted together. There was nobody with whom he would rather spend the rest of his life.

His thoughts drifted off once more. To Rosie. 'Goodbye, my love,' he murmured. 'And thanks for everything.' And as he did so, all he could hear was the music from *Dr Zhivago*.

**SIMON &
SCHUSTER**

The Last Lighthouse Keeper

Alan Titchmarsh

Will Elliott is out of a job. The lighthouse he's been
manning on Prince Albert Rock, off the wild Cornish
coast, is about to become automated. So Will decides
to fulfil his lifelong ambition – to sail round
the coastline of Britain.

But he hasn't reckoned on the arrival in sleepy
Pencurnow Cove of Amy Finn, a beautiful artist
and fellow loner . . . And as if that isn't distraction
enough, suddenly his sleepy Cornish village is
rocked by the biggest scandal to hit Cornwall
since Guinevere ran off with Lancelot.

It seems as if Will will never get away, and even if
he does, will his journey be solo or a two-man
voyage of discovery?

ISBN-13: 978-0-7434-7845-8
£6.99

SIMON &
SCHUSTER

Mr MacGregor

Alan Titchmarsh

When Rob MacGregor is picked as the new presenter of a struggling gardening programme, he quickly becomes a favourite with everyone. And that's half his trouble . . .

Having a gardener who's also a sex symbol might be a godsend for TV bosses, but there are plenty of others who are not so happy: Bertie Lightfoot for one, the expert Rob replaced; Guy D'Arcy, another TV rival and insatiable womaniser; and most importantly Rob's fiery girlfriend, Katherine – an investigative journalist on the local paper. As Rob becomes more and more wrapped up in his career, and she is involved in a big story for the paper, the relationship comes under strain. Especially when a misunderstanding causes sparks to fly and things get really complicated . . .

ISBN-13: 978-0-7434-7847-2
£6.99

SIMON &
SCHUSTER

Only Dad

Alan Titchmarsh

According to their friends, Tom and Pippa Drummond
have the perfect existence – an enviable lifestyle,
a happy marriage, and a great kid in Tally.

A rare summer holiday is planned – an idyllic retreat in
the Italian hills. Tom takes time off from running his
restaurant, Pippa leaves her herb garden in the charge
of a dotty neighbour and Tally takes a break
from the two men in her life.

Tuscany is everything they hoped it would be – cicadas
in the trees, the scent of sage and citrus and suppers
under the stars. But their joy is short-lived. Overnight
their lives, their circumstances, their very identities are
altered, and life will never be the same again.

ISBN-13: 978-0-7434-7846-5
£6.99

Reason I jump

Fall down 7 times get up 8.

SIMON & SCHUSTER

Animal Instincts

Alan Titchmarsh

When Kit Lavery's father dies, he is forced to return home after a ten year stint in Australia to sort out his affairs. A well-known conservationist and champion of wildlife, Rupert Lavery has left behind a nature reserve in Devon, staffed by two very determined women; Elizabeth Punch and Jess Wetherby, both of whom are committed to keeping his work alive.

As if these two women weren't enough, Kit falls under the spell of the beautiful Jinty O'Hare, niece of the local Master of Foxhounds.

When a buyer is found for the estate, Kit is torn. Will he stay or will he go? Perhaps Wilson the Gloucester Old Spot pig has the answers.

ISBN-13: 978-0-7434-7848-9
£6.99